"Scout's part of my life," he said.

"That's why I find it hard to take him to the department to stay in a cage," Cal went on. "I know it'll be hard on him."

Jessica's heart warmed for the big, gruff cop. To her way of thinking, how could someone *not* care about kids and dogs? But Cal seemed to, more than the average person.

He was a stranger, and she was thinking about turning her life upside down for him by offering to take care of Scout. How would she manage with a high-maintenance dog—and keep doing her job with the long hours, odd shifts and unpredictable emergencies? She reminded herself again why she didn't have a pet, despite her love for animals.

But then she looked at Cal, saw the concern in his eyes, and her heart melted completely. She wanted to help them. She really did. But she couldn't deny that part of the reason was the fact that she'd be able to see Cal.

Dear Reader,

This is the first book in my K-9 squad trilogy, and it's the story of trauma surgeon Jessica Hansen and San Diego Police search and rescue officer Cal Palmer. Although I have always had a profound sense of gratitude for the men and women who dedicate their lives to law enforcement, through my research for this trilogy I gained an even greater appreciation for the bravery and dedication of canine officers and the intelligence and resourcefulness of police dogs.

Thank you for choosing to read Jessica and Cal's story. I have frequently been asked with respect to my previous books if I planned to tell the story of any of the secondary characters in a sequel. The beauty of writing a trilogy is that we already know there will be two more books. If you enjoy *When the Right One Comes Along*, you won't have to wait long for the second book in the trilogy, *When Love Matters Most*. The story of K-9 unit sergeant Rick Vasquez and veterinarian Madison Long is scheduled for release early in January 2016.

As always, I would love to hear from you! You can connect with me through my website, Facebook page, Twitter or regular mail.

Happy reading!

Kate

Website: Kate-James.com

Facebook: Facebook.com/KateJamesBooks

Twitter: @KateJamesBooks

Mailing address: PO Box 446, Schomberg, ON, L0G 1T0, Canada

HEARTWARMING

When the Right One Comes Along

—

Kate James

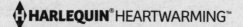
HARLEQUIN® HEARTWARMING™

Recycling programs
for this product may
not exist in your area.

ISBN-13: 978-0-373-36745-0

When the Right One Comes Along

Copyright © 2015 by Kate James

All rights reserved. Except for use in any review, the reproduction or utilization of this work in whole or in part in any form by any electronic, mechanical or other means, now known or hereinafter invented, including xerography, photocopying and recording, or in any information storage or retrieval system, is forbidden without the written permission of the publisher, Harlequin Enterprises Limited, 225 Duncan Mill Road, Don Mills, Ontario M3B 3K9, Canada.

This is a work of fiction. Names, characters, places and incidents are either the product of the author's imagination or are used fictitiously, and any resemblance to actual persons, living or dead, business establishments, events or locales is entirely coincidental.

This edition published by arrangement with Harlequin Books S.A.

For questions and comments about the quality of this book, please contact us at CustomerService@Harlequin.com.

® and TM are trademarks of Harlequin Enterprises Limited or its corporate affiliates. Trademarks indicated with ® are registered in the United States Patent and Trademark Office, the Canadian Intellectual Property Office and in other countries.

Printed in U.S.A.

HARLEQUIN®
™ www.Harlequin.com

Kate James spent much of her childhood abroad before attending university in Canada. She built a successful business career, but her passion has always been literature. As a result, Kate turned her energy to her love of the written word. Kate's goal is to entertain her readers with engaging stories featuring strong, likable characters. Kate has been honored with numerous awards for her writing. She and her husband, Ken, enjoy traveling and the outdoors with their beloved Labrador retrievers.

Books by Kate James

A Child's Christmas
The Truth About Hope

Dedication

To Veronica Cohn
She lives on in countless hearts

Acknowledgments

As always, I have to acknowledge my brilliant editor, Paula Eykelhof. I am grateful to her for her invaluable contributions to all my books. And much thanks to Victoria Curran for challenging me and all the Heartwarming authors to tell the very best stories we can.

I owe special thanks to York Regional Police (Ontario, Canada), and Constable Jim Hilton, in particular. Constable Hilton, a YRP canine unit officer and trainer, was generous with his time, resource materials and limitless knowledge as I conducted my research for this trilogy. I also thank him for introducing me to his explosives detection dog, Max, and demonstrating to me some of Max's skills.

Finally I offer my sincere gratitude to all the men and women who dedicate their lives to law enforcement, to keep us safe and secure in a world where their jobs are becoming ever more complex.

CHAPTER ONE

CALEN PALMER'S POLICE-ISSUED Ford Explorer veered sharply to the left, barely missing the large chunk of concrete, twisted rebar and other detritus strewn across the road. As he straightened the steering wheel, a blur of motion had him hitting the brakes hard.

The SUV skidded sideways on the dust-slicked road, shuddering to rest just inches from a wide-eyed woman. Her face and clothes were streaked with grime and blood, and she clutched a small bundle to her chest.

At the soft whine behind him, Cal looked over his shoulder. "It's okay, Scout. You're okay, pal," he told his canine partner while he opened the driver's door.

"Earthquake! We got an earthquake!" someone yelled. As if he didn't know that already. But people were panicked and the guy must have been reacting to the San Diego Police Department markings on his vehicle.

Voices erupted all around as he ran to the woman.

He felt the surge of adrenaline. It was a baby she was holding. And the blanket was saturated with blood.

"How badly are you hurt?" he asked, as he gauged the severity of the cuts on the woman's forehead and her right forearm, and checked her pupils for dilation.

"I… I'm okay," she choked out through her sobs. "My baby. Lila…" She cast a terrified glance at the child she cradled against her.

"Let me see." Cal eased back the blanket and scrutinized the tiny, scrunched-up face, the furiously working little mouth and the tightly fisted hands. The baby was alive. He did a quick, careful check. There were no obvious signs of trauma. The blood on the blanket was the woman's, not the child's.

"Your daughter appears to be fine," he assured her. She didn't respond, and he hoped she wasn't going into shock. He had to leave. People's lives depended on him and Scout, but he had to do what he could for the woman and her child.

A siren wailed, and Cal looked over at the ambulance barreling toward the intersection of University and West Washington. Dispatch had told him the triage area was set up in the parking lot of a nearby mall.

"Listen to me." He shook the woman gently. "Listen, okay?" Finally, her gaze met his. "See where that ambulance is headed?" She nodded. "Go there. The hospital's sent medical personnel. It's not far. Maybe a five-minute walk. Have a doctor look at your baby. They'll need to stitch up your arm, too."

She stared at him, tears welling in her eyes.

"Do you understand?"

She nodded again, and was about to move away, but Cal glanced at the baby again and put a hand on her uninjured arm. "Wait a minute."

He sprinted over to his truck, opened the passenger-side door and pulled a cotton sweat-shirt from his duffel. Using a pocket knife, he tore off a sleeve as he ran back to the woman, and tied it around her arm as a makeshift bandage. He then quickly helped her remove the soiled blanket from her child and replaced it with the clean sweatshirt. The woman rested her forehead against her child's, and mur-mured a thank-you. Cal tucked the cloth more snugly around the small form, and nudged the woman in the direction of the triage area. "Now go. Lila'll be okay," he said, and prayed he was right.

Jumping back into his vehicle, Cal continued to the incident command location he'd been given by dispatch. He veered around a crushed concrete column, toppled on its side. It was blocking part of the roadway, its upper half shattered, the exposed rebar bent and tangled. He knew the amount of force it took for concrete to fail, which didn't bode well for what he'd see closer to the epicenter.

Cal was the newest member of the San Diego Police Department's K-9 Unit, and wasn't it just his luck that although San Diego was one of the California cities least prone to earthquakes, it had been hit by a massive one. He'd heard that the quake was 7.6 on the Richter scale. He could see the devastation all around him as he approached Incident Command. An elevated section of the highway had collapsed, and portions of the road surface had heaved and buckled. A rippled concrete parapet wall leaned precariously over the roadway. Two low-rise buildings and a parking garage had also collapsed.

Cal pulled into the cordoned-off area that

had been designated as Incident Command, and parked behind another SDPD vehicle.

Cops, firefighters, paramedics and panicked civilians were everywhere.

Cal recognized Riker, another officer with the department. He was in a huddle with a tall, plain-clothed man and a firefighter. Cal surmised that the man in plain clothes was the incident commander. He left Scout in the vehicle and went to join them. Introductions were made; he'd been right about the third man. His name was Williams and he was in charge.

"It looks bad," Cal remarked. "Do we have any idea of the numbers yet?"

Williams shook his head. "Too soon to tell how many injuries and fatalities we'll have. The fact that it's late on a Friday afternoon might work to our advantage." He jerked his head toward the collapsed structures. "They housed offices mostly. Let's hope a lot of the workers cut out early."

Cal scrutinized the buildings. One had collapsed in on itself. Most of the floor appeared to be intact, if skewed. Best-case scenario, the people inside had time to find shelter near the load-bearing walls and would have survived. The condition of the other building was far worse. A couple of the lower floors had crashed down on top of each other. There couldn't have been much room for people left inside.

Cal heard Scout's muffled bark and knew his partner was anxious to get to work. He was always impressed by how intuitive police dogs were, sensing when they were needed. "Is it safe to go in?" Cal asked the commander. He'd done lots of search-and-rescues in the five months he'd been in San Diego and in his decade on the job with the Lincoln Police Department in Nebraska before then, but he'd never had to deal with an earthquake before. Sadly, there was a first time for everything.

"I think they're clearing it now." The firefighter motioned to a group of men near the entrance to one of the buildings. "But there's always the possibility of aftershocks." He glanced over at Cal's SUV, clearly marked as part of the K-9 Unit. "You plan to go in?"

Cal studied the buildings, considered the risks involved. He thought about Haley and forced the image of his little girl with her blonde ringlets out of his mind. She wouldn't know if he lived or died. He shrugged. "It's why we're here. It's what Scout and I do."

The commander gestured to one of the men by the building "We've got the all clear."

"Thanks." Cal shook hands with Williams, Riker and the firefighter before jogging to his vehicle. He opened the back door and signaled for Scout to jump out. Scout yipped excitedly and Cal took a moment to rub the dog's head and ruffle his fur, then attached his leash to his collar. Knowing it would be dry, dusty work and with no idea how long it would be before they could take a break, he gave Scout a drink from a water bottle.

With another hand signal, he alerted Scout that he was now officially on duty, and they headed toward the collapsed buildings and the men gathered on the roadway in front of them.

JESSICA HANSEN HAD been at Ocean Crest Hospital when the earthquake hit. Because of its severity, the hospital had immediately activated its critical incident response plan, including the deployment of the trauma team. The trauma team was responsible for onsite triaging and treating the injured, and dispatching those who needed additional care to the hospital. As a trauma surgeon, Jessica would've been called in regardless, but being at the hospital made it easier for her to mobilize a team and get to the site.

Ocean Crest was the closest hospital to the earthquake's epicenter, where most of the injured would be, and no more than a few miles from where they were setting up the triage area. A 7.6 quake was virtually unheard of in San Diego, but as a trauma doc she'd experienced quakes of a much lower magnitude that still had significant consequences. She knew this would be serious.

Thank heaven the hospital itself was largely unaffected by the quake. But then it had been designed to higher standards to ensure that it did. From the reports already coming in, they'd need all available resources, both human and physical.

In the hour since Jessica, the other trauma docs and a few of the emergency room nurses had set up at the designated triage site, she'd already seen at least a dozen people, and there were many more waiting.

She swiped impatiently at the sweat and loose strands of hair on her forehead as she finished splinting an elderly man's badly fractured forearm, and sent him off to the hospital.

Pinching the bridge of her nose, she counted slowly to ten. She had to stay sharp, she reminded herself. She couldn't be unsettled by the young boy she'd treated and sent to the hospital just before the older man. The boy had lost a lot of blood. Too much blood. Her vision blurred and she swallowed hard against the nausea. If she gave in, she'd be no good to anyone.

She felt a gentle touch on her shoulder. "You okay, Jess?"

Jessica slid her clammy hand over her brow and turned. Marcia Rodrigues stood behind her, the furrows on her forehead more pronounced than usual, concern evident on her face. The gray-haired nurse, now in her sixties, had worked in the emergency room at Ocean Crest longer than Jessica's thirty-one years, but they'd formed a strong bond—both professional and personal. "It was the boy, wasn't it?" Marcia asked.

Jessica passed her hand lightly over Marcia's. "Yes, and thank you. I'm okay now." She glanced around. "Did anyone else notice?"

"No. Of course not. I just know you well."

Jessica was certain that her episode and the subsequent exchange with Marcia took no more than a minute. But a minute could mean life or death in a crisis situation. She silently berated herself for her lapse. After all, this was why she'd given up pediatric surgery in favor of trauma. If she couldn't maintain her composure under these conditions, she had to ask herself if she was fit to practice medicine at all.

Jessica barely had time to finish the thought when Marcia brought her the next patient. It wasn't a child; she knew Marcia well enough that she didn't think she'd be seeing more children that day, but she was still relieved.

But *she* was in charge. She shouldn't have to be protected.

Most importantly, she could not, *would not*, fall apart. "Focus, Hansen," she ordered herself under her breath as she examined the mangled leg of the woman in front of her.

CHAPTER TWO

AFTER A GENERAL outline of strategy with the other first responders, Cal and Scout went to work. They started with the least damaged building first. They were gratified to have some quick wins—people relatively uninjured and easily extracted. They cleared the first building, then did a fast sweep of the perimeter of the other building and adjacent parking garage. When they were done, no fewer than two dozen people had been helped out of the rubble, most requiring only minor medical attention.

But now it was time for the hard work. Scout and Cal had to go into the more severely damaged building. Cal knew, too, that his unit mate, Hal Robinson, and his cadaver dog, Max, were on scene. Cal hated that. He and Robinson got along well enough, but he hated to lose a person to Robinson and Max. Cal wanted to find people alive and rescue them. It was still their turn, his and Scout's. He intended to make it a slow day for Robinson and Max.

He and Scout now had to locate the people trapped deeper inside the building and likely requiring more assistance, whether because of injury or where they were. Those they'd been able to rescue said they had coworkers and friends still inside.

Cal and the other first responders had a quick huddle with the incident commander and the city's engineers, and mapped out a course of action.

Cal gave Scout some more water, stroked the fur on his head. "Okay, pal. Ready to go?"

A short bark confirmed Scout's willingness. Along with two firefighters, they headed off toward the more damaged building once more.

Since they couldn't access the interior from street level due to the collapsed floors, they were lowered through the central core by a boom. The city engineers had advised Cal that the building was nearly identical in design to the other, with a central atrium, but in this case, the atrium had held and the floors had collapsed. It wasn't going to be an easy rescue. Even after all his years as a cop, he still found it exceedingly difficult to deal with death. He hoped he wouldn't have to encounter it today.

They were in the bowels of the building and had cleared an area that must have been a coffee shop. They headed to the next space when Scout alerted, and started to dig at an area where a doorway had collapsed. This was not a passive indication. There was someone trapped on the other side. Cal shone his headlight around. They were near the center of the floor plate where the building seemed to have crumpled. The upper floors had caved in. He couldn't see any way into the area Scout had indicated. He ordered Scout to lie down and stay, dropped onto his knees where the dog had been digging and called out. In the relative silence he listened for a response. Gave it a moment.

Nothing.

He tried again. And waited.

Scout's agitation was obvious. The dog sprang up despite Cal's command and started digging at the rubble again. Scout's training was such that he would've kept digging until he got through, but he would have injured himself badly on the shards of glass and other sharp edges in the debris. His behavior was a sure sign that there was someone in there. Cal ordered Scout to stand down again. Just when he was about to call out once more, he heard a noise. A cough.

It was a child. A young child. He called out again. Calmly, reassuringly, despite his fear.

He heard a couple more scratchy coughs before the sound turned into hiccupping sobs.

"Can you hear me?" Cal shouted.

After some soft sniffles, he heard a hesitant, "Yes."

"Okay. I'm with the police and I'm going to help you."

Cal heard whimpers this time.

"What's your name?"

There was a pause, another sniffle. "Kayla."

"Okay, Kayla. Are you hurt?"

"I… I don't know. But my mom…"

"Your mother is with you?" Cal felt a chill permeate his bones.

"Yes. She…she's sleeping."

Oh, God. "All right, Kayla, try to stay calm, and I'll get you out."

"When?" she asked hesitantly. "It's dark in here. I'm scared." Her voice quavered. "And

Mommy… Mommy's sleeping. I can't…can't wake her up."

"Listen, Kayla. I'll get you out," he repeated. "Real soon." Cal hoped he could keep his promise.

He yanked his radio off his belt. "I've got a child here. Condition unknown. With her mother. She says her mother is asleep." He lowered his voice to a whisper. "She hasn't been able to rouse her. I'm betting unconscious." He paused. "At best." He flashed the light around. "It doesn't look good down here," he reported to Command.

"Can you get to them from where you are?" Williams asked.

"No. I don't think so."

"All right. We're sending you help."

"Make it fast. I don't know how much time we have." He was worried about the oxygen supply where the kid and her mother were. He had to do what he could to get some airflow in. He scanned the area around him and found a couple of metal scoops. Based on their size, he assumed they were decorative, but they could've been used for beans in the coffee shop. The good news was they were sturdy enough to be functional. He gave Scout another firm command when the dog started digging, then he used a scoop to clear away debris in an attempt to make an opening. All the while, he tried to keep up a conversation with Kayla.

His radio crackled, and the incident commander's voice came on. "A firefighter is on his way down to you. Have you made any progress?"

"No." He heard the frustration in his own voice.

"Can you get to her with help?"

He almost groaned from exertion and exasperation. He heaved away a large chunk of concrete. "I doubt it. Not from here," he growled. He'd hardly scratched the surface.

"Do you have an update on her condition?"

Cal lowered his voice. "Alive. Other than that, I don't know." He moved away, just in case the girl could hear him. "Her voice is fading. I don't know how much oxygen there is. The doorway here is sealed solid, and wouldn't be a source of air for her and her mother."

Cal heard some background chatter.

"Okay," the incident commander said, "we've got the building plans. Let's locate her so we can determine if there's another way in."

After a hurried conversation, they decided that the girl and her mother were likely trapped in an interior corridor, and the elevator shaft would be the only feasible way to get to her. The firefighter they sent in arrived while Cal was still on the radio.

"We'll need you and your dog to help us locate her from the other end," the commander said. "Come on out and leave Mark—" referring to the new arrival "—to keep the girl calm."

"Ten-four." Cal moved back to the doorway and signaled for Mark to join him. "Kayla?" he called out.

Nothing.

"Kayla," he shouted, trying to keep the rising panic from his voice. "Can you hear me?"

"Uh-huh," came the subdued answer. "I'm sleepy. I'm going to lie down and go to sleep with Mommy."

Cal's eyes locked on Mark's momentarily, and he knew they shared the same fear. Kayla was running out of oxygen. "I know you're tired, Kayla, but please try to stay awake for me, okay? Don't move around but try to stay awake. Can you do that?"

"I'll try." The words were so faint they could barely hear them. They were slurred, too, which worried Cal greatly. She was close to losing consciousness, he was certain. And that was just one step away from... A vision of his sweet Haley flashed through his mind again. He began to dig furiously. *No.* He would not let Kayla die. Mark rested a hand on Cal's shoulder. "You're needed to locate her from the other side. Leave this to me now."

Cal didn't want to stop, but he knew the firefighter was right. "Okay," he said. "Kayla, I'm going to come and get you, but I have—" he glanced at the badge on the firefighter's shirt "—Captain Eagan with me. He'll be here if you need anything, okay?"

"Yes." She'd clearly worn herself out or was already losing consciousness. She didn't have the energy to cry anymore.

In hushed tones, Cal explained the situation to Mark. "You have to create an opening," Cal said. "I doubt she has enough time for us to get her from the other side."

Mark had both a pick and a shovel with him and continued where Cal had left off.

Cal signaled to Scout, and they went back in the direction they'd come. Outside, he met up with two more firefighters and a building engineer, and was directed to where they could access the elevator shaft. The elevator had failed in its normal mode with the counterweight plummeting, meaning the elevator itself was at the top of its trajectory, so the shaft was clear. The two firefighters entered the building with him, and he, Scout and one of them were lowered down the shaft to the ground floor. With the firefighter's key and some effort, they were able to open the elevator landing doors.

Cal could immediately see what had happened. As he'd suspected, when the floors of the building had collapsed, they'd blocked off the entrance to both corridors leading off the lobby. The entrance to the corridor where Kayla and her mother were trapped looked even less accessible from this side.

Cal feared that if the corridor was the only way to get to Kayla, they wouldn't reach her before she ran out of oxygen. He had to believe that with the tools Mark had, he'd be able to create an opening sufficiently large for air to get in. When Cal gave Scout the hand signal to locate the girl, Scout bypassed the corridor entrance altogether. The rubble must have masked Kayla's scent. In seconds, he was barking and scratching along what would've been a side wall.

Hope surged through Cal as he and the firefighter rushed over to where Scout was digging. They might still have a chance. He instructed Scout to move back and wait, and squatted to get a better look. A structural column had collapsed, and the beam it was supporting had tumbled down on top of it, but there was a small triangular opening at its base. The gap was filled with crushed concrete and other debris, but it appeared to be loosely packed. Cal and the firefighter worked feverishly to open up the space. If the little girl had depleted the available oxygen, every second counted.

The time seemed interminable, but it actually took them less than a minute to create an opening under the column. The good news was that air was now flowing freely into the space. Cal hoped fervently it wasn't too late.

Crouching down by the opening, he shouted, "Kayla, it's Cal. Can you hear me?"

There was no response. No sound of movement.

He called out again, then asked the firefighter to radio Mark Eagan on the other side to see if Kayla was still communicating with him. Lowering himself to his stomach, he tried to crawl into the gap. He could aim his flashlight in, but there was no way his shoulders were going to fit.

The firefighter reported that Kayla had been non-communicative for nearly five minutes.

That sent a chill up his spine but, he wouldn't give up on her.

He considered the small opening. It would be tight, but Scout should be able to crawl through, he decided. Before giving the dog commands, he shouted, "Kayla! I'm here and I'm going to get you out, like I promised. I'm sending my dog in to get you. His name is Scout and he won't hurt you. Don't be afraid, okay?"

Still no response. The firefighter shook his head dejectedly, but Cal refused to accept that they were too late.

Although search-and-rescue dogs generally didn't perform extractions, Cal had made it a game with Scout during training. He wasn't sure it would work, but it was Kayla's only chance right now and worth a try.

He removed Scout's collar; he didn't want to risk having it get caught on something in the tight space. If that happened, both Kayla and Scout would be trapped. He gave Scout the play signal, and pretended to throw a toy into the opening. The shepherd cocked his head and looked at Cal questioningly. Cal pointed to the opening. "Go get her, Scout," he said with as much enthusiasm as he could. "Go on. Go get her."

Scout obviously understood there was no toy involved, but crawled into the void on his belly. Down on one knee, Cal continued to aim the flashlight into the space and listened intently. He heard scrambling as Scout must have reached the cavity on the other side. A series of staccato barks indicated to Cal that Scout had located his target. He heard more scrambling, then Scout was backing out through the opening. From the way he was laboring, Cal knew he had the little girl. If only the child was still alive.

As soon as Scout's back end cleared the opening, Cal gave him the command "out" to release. The dog been dragging the girl by the hood of her sweater, which luckily had been buttoned up in the air-conditioned cool of the building.

Cal handed the flashlight to the firefighter and wriggled in as far as he could to get hold of the little girl under her armpits, gently pulling her out. Once she was clear of the opening, the firefighter checked her for vital signs. Nodding to Cal, letting him know she was still alive, he started rescue breathing.

Cal felt an immediate sense of relief. His next priority was to locate Kayla's mother— or anyone else who might've been trapped with them. He signaled to Scout again, and said silent thanks when he heard the little girl cough behind him. He knew the firefighter would take care of Kayla and have her lifted out. His focus was now on the mother.

Cal illuminated the cavity with his flashlight. From his vantage point, he couldn't see anyone, or anything of significance. But he assumed from what Kayla had told him that her mother was in there somewhere, unconscious. He tried again to get his shoulders to fit through the opening. It was a no-go.

"Palmer," the firefighter called to him.

He backed out of the opening. "Yeah. What?" he snapped in frustration.

"We need you here."

Cal's irritated gaze met the other man's.

The firefighter gestured to Kayla. "She needs you."

Cal glanced at the girl with her long black hair and huge dark brown eyes, and everything in him softened. The kid couldn't have been more than four or five. It was obvious that she was making a heroic effort not to cry.

Cal squatted down in front of her.

"Mommy...?" she croaked, tears shimmering in her eyes and spilling over to trail through the grime on her cheeks.

"Kayla, your mother was with you?" He pointed toward the opening. "In there?" She'd already said so, but Cal hadn't been able to see anything, nor had he heard any further noise from inside.

The child swiped the back of her hand under her nose. "Uh-huh," she said before she started to cough once more.

The firefighter offered her some water

from his flask. She took a sip, gagged, then coughed again as Cal patted her back. "You're okay," he reassured her. "I'm going to look for your mother. We need to get you out of here."

"No!" The word exploded from her and she grasped his wrist with her small hand. "I want my mommy."

"We're going to get her next, but you have to go out of the building."

"No. I don't want to. I want Mommy." She thrust out her lower lip.

"You have to. Your mother would want you to be safe. This man will take you out and I'll look for your mother."

"Can't the other man get Mommy?" Her chest was heaving and she clutched Cal's arm harder. She was obviously near her breaking point.

Cal glanced up at the firefighter, who shrugged.

"That's why I called you. She wouldn't leave. She wanted you."

Cal gripped Kayla's shoulders and stared into her tear-drenched eyes. "I'm going to look for your mother now."

She started to sob and threw herself in

Cal's arms. "I'm afraid. I don't want to go without Mommy. Or you."

Cal held tight, clasping one hand over the back of the child's head, smoothing down the tangled, matted mass of dark hair. He assessed the circumstances quickly and decided the extra couple of minutes it would take him to lift the girl out would likely make no difference to her mother. Air was getting in. If the woman was unconscious, she wouldn't run out of oxygen. And if it was worse…well, he didn't want to think about it.

A loud grinding noise reverberated around them—metal abrading against metal—as if the building was settling. Cal and the firefighter froze, waiting for the noise and the vibrations to cease.

"I'll take you out, but after that you'll stay with this man, so I can come back for your mother."

She sniffled a bit, then nodded, her head resting against his shoulder. "Okay."

Cal rose, with Kayla in his arms. They made their way over to the hoist and the firefighter radioed to let them know up top what was happening. They decided the firefighter should go first. He would take Kayla to the triage area once Cal got her out. Cal ordered Scout to wait. The firefighter was lifted out, then the harness was lowered again. Cal strapped himself in. Holding Kayla firmly against his chest, he wrapped the final harness strap around both of them. He signaled for the crew to start the extraction.

As they began to move, the little girl held on tight, her arms wound around his neck, her face still buried in the crook of his neck. They ascended slowly and cleared the building. He blinked rapidly to adjust his eyes to the late-evening sunshine, blinding after the darkness inside.

He wondered fleetingly how the sun could shine so intensely with all the destruction below, but he didn't have long to dwell on it. They were swung away from the opening and Cal unfastened them, handing Kayla to the firefighter.

Just as Cal was strapping himself back in, he felt a strong breeze and spread his legs to brace himself. Even so, when the building beneath him shook, he was nearly knocked off his feet.

"An aftershock," he heard someone yell, and the building shifted, then tilted perilously.

This time Cal did lose his balance. Landing on his backside, he was catapulted down the inclined rooftop headfirst. The harness he hadn't fully secured snapped free. He tried to twist around as the edge of the rooftop rushed toward him. He managed to turn enough so that he wasn't leading with his head when he hit the parapet wall. He lay still for a few moments to catch his breath. His left shoulder screamed but he didn't think it was broken. He hoped it wasn't dislocated, either. Nothing else seemed to hurt enough to worry about.

People on the rooftop and at street level were shouting and rushing about. Cal unfolded himself and, bracing against the parapet wall, he rose to stand on the steeply sloping rooftop. He took one quick glance over the edge and knew that if the parapet wall hadn't been there or hadn't held, it would have been game over for him.

He pushed that thought aside and turned to search the area for the firefighter and Kayla. They were huddled together against the railing by the rooftop stairwell and looked unharmed. His next thought was of Kayla's mother and Scout. He had to get back into the building. Massaging his shoulder, he walked at an angle along the steeply sloping roof toward the elevator shaft opening and the hoisting mechanism.

"Let's get this done," he said to the firefighter operating the hoist as he strapped himself back into the harness.

"You aren't going down there."

"Darn right I am." He gestured toward Kayla. "Her mother is down there, and so is my dog."

"I don't have permission to let anyone back in."

"Then get it," Cal snarled, forestalling any further argument.

The firefighter had a hurried conversation on his radio with the incident commander, and shook his head. "No go. The building might be unstable now and they're worried about another aftershock."

Cal cursed under his breath and yanked his own radio off his belt and contacted Incident Command. "Yeah, I *have* to go back in," he said. "Why? Because there's a person still in there. The mother of a child I just brought out. Yes, I realize she's probably deceased. And Scout—my partner—is down there."

"Your partner is in there?" the incident commander boomed into the radio. "Have you contacted him? Is he okay?"

Clearly Williams had forgotten that Cal was with the K-9 Unit and his partner was a dog. Cal ran a hand over his hair. He didn't bother to set him straight. "I have to go in."

"No."

"I have to—"

"I said no."

"But—"

The voice on the other end became more human, less like the commanding officer at a serious incident. "Look. I understand your position, but we have no idea if anyone still down there is alive. It was a significant aftershock, and the building shifted considerably."

"Yeah. But I have to make sure."

There was a long pause. "No. It's too dangerous. We haven't ascertained the structural integrity of the building, and the probability of another aftershock is high. I'm sorry, but I can't risk it. I can't clear you to go in."

Cal heard the click of the radio disconnecting and was tempted to hurl the device over the edge. Instead, he glanced around. He saw the firefighter who'd been in the building with him preparing to take Kayla down to street level on the articulated boom lift of a fire truck. She was holding on to him, her chin resting on his shoulder. When his eyes met hers, she raised a hand and waved to him, and he was sure her mouth formed the word *mommy.* That decided it for him. He had to go in. He'd promised her he'd go back to find her mother. The odds might be against it, but he couldn't ignore the possibility that Kayla's mother was still alive.

And he wouldn't leave Scout.

There weren't many people left on the rooftop, and those who remained were in the process of making their way back to street level.

Soon it would be him and a firefighter who'd been helping with the hoisting mechanism. Cal didn't know where the firefighter he'd argued with had gone, but this guy was young—no more than twenty-four or -five—and in the process of dismantling the contraption.

"Hey!" Cal called as he did his best to jog

up the slanted roof toward him. "Hold on a minute. I need to go back in."

The kid looked around, seemingly confused. "I was told no one else is going in. I'm supposed to wrap up here and get off the rooftop."

"Well, I have to go back in." When the kid just stared at him, Cal sighed. "Hey, my partner's in there…"

"Your partner?" The kid sounded horrified. "But we lifted everyone out before the aftershock hit. We tracked everyone going in and out."

Cal's mind was made up. He doubted he could do anything for Kayla's mother; he had to face reality. But Scout was still down there, his condition unknown. He was going in, with or without Command authorization, whether this kid was going to help him or not. He raised himself to his full six feet two inches and tried to look intimidating. "I don't have time to argue. You saw that little girl?" The kid nodded. "Her mother's down there. I don't know what kind of shape she's in, but I can't leave her without determining her condition. What if she's still alive? You want to tell that little girl that we abandoned her mother to die? And my partner is the search-and-rescue canine hoisted down after me. I'm not leaving him, either."

"Okay," the kid said hesitantly, and reached for his radio. "I'll just get it cleared."

Cal shot out a hand and placed it over the kid's, held his gaze. "You're not going to get clearance. I've tried and Command refused it."

"But…"

Cal felt the guilt trickle through him. It was one thing for *him* to disregard a direct order from Command, especially with the blot on his past. It was something entirely different for him to coerce someone else to do so—and that someone still young and inexperienced. "Look—" he checked the kid's nametag "—Adam, I'm disobeying an order by going back in, but I have to do it. Like I said, there's no way I'm leaving my dog. And I want to verify the condition of the girl's mother. I owe it to Kayla to make sure. What if she *is* alive and I can save her?"

Cal examined the ropes and pulleys of the hoisting mechanism. His voice was solemn. "I don't want to implicate you in what is essentially insubordination. Go. But if you could leave this stuff behind, I'd appreciate it."

Cal could see that Adam was trying to work things out in his own mind. When Adam spoke, his voice was a little shaky but he seemed resolved. "You can't do this on your own. I'll help you."

"You understand what it means if you do?"

Adam nodded.

Cal had a silent debate with himself. He was involving the rookie in something that could cost the kid his job, his career. But he acknowledged that he needed Adam's help. If sparks flew, he'd just take all the heat, accept all the blame. He'd say he'd pressured the kid. It would be even worse for him, but Adam would get written up for a mild misdemeanor without the risk of losing his job.

"Then let's do it," Cal said.

The elevator shaft no longer provided a straight vertical descent. Their progress was slower and Cal had to guide himself down, using his feet to push away from the obstructions and around protruding structural elements. They couldn't use their radios or they'd be discovered; they communicated by a pre-arranged sequence of tugs on the guywire.

When Cal reached the third floor, he could no longer follow the elevator shaft. The force of the aftershock had created a hundred and thirty-five-degree elbow in the passage. He was lowered through the elevator door opening, directly into the tilted two-story atrium of the main lobby. When he emerged from the elevator shaft, he was suspended a good twenty feet above floor level. Two thoughts flashed through his mind. First, that the space had shifted considerably with the aftershock, just as he'd been warned. And second, that Scout was nowhere in sight. As his feet touched the floor and he unbuckled himself, he swept his gaze around the room and called Scout. Relief flooded through him when he heard the short, sharp barks signaling the dog's location. Following the sound, he could tell that Scout was in the same cavity from which they'd rescued Kayla. He must have tracked the scent back to Kayla's mother, but the opening they'd cleared was blocked again.

"I found you. You're okay!" Cal called to Scout as he rushed over. Fortunately, the opening, enlarged by the way the building had skewed during the aftershock, was blocked only with loose rubble. When he removed it, the dog bounded out and directly to Cal. Scout's coat of black and brown was covered with so much concrete dust he looked nearly white. Even his eyelashes and whiskers were coated in white. While Scout licked Cal's face and pranced around, Cal did a quick exam to satisfy himself that the dog appeared to be unharmed. He took a moment to reattach Scout's collar, and instructed him to sit-stay.

Because of the enlarged opening, Cal was able to shimmy into the cavity on his stomach, using his elbows to propel himself, his flashlight gripped between his teeth.

Sweeping the beam of light around the confined space, he saw her, lying on her back. Her face was stunningly beautiful. Dark olive skin, delicate features and the long cascade of ebony hair, so much like her daughter's. His throat clogged and he had trouble breathing. He crawled over to her to check for vitals, but he was certain it was just a formality.

He understood why Kayla would have thought her mother was asleep; she must not have noticed—understandable with the absence of any light filtering in—that her eyes were open. She had one arm slung above her head and the other extended at her side. The way her hand was positioned and her fingers curled, Cal concluded Kayla would've been holding it.

The woman looked flawless and uninjured from her abdomen up. A portion of the collapsed wall lay across her lower torso. The black jacket she wore appeared to be soaked in blood. None of it would have been evident to Kayla in the dark. Thankfully, the child would not be haunted by images of her dead mother for the rest of her life.

There was nothing Cal could do for her. This woman would now be the responsibility of the coroner. He made another thorough sweep of the area with his flashlight, then backed out through the opening.

He signaled to Scout, ordering him to do a quick search to make sure they weren't leaving anyone behind. The dog didn't give any indication that there was anyone else present.

A light vibration had Cal bracing himself again and grabbing for Scout's collar. The rumble passed and he exhaled.

Back in the atrium, he strapped Scout into

the hoisting harness and tugged on the guywire, signaling to the firefighter to lift him
out. When the harness came back down, Cal
secured himself in quickly, and gave the two
tugs to let Adam know he was ready. He
could hear the winch kick in and he began
his slow ascent.

He was almost at the top of the atrium,
nearing the elevator shaft, when he felt what
seemed to be a gust of air whoosh down the
opening. Simultaneously, the building shud-
dered again, and Cal started to swing and
twirl on the hoisting rope. With the next
tremor, he was catapulted toward a solid interior wall. He leaned back to try to control
his motion and was able to maneuver sufficiently to cushion the impact with his legs
when he collided with the wall. The force
sent him hurtling backward. Just as he was
twirling around once again, another rumble
came from the ground beneath and seemed
to rise up to engulf him. An ominous grating
sound followed.

Cal's blood ran cold as he watched a ceiling
beam tear loose to his right. Still anchored to
a column by some rebars, it crashed toward
him like a battering ram.

He thrust back and as far out as possible, and flailed his legs to increase the swing of the rope. Unable to control his spin, he was propelled in the opposite direction from the one he'd intended, right into the path of the beam.

CHAPTER THREE

JESSICA ACCEPTED THE scissors from Marcia and snipped off the ends of the surgical thread she'd used to suture the long gashes on the face and neck of a middle-aged man. She thought about how close one of the lacerations had come to the man's carotid artery, and how different the outcome could have been.

"You're going to be fine, Mr. Bowen," she assured him. She cleaned another cut on his left arm and applied a gauze bandage. "You'll have some scarring unfortunately. Treating the wounds with vitamin E cream while they're healing will minimize the effect."

"Fortunately, my wife loves me for more than my pretty face." He smiled weakly as he pulled his shirtsleeve back down.

"There's no need for you to go to the hospital, but your family doctor should have a look at that wound in a couple of days. Nothing to worry about. I just want to make sure you don't develop an infection. Your stitches will have to come out in a week's time." She gave him an encouraging look as she removed her latex gloves and tossed them in a waste receptacle.

"Thanks, Doctor," he said as he slid off the treatment table. Their smiles faded as they watched two paramedics carry a black body bag to a waiting transport vehicle. "I'm lucky to be alive," he murmured.

Yes, he was, Jessica thought. She made some hurried notes on a chart and glanced up in time to see Marcia taking a little girl from the arms of a firefighter. She felt a chill descend on her and a voice inside her head screamed, "No!" Still, she did a quick visual scan of the girl for obvious signs of trauma, and was relieved to find none.

The girl was maybe five. She was wearing lemon-yellow shorts and T-shirt, and had a small white sneaker on her left foot and only a white sock on her right. She had long dark hair. Her hair, like the rest of her, was covered in concrete dust.

Jessica noticed Marcia looking around fretfully, and she knew the nurse was searching for another trauma doc who could attend to the little girl so she wouldn't have to.

Jessica sighed. Hadn't she vowed earlier not to let herself be protected? What kind of trauma surgeon was she if she couldn't deal with any patient that came her way? She could feel the anxiety build inside her—tempting her to let Marcia find another doctor.

No, she wouldn't give in.

"Marcia," she called. "I'm done here. I can take her."

She could see the reluctance in Marcia's eyes as she approached with the softly crying child in her arms. "Are you sure?" The worry was evident in her voice, too.

Jessica almost snapped that of course she was sure. Knowing full well the anger was directed at herself and not her colleague and friend, she swallowed the harsh words. She hadn't realized she was wound so tight. She understood that Marcia was trying to help… and she couldn't deny that it wasn't without good reason. "Yes, I'm sure," she responded with a calm she didn't feel. "But thank you for trying to look out for me." She forced a cheerier tone into her voice as she reached for the young girl. "Who do we have here?"

Marcia helped Jessica position the girl on the exam table. "Her name is Kayla. She said it's Kayla Hernandez," Marcia supplied when the child remained silent, staring at Jessica with large somber eyes brimming with tears. "She said she can't find her mother, Marina Hernandez," she added in a whisper.

Jessica hoped the child's mother was all right. She smoothed the matted hair back from Kayla's forehead and did another quick perusal, still not seeing any discernible injury. "How old are you, Kayla?"

"I'm five," the girl said, holding up her hand with all fingers and thumb spread. Then her lip trembled, and her eyes filled with more tears. "Where's my mommy?"

Jessica gave her a tissue and she blew her nose, while Jessica cast a questioning glance at Marcia. The nurse indicated with a slight shake of her head that she had no knowledge of the woman's whereabouts.

"I'm certain people are looking for your mother, but for now I'm going to listen to your heart and check your temperature, okay?"

She could handle this, Jessica told herself. After all, the little girl appeared fine, and she appealed to the powers that be that she wouldn't find any sign of internal injuries.

THE I-BEAM HURTLED toward Cal. His trajectory, swinging from the hoist rope as he was, would put him directly in the path of that beam. He caught an interior column with his right foot just enough to shove back and marginally away from the beam as it crashed by him.

A searing pain ripped through his right thigh, so intense he couldn't stifle a yell. He glanced down. The jeans he'd been wearing when he was called in were torn open and a deep, angry gouge welled with blood. He pressed a hand to his thigh in an attempt to ease the pain and control the flow of blood, but neither seemed to subside. Balancing unsteadily on the hoisting harness and trying not to jar his injured leg, he yanked off his T-shirt. He used it as a tourniquet for his leg. When he tightened it, the pain tore through him again.

The rumbling gradually subsided, and the building around him groaned as it settled. Cal held his breath, praying there'd be no further collapses. When it seemed the structure had stabilized, he gave the guywire a couple of tugs, hoping the firefighter was still up top and uninjured—and the hoisting mechanism was operational. When nothing happened, he tugged again.

After interminable minutes, he reached for his radio. If Adam had been hurt, he'd have to come clean with Command about what he'd done. Williams would be displeased but they'd send someone to get him out. There was no way he could climb up with his injured leg.

His movement caused the harness to tilt and he reflexively used his legs to balance himself. The pain that shot through him caused his body to jerk. He grabbed for the rope to keep from falling backward, and the radio went spiraling down to shatter on the ground.

Cal cursed himself as he waited for the agony to subside, and tried to assess his options. He couldn't jump down. He was over two stories up, and even with two good legs it would've been dangerous. With his right leg in such bad shape, he'd be breaking bones and probably his neck. He couldn't scale the rope, and there was nothing around him he could swing to, to help him climb up or down.

Without his radio, he was stuck with no way to communicate to the outside world.

Still, he'd have to try to pull himself up the rope somehow. There was no viable alternative. He had a strong upper body—thanks to rigorous workouts to stay in shape, a requirement for his job—but it was a long way up. He tested his strength by reaching up and pulling on the rope. If he got into the elevator shaft, which wasn't that far above him, he might be able to…

As he suddenly dropped three feet, he held on tight with both hands.

Twirling again from the force of the drop, he didn't know what to make of it. He was terrified to move. If his testing of the rope had caused the plunge, he didn't want to chance it again. He was still more than twenty feet above the ground. As he'd already concluded, it was unlikely he'd survive a twenty-foot drop.

When he felt the rope give again, he held on, closed his eyes and thought of Haley, certain he was about to fall to his death.

CHAPTER FOUR

CAL'S EYES FLEW open when he felt himself rising, slowly but steadily.

Holding the hoisting rope with his right hand, he used his left to keep himself from careening into protruding obstructions as he ascended through the elevator shaft. Soon he could see the night sky above and he was clearing the top of the shaft.

Adam was reaching for him. "Sorry, man. The aftershock caused a piece of siding to get stuck in the flywheel. I had to lower you manually and clear it before I could hoist you…" His rapid-fire speech halted as he steadied the harness and helped Cal balance on the roof. "What happened to your leg?"

"An I-beam." Cal looked around, saw Scout running toward him, unharmed. With a hand signal, he got him to drop down and hold his position. The last thing he needed right now was an enthusiastic greeting from his dog.

He looked at his thigh, too, as he carefully put most of his weight on his left leg. "I was able to get out of its way, or mostly. Otherwise, I'd be even more of a mess." Taking in the rusty marks on his blood-soaked jeans, he added, "It must've been a piece of rebar sticking out that sliced through me. How bad was the aftershock?"

"It could've been a lot worse, but it might not be the last. They've confirmed that the quake was a 7.6. No wonder we've had so much damage. Well, let's get you down and checked out." Adam threw his arm around Cal, and Scout followed at Cal's side.

"We're in for it," he said to Cal as he assisted him into the bucket of the articulated lift. "They know what we did. When the aftershock hit, I had to report in. This—" he pointed to Cal's thigh "—isn't going to help us. I don't think you'll be able to play the sympathy card. Williams is really pissed."

"Yeah, I bet."

The boom lowered Cal and Scout to street level. With no other way to get there, Adam helped Cal hobble over to the triage area on one leg. Excruciating pain shot through him each time his right leg moved, let alone if his foot inadvertently touched the ground. They advanced slowly, in stark contrast to other people still rushing around.

"Do you know how the little girl, Kayla, is?" Cal asked, head down, watching for trip hazards on the pavement as they neared the medical area.

"You can find out for yourself," he responded. "She's with a doctor right now."

Cal looked up and saw Kayla sitting on a makeshift examination table. The little girl held hands with an older woman who was crouched down in front of her and was obviously consoling her. Another woman in scrubs was examining her.

Kayla's clothes were filthy; her hair was matted and dirty and tucked behind her ears. But there was no denying whose daughter she was. In the overhead lights, he could see she was a miniature version of her very beautiful mother.

Cal wondered if they'd had a chance to contact her father yet. He hoped that knowing his daughter had survived would alleviate some of the grief the man would feel when he learned about the death of his wife. And Kayla had lost her mother. It occurred to Cal again that if he'd been the one to die, his little girl, Haley, wouldn't even know it.

As they approached the doctor, he really looked at her for the first time. He felt an immediate and visceral tightening in his gut. It astonished him, especially under the circumstances. The devastation around them, his severe pain and his view of relationships—yet there it was, no denying it.

She wasn't classically beautiful. Not like Kayla's mother. She was tall and lithe. On the slim side. Her face was a little longish, dominated by huge wide-set eyes; he couldn't discern the color. Her nose was average, her mouth perhaps a bit too wide. But there was something about her that just grabbed him and wouldn't let go. Then there was the hair. Pulled back in a ponytail, untidy and sweaty as it was, he could tell it was a thick, heavy, straw-colored mass.

The thoughts running through his mind made him suspect he'd hit his head without being aware of it. After Anna, he wasn't interested in women. His reaction to the doctor annoyed him, and it showed in his demeanor.

"How is she?" Cal asked irritably and without preamble as they reached the triage area. Silver-gray eyes shot up, the doctor's gaze meeting his.

JESSICA NARROWED HER eyes as she glared at the man standing before her, shirtless and leaning heavily on the shoulder of a firefighter. His simple question sounded both gruff and belligerent. Her gaze dropped to the well-muscled chest and arms, before sliding lower and seeing the makeshift tourniquet, understanding why he wasn't wearing a shirt. "Marcia," she called, keeping her eyes on the man but a steadying hand on the girl. "Can you please get Mr....?" She looked at the man inquiringly.

"Palmer. I'm a cop. Or just Calen. Or Cal."

"Marcia, please help *Officer* Palmer sit down and get the weight off that leg and check his vitals until I can see him."

"I asked how Kayla was," he repeated, unmoving.

At the sound of her name, the little girl looked up and her crying eased. Her eyes brightened for the first time since Jessica had seen her. "Cal," she squealed, twisting sideways and raising her skinny arms up for him.

He obliged her with a hug. "You're hurt," she exclaimed.

"It's nothing. I'll be fine," he said.

"Where's Mommy?" Kayla asked, trying to see around the cop.

"Let's worry about that later, okay?" he said evasively. "How're you?"

Jess was shocked by the complete transformation in his tone and deportment, but sadly she could see the answer to Kayla's question in his eyes.

"Dr. Hansen says I'll be fine." She reached back for Jessica's hand. Jess took it in her own and gave it a squeeze. For a moment, they formed a unit—linked through the child. For some reason, that realization made Jessica uncomfortable. She slid her hand out of Kayla's and placed it on the little girl's knee to get her attention.

"Yes, you'll be fine, Kayla. But just to make sure, I want you to go to the hospital. Get checked out. Okay?" She'd triaged Kayla as "delayed." Her injuries were likely relatively mild, concussion being the most serious concern, but she needed to be examined more thoroughly for possible internal injuries.

"Um. 'Kay. Will my mommy be there?"

Jessica met Cal's eyes again over the top of Kayla's head. The man was an enigma. His eyes were filled with anguish, and Jessica surmised that she'd been right—he knew more about Kayla's mother than he'd said. She was worried about how the girl would handle the bad news and wanted to postpone it, at least until she had family with her. "We'll see," she murmured, and rethought her course of action. "But Mrs. Rodrigues," she said, turning to Marcia, "will go with you. How about that?"

"Okay." Kayla sounded unsure. "Can Cal come with me, too?"

"Unfortunately not." When Kayla's lower lip protruded, Jessica rushed on. "I need to examine him, too." Jessica looked at Calen's injured leg and Kayla's gaze followed. She saw the distress on the little girl's face and drew Kayla's attention back to her. "But you might see Officer Palmer there. And Marcia—Mrs. Rodrigues—will be with you."

"But…" Marcia began, and Jessica turned imploring eyes on her.

"I know what you're going to say." Jessica spoke in a hushed whisper. "We're not finished here yet. Well, we nearly are." She touched Marcia's arm. "And this little girl needs you." She dropped her voice even further. "If the cop's face is any indication, she just lost her mother."

Jess could see Marcia's internal struggle. It showed in every line of her face, in the depth of her eyes. She understood that Marcia probably feared she was getting too involved with this child. But how could she not? Kayla's mother had almost certainly died in the earthquake.

"Please," she entreated.

"Fine."

Kayla was still grasping Jessica's hand and didn't seem to want to let go. Jess gave her hand a tug. "You're going to the hospital now, and Mrs. Rodrigues will go with you. The doctors there will do some tests, but Mrs. Rodrigues will stay with you the whole time." She looked at Marcia, who nodded resignedly.

"And my mommy?"

"Let's get you taken care of first, okay?"

"Will you be there? Will you do the tests at the hospital?"

"No, I won't, but if you're still there when I get back, I'll come see you." Jessica could have bitten off her tongue the minute the

words were out of her mouth, and she could
see the disapproval on Marcia's face. She
would *not* see Kayla at the hospital. She was
a trauma surgeon. She'd chosen that field so
she could treat patients and then be done. No
attachment. No follow-up.

Kayla nodded. She hugged Cal again, and
let Marcia lead her away.

Jessica turned to her next and apparently
last patient, the man leaning heavily on the
firefighter who'd helped him to the triage
area. At first she'd wondered if he might
have been Kayla's father, but she'd quickly
dismissed that thought. If he was, he would've
said so. He was injured, but she sensed that
wasn't all that contributed to his surliness. A
hard day all around, she supposed.

She took in his tall, muscular frame, his
brown hair, ocean-green eyes, the jeans and
absence of a shirt, the strong face with the
slightly crooked nose, the frowning mouth.
She noticed the dog by his side for the first
time. She loved dogs and knew them well,
having grown up with them. This one was a
beauty. A near-black shepherd, although his
coat was covered in dust. From the size of
him, probably a king shepherd, with large

paws and alert, intelligent, appraising eyes. He had to be a police dog.

"You're next." Jessica gestured to the cop to sit on her exam table.

The firefighter helped Cal shuffle over. "I guess I'll be seeing you later over that…matter that'll need to be addressed," he said.

Jessica saw the cop's expression soften again as he patted the firefighter on the back. "Don't worry about it, Adam. I'll take care of it." He held out his hand. "Thanks," he said as they shook hands.

The moment the cop turned his attention back to her, Jessica felt uncharacteristically self-conscious in her baggy scrubs. The anger was back in his eyes, but Jessica had no idea why she seemed to elicit hostility from him. It had to be her, though, since there'd been no sign of it when he'd interacted with the girl or the firefighter.

Her only concern with the cop, she reminded herself, was dealing with his leg wound and getting him to the hospital. She snapped on a new pair of thin blue gloves. "How did this happen?" she asked briskly. If he could have an attitude, so could she.

"As I said, I'm a cop." He pointed to the dog. "Scout and I were part of the rescue team."

Jessica checked Cal's vitals, as Marcia hadn't had a chance to do it, and focused on his injury. The wound looked bad. He had every right to be angry, she decided. Tired, too. She wasn't feeling much friendlier herself. She'd been at it for hours now, all through the night, and the number of injured was significant. That could excuse his surliness, but it didn't explain why it seemed to be directed at her.

"You rescued Kayla?"

He nodded.

Jessica turned to the tray behind her for a pair of scissors. "Kayla's mother died in the quake, didn't she?" She turned back in time and knew the answer before he vocalized it. She saw the sorrow flash across his face, cloud his eyes. Jessica met a lot of cops as a trauma unit doctor and while taking shifts in the emergency room. She knew it was a hard job and they saw unimaginable horrors, and yet she worried most about the ones who seemed to have become hardened against it. This one didn't look like a rookie, but he wasn't calloused, either.

"And the father?" she asked as she removed

the makeshift tourniquet around his thigh and began to cut away the soiled denim. She tried to sound casual, all the while berating herself. Here she was, still worried about Kayla, and she knew too well what that could lead to.

Cal shrugged. "No idea."

"Okay." Jessica tried to force Kayla out of her mind. The little girl would probably be gone by the time she got to the hospital and she'd never see her again. That was the way she wanted it. "How did this happen?" She repeated her earlier question as she continued to cut away the jeans, noting the dirt and rust stains on the denim. "Exactly?"

Cal gave her a short account.

Jessica paused, glanced at the beautiful German shepherd sitting quietly next to the table, completely focused, not missing a thing. She found herself reassessing her opinion of the cop. "You went back into the building following the aftershock to get your dog?"

Cal leaned over to drop a hand possessively on Scout's head. "I needed to ascertain Kayla's mother's condition, too, but yeah. Scout's my partner. I couldn't leave him. By the way, do you have any water I can give him?"

"Sure." Jess considered the tough exterior

of the cop as she poured some water into a plastic container. He came across as harsh and surly, but he clearly cared about kids and dogs.

She'd worked with enough cops to know that police dogs were considered a tool by the department, and she'd never understood how their handlers could spend so much time with their dogs and think of them that way. Obviously this cop didn't. There had to be a soft center under that hard shell.

She expected she'd have done the same thing. Gone after the dog, if he was hers. But then again, she tended to lead with her heart. That had been her downfall as a pediatric surgeon, and likely would've made her a lousy cop, too.

With the full shift she'd put in at the hospital before she was called out to the field, she was worn out. It was hardly surprising that her mind kept wandering; still, she needed to focus.

She had to clean the wound and apply a temporary dressing for pressure before she sent the cop off to the hospital. He'd probably gotten dirt and rust deep in the wound, and that concerned her. She'd clean it the best she could, but he'd have to be looked at. They were out of local anesthetic in the field because they'd treated so many people. As nasty as the wound was, she had to clean it. She knew it would hurt, but she couldn't wait until fresh supplies arrived.

"How'd you break your nose?" she asked, trying to distract him as she peeled back more of the denim that was stuck to his leg.

"It happened when I was a kid," he responded tersely.

"How?" she persisted.

"I was teaching my brother karate."

"Yeah?" She wanted to keep him talking.

"I was showing him how to split a board. Frankly, he sucked at it. Drew was always a geek." She detected the smile in his voice, but the affection, too. "I was holding the board for him when our mother called us for lunch." He chuckled. "I lowered my arms. Drew took his shot. For once his aim was right on, and he connected with my nose, where the board would have been."

When she glanced up at him, he was grinning. There wasn't any resentment, which surprised her. The hard, angular lines of his face were transformed by the appealing, almost boyish smile. She was tempted to shake her head. She must really be exhausted if she was thinking how attractive one of her patients was. "You're kidding?"

"No. It's true."

Jess raised an eyebrow, but went back to her task. "This is going to hurt," she cautioned. "There's not much I can do about it. We're out of anesthetic." She looked up again. His smile had faded, and he nodded. He knew what was coming and seemed ready for it.

Even so, as soon as she started to clean the wound with the iodine-based cleanser, he threw his head back and groaned loudly.

At Cal's obvious agony, the big dog sprang up and let out a throaty, menacing growl directed at her. It all happened so fast. Cal was still absorbed by the pain and hadn't noticed, but Jess was well aware that most police dogs were trained to protect their handlers. That was obviously what the shepherd was intent on doing. If she showed fear or appeared to be a threat, she suspected the dog would attack her. She only had an instant to consider. She took a step toward the dog, drawing her shoulders back. The dog bristled, growled and stood his ground but didn't advance.

Calm, assertive, she reminded herself. "Sit," she ordered in a no-nonsense voice, using her hand to reinforce the command. The dog glanced over at Cal, who was still preoccupied with his pain. The dog cocked his head and hesitated, but Jessica didn't back down. He made an oddly human huffing sound. Still alert, still on guard, he nonetheless obeyed her command and plopped down. His eyes remained watchful and trained on Jess.

Jessica exhaled. The dog must not have perceived her as an imminent threat to the cop, or he wouldn't have listened to her. Still, she was relieved that she hadn't been attacked by him in the process. He was a beautiful dog, but large and she had no doubt those shiny white teeth could mean business if he was provoked.

Turning her attention back to Cal, she saw astonishment on his face, and something else. Could it be respect from the cantankerous cop?

He eyed his dog. The dog angled his head and waited. "Down," he ordered, then looked back at Jessica. "I can't believe he responded to you. How did you do that?"

She couldn't resist the small smile that tugged at the corners of her lips. "He's your dog. You tell me."

The dog was lying down with his head between his outstretched paws, shifting his gaze back and forth between the two of them. "Obviously he didn't think you intended to hurt me," he murmured.

"I'd appreciate it if you could assure him of that. I'm going to continue to clean your wound, and I wouldn't want him to get the wrong idea."

"Scout, stay. Friend," he added.

"Now can we get back to this, if... Scout, is it?"

He nodded.

"If Scout doesn't object?"

Jessica worked quickly and efficiently to clean the wound and apply a temporary dressing. She tried not to be distracted by the large dog. She could see from her peripheral vision that he was watching her every move. She'd shown him who was alpha, but he was the cop's dog, and based on his earlier reaction, she supposed he'd protect his handler if he thought she was hurting him. She was glad the cop was taking her ministrations stoically, and was thankful he handled the pain as well as could be expected. She didn't want to test her mettle against his dog again. She knew he must have been in excruciating pain while she cleaned the wound, but after the initial outcry, the only sounds he made were deep hissing breaths during the worst of it. She didn't take the time to look up at him, but she could see his white-knuckled grip on the edge of the table.

"We're done here," Jessica said as she applied a bandage to Cal's leg, tossed the blood-stained cloths into the waste receptacle and took off her gloves.

"Great. Thanks," Cal said through gritted teeth as he slid off the table to balance on his left leg.

Jessica placed her palm lightly on his chest. "Not so fast." She shouldn't have been surprised at how firm his chest felt under her fingers. She was tempted to keep her hand there, but pulled it back quickly.

"Why?" Cal asked, testing to see if he could put weight on his right leg, only to wince and nearly collapse.

Jessica gave him a humorless smile. "Well, that, for one. I doubt you'll be able to put weight on that leg for the foreseeable future. It's not just a surface wound. It's a fairly deep soft-tissue injury. I wouldn't rule out that you might have chipped some bone, too. Worst-case scenario, you might have fractured your femur. In any case, you'll need crutches, and you'll have to stay off the leg for at least a couple of weeks."

Cal threw her an annoyed look but she continued. "Secondly, you need to go to the hospital. Not just for an X-ray to determine if there is a fracture. The rebar that gouged you was dirty and rusty. I cleaned your wound as well as I could here, but it'll have to be cleaned more thoroughly and there's no telling whether some of the rust and dirt might have gotten into your bloodstream. That would mean you'll—"

"Yeah. I know. Have to watch for sepsis."

Jessica nodded. "Correct. So, you'll be making a trip to the hospital."

She could feel him watching her as she made notations on the chart.

"I don't have time to go to the hospital."

She raised her eyes and gave him her best authoritative look. "Before you argue that point, tell me when you had your last tetanus shot?"

"Cops have to get regular shots. You should know that."

"I do, but that doesn't answer my question." Since there was no reply, Jessica glanced up again.

"I don't know. A few years back."

Having completed the charting, she put down the clipboard. "Would a few be more or less than five years?"

Cal threw his hands skyward in annoyance. Scout immediately sat up, ears pricked. Cal sent him a hand signal and calmed himself. "I don't have time for this. I have work to do."

"Unless you want serious complications, you *will* make the time." Cal's brows drew together in a menacing V. Before he could say anything, she raised a hand. "I wouldn't send you to the hospital if it wasn't absolutely necessary. We're going to be swamped, and I want to make sure we provide care to those who need it most. You understand the triage process, correct?"

The V deepened, but he nodded.

"I triaged you as 'urgent.' You know that means you need medical attention at Ocean

Crest, for treatment, stiches and—if you can't be more specific about when you had your last one—a tetanus shot, as well. Finally, I want X-rays. As deep as that wound is and based on how it occurred, as I said I can't discount a possible hairline fracture of your femur."

"Okay. I get it." He reached into his pocket and pulled out his keys.

"You can't be serious!"

"What?"

"You're planning to drive yourself to the hospital?" She was incredulous.

"Yeah," he responded, hesitancy in his voice. "I can drive." He sounded a bit like a petulant child.

"Right. Try again to put some weight on that leg. Your *right* leg, I might add."

Cal's brows remained furrowed and he kept his eyes on hers—the green even brighter now than when she'd first locked eyes with him. She knew the instant he put some weight on the right leg, because he squeezed his eyes closed and his mouth formed a hard, straight line.

She reached out to steady him as he wobbled. "You were saying?" A hint of humor crept into her voice. She couldn't help being a little smug. She was tired, cranky—and she was only human. "I know you're a tough guy, but even you have your limits. Here's an ambulance now. They'll take you." She signaled to the paramedic.

"Wait. What about Scout? They won't let me take him in the ambulance, will they?"

Jessica frowned. She hadn't thought of that. "No. That's not possible."

"I can't leave him in my vehicle. It's going to heat up again. It's got a temperature-activated cooling system, but during the time I'll be in the hospital, the truck will likely run out of gas and power." He reached for the holster on his belt and found it empty. He looked around, apparently searching for someone. Police department personnel and other first responders at the site were still rushing around, all of them occupied in dealing with the aftermath of the earthquake.

He looked back at Jessica. "I need help."

"You just had it. The hospital needs to take over now."

"No. That's not what I mean. Not medical aid. I need your help with Scout."

She bent down, let Scout sniff her hand. "May I?" she asked. When Cal nodded, she rubbed his head. "In what way?"

"Well, I can't take him to the hospital with me. I can't leave him in my truck here in this heat. I lost my radio in the building and, as you can see, everyone from the department is busy." He made a sweeping motion toward where the frenetic activity still continued. "I can't impose on them."

Jessica continued to stroke Scout but looked up at Cal. "What about someone else? A volunteer, maybe? Someone who lives close by? A friend?" She broke eye contact and turned her attention back to Scout. "Aren't you a handsome boy," she murmured. "So smart and handsome."

"It won't work," he said, replying to her question. "Police dogs have their behavioral idiosyncrasies due to their specialized training. They need firm alpha handlers. Scout's no different. I only moved here recently. Besides the other cops, I don't have friends close enough for me to turn to." He was silent for a moment. "How about you?"

Jessica glanced up at Cal. "Me? What about me?"

"Would you take Scout until I'm done at the hospital?"

"That's impossible."

"You said you were finished here." A smile spread across his face, and Jessica felt an uncharacteristic pull of attraction. That was totally inappropriate with a patient, she chastised herself.

"You've already proven you can handle Scout," Cal continued. "And Scout's demonstrated that he's willing to accept commands from you." He chuckled. "Not a common occurrence for a police dog."

Jessica straightened. At her full height and in her comfortable work flats, she was only a few inches shorter than the cop. She gaped at him. "You're asking me to take Scout *home* with me?"

The smile faded. "Well, you're not giving me a lot of options, Doc, triaging me as 'urgent.' So, yeah."

She started to shake her head, but he broke in before she could speak. "I have no other alternative on such short notice. You triaged me, treated me and said I have to go to the hospital. If I can't get someone to take care of Scout, that's not happening. I'll just have to drive myself and Scout home, using my left leg."

She'd been working the better part of nineteen hours now. She just wanted to get a few hours' sleep before she was due back at the hospital. She didn't have time to deal with a rude, pushy cop. Jessica was tempted to call his bluff, but then she remembered what had gotten Cal into this predicament to begin with. He had saved people, including the little girl, Kayla. He'd risked his own life to rescue Scout. If he cared that much about his dog, she had no doubt that he'd follow through on his threat and try to drive. If anything happened to him and the dog as a consequence, she would blame herself. She swiped impatiently at her bangs to get them out of her eyes.

She nearly agreed, then realized what she was about to do. Get personally involved and care too much about another patient. Granted, this patient wasn't a child. And, okay, it was actually the patient's dog. But she was a trauma doc. Her job was done. Cal could figure out what to do himself. It seemed impossible that he didn't have anyone to turn to, someone from the police department certainly, but it wasn't her problem.

Then Cal gave a soft command to Scout. "Ask nicely."

To Jessica's astonishment, the big dog sat back on his haunches and raised his forelegs in the air. He crossed his front paws, tilted his head and whined in a manner that sounded a lot like "Please."

Jessica chuckled. "That'll get the bad guys to drop their guns and surrender."

"Just wait. Scout, say your prayers."

The dog bowed his head, and covered his eyes with his front paws.

Jessica laughed outright.

"How can you say no to that?"

Jessica crouched down again and scratched Scout's ears. "I'm sure I'm going to regret this, but okay."

CHAPTER FIVE

CAL RESIGNED HIMSELF to the fact that he had to go to the hospital and needed to be transported by ambulance. The doc had been right; there was no way he could drive. He couldn't even touch the ground with his right foot without agony. Since there were no crutches available, one of the paramedics had to help him hop over to the ambulance. Getting in the vehicle was no easy feat, either.

"Hell of a night," the paramedic commented to Cal as they made their way through the broken streets to Ocean Crest Hospital. The sun had just started to rise.

"Yeah." Cal gazed out the window. He absorbed the chaos and destruction around them as they sped toward the hospital. Having lost his radio in the building, he hadn't been able to hear the reports. Now he listened to the scanner in the ambulance as the salient facts were recounted.

The Rose Canyon Fault ran in a north-south direction through San Diego County. But it had never been a major concern, to the best of his knowledge, because San Diego was relatively low risk for earthquakes. The fault was known to be capable of generating a 7.0 magnitude quake, with 8.0 at its upper range.

The quake they'd experienced was nearly at the fault's limit. Cal knew that anything above 7.0 was considered a major earthquake, likely to cause serious damage. Anything over 8.0 could totally destroy communities near its epicenter.

As he continued to survey the damage, he could readily grasp how extensive it was. Even so, it could've been worse. There could've been a lot more damage…and many more casualties. The quake had been felt across great distances—as far away as Los Angeles, he'd heard—with damage mostly limited to a hundred and fifty miles from the epicenter. And the death toll? An update stated it could have been in the tens of thousands, but they'd been fortunate to have had reported fatalities of less than a hundred.

And Cal had found one of those. He thought of Kayla and wondered who would tell the little girl that her mother was gone. Would it be the doc who'd treated both of them?

He couldn't remember having the sort of reaction to a woman that he'd had to the doctor, not in a long time. Very long, in fact, as it would've been before he was married to Anna. He'd barely looked at a woman since Anna blindsided him by leaving, taking Haley with her. His brother, Andrew, kept telling him he had "trust issues." It almost made him laugh. You didn't have to be a genius to figure *that* out or what had caused it.

He realized he'd been unpleasant to the doctor and she'd done nothing to provoke it. He supposed it had been a combination of the day he'd had and an involuntary defense mechanism against his attraction. Even with his nasty attitude, the doc had agreed to take care of Scout. He had to hand it to her. He didn't think he would've been as magnanimous if their roles were reversed. He reached into his pocket to make sure the slip of paper with her cell phone number was there, then tried to block both Dr. Jessica Hansen and his daughter, Haley, out of his mind. Instead, he focused on the havoc around them.

Although Cal was a seasoned police officer, a ten-year veteran of the Narcotics Unit of the Lincoln Police Department in Nebraska, he was relatively new to the San Diego Police Department. In his short time with the SDPD, he and Scout had successfully concluded a variety of searches involving missing children, lost hikers and wandering hospital patients. They enjoyed what they did and worked well together, but he hadn't expected to deal with a catastrophe of this magnitude. What should have been a relatively quick drive to Ocean Crest was taking quite a while because of the damage from the earthquake and resulting traffic jams. With time on his hands, he let his mind wander back to what had brought him here to begin with.

Cal had a beautiful five-year-old daughter, Haley, and he'd been happily married—or so he'd thought. He'd been thrown for a loop—stunned, really—when Anna had announced over a year ago that she could no longer tolerate being the wife of a cop. Maybe the trigger had made sense, since her declaration was prompted by the ransacking of their home by an associate of a drug dealer Cal had been instrumental in apprehending. Fortunately, Haley and Anna weren't home at the time, but the occurrence had pushed Anna over the edge. She wanted out of the marriage. Even so, Cal could never have foreseen the sequence of events that resulted in an internal police investigation of his conduct—and all ties with his little girl severed. Anna had not just taken Haley, but had turned their daughter against him.

He'd felt angry, bitter and alone, and that hadn't changed in the time since. The last thing he'd wanted during the year that had passed was another relationship. No wonder he'd reacted the way he had to the doctor after feeling that treacherous pull of attraction.

The messy split from his ex-wife had left Cal swearing off relationships. And the internal police investigation into his conduct caused him anger and disillusionment with his job. So he'd resigned from the Lincoln Police Department and relocated to San Diego, for no other reason than this was where his brother, Andrew, a schoolteacher, lived. He hadn't much cared where he went. With no hope of seeing Haley in the near term, he just wanted to start a new and solitary life.

With Cal's experience and solid references, the San Diego Police Department offered him the position of sergeant in their Narcotics Unit, but Cal had had enough of that area of policing. He'd worked closely with the narcotics dogs in Lincoln and he'd actually started his career in search and rescue; because of that, he accepted a lower-ranking position as a search-and-rescue officer in the department's K-9 Unit. The role suited him well, he mused. With his recent experiences he'd come to prefer animals to people.

The morose thinking had him in a nasty mood again by the time they reached the hospital.

The paramedic got him settled in a wheelchair and turned him over to the emergency room staff. Based on his condition and the site doc's assessment, he was fast-tracked.

Since the medical staff had cut off what had been left of his jeans, a nurse was kind enough to give him a pair of scrubs. Lavender might not have been his color of choice, but it was better than parading around in his underwear.

When they were done with him, he gingerly pulled on the scrubs. Loose though they were, he still winced when the light cotton brushed across his bandaged right thigh. He toyed with the crutches before leaving the treatment room. On his way out the front door he halted, remembering he didn't have his truck. It was still at the scene of the earthquake.

He mumbled an expletive and hobbled back to the information counter. The young blonde gave him a big smile as he approached. He didn't have the time or the inclination for her flirting. He asked her, in a less than pleasant manner, to call him a cab. Her smile faded and, perhaps not surprisingly, she seemed to get some satisfaction out of telling him that because of the earthquake, it might take up to forty minutes for the taxi to arrive. With a brittle smirk, she suggested he have a seat in the waiting area, and pointed to a grouping of uncomfortable-looking plastic chairs. He was about to move away when he pivoted back.

"One more thing."

"Yes?" the receptionist asked without enthusiasm.

"A little girl was brought here from the earthquake site. Shortly before I was."

"You'll have to be a bit more specific."

"Her name's Kayla." He lapsed into cop mode. "She's approximately three feet five inches, near-black hair, dark brown eyes. Probably four or five years old."

The woman had turned to her computer but looked at him expectantly. "May I have her last name?"

"Oh." He searched his memory. He hadn't asked, but thought back to when he was waiting in the triage area. "Ah... Rodrigues? No, that was the nurse. Hernandez? Yes, it's Hernandez."

"Are you family?"

"No."

"Then I'm sorry, but—"

"I'm a cop," he interrupted. "I brought her out of the building that collapsed on her." His explanation seemed to mollify the woman. "I just want to make sure she's okay."

"Let me check...yes, she's here. She's been admitted...oh..."

"Is there a problem?"

"I was just checking family..." She looked up at Cal with a woeful expression.

"Are you saying they haven't located any?"

The woman nodded.

"Can you tell me which room she's in?" He gave her a brief smile. "It seems I have some time on my hands."

Her smile wavered. "Pediatric ward. Room 4-235. The elevators are down the hall and to your left."

As Cal shuffled in the direction the blonde had indicated, he felt discomfort in his chest and, with every step, a sharp pain in his shoulder.

He realized he must have sustained injuries beyond the obvious. Soft-tissue damage to his shoulder, probably when he'd hit the parapet wall on the rooftop, and maybe a cracked rib or two. Not much could be done about either, he mused as he adjusted his crutch to ease the pain.

He took the elevator to the fourth floor and found room 235. It contained four beds; three were occupied. The one closest to the door had a curtain drawn around it and Cal heard the murmur of voices. A girl, with her head, face and left arm bandaged, lay in the bed adjacent to it, her eyes closed. A man and woman clustered in chairs close to the bed, the woman holding the child's hand. The man looked up at Cal, his face ravaged and grief-stricken, before turning to his daughter again.

On the farthest bed, next to the window, was Kayla. She had tubes and monitors attached to her. Other than that, she looked healthy and uninjured. Someone must have brushed the dust out of her hair, which was spread out, glistening, across her pillow. She wore a pink hospital gown with a teddy-bear print. Her head was turned away from him, toward the window. He could see her small chest rise rhythmically with her breathing.

Although they were complete opposites in appearance, watching Kayla brought back painful memories of his own sweet Haley. He took a step into the room, then hesitated. If Kayla was asleep, he didn't want to wake her. As he debated what to do, she turned her head. Quiet dark eyes met his.

"Cal," she said softly. "You hurt your leg. Are you okay?"

He limped to her bedside. "Yeah. I'll be fine. More importantly, how are you?"

She gave a shrug. Examined the hand with the IV tube inserted. "Okay, I guess." She shifted her gaze to meet his. "Did you find Mommy, like you said?"

Cal didn't know what to say. His instinct was to see if there were nurses or doctors around, but he knew they couldn't help.

Kayla spoke again before he had a chance to answer. "Mommy's gone, isn't she?"

There was something achingly wise in her deep brown eyes, and she sounded much older than her years. Cal rested one crutch against the footboard and took Kayla's hand in his. "Yes, she is. I'm sorry."

"I don't have a daddy," Kayla said matter-of-factly. A quiver in her lower lip was her only show of emotion. "Can I live with you, Cal?"

"Ah… I don't think that would work."

"Then who will I live with now?"

CAL SAT IN the back of the taxi on his way home. He stared out the window, but all he could think of was Kayla's small serious face, and the plaintive question she'd voiced. She hadn't cried; she hadn't broken down. She'd simply stared at him, waiting for an answer he couldn't provide.

She said she didn't have a father, and he wondered if that was true, or if he was absent from her life the way Cal was from Haley's. If it was the former, where *would* she live? he wondered. She must have other family.

Since he wasn't related to her, the nurse

wouldn't tell him what Kayla's condition was, but he knew they'd admitted her for observation.

He tried to convince himself that it wasn't his concern, and yet he couldn't get her out of his mind the entire way home.

Damn, he hadn't realized how many steps there were up to his front porch. He didn't want to even think about trying to navigate the longer set of back steps down to the beach. Not that he'd be doing a lot of walking on the beach for a while...

He let himself inside, grateful to be home, and almost tripped over a rubber bone Scout had left lying on the hallway floor. One crutch clattered to the ground as he braced himself against the wall. Now he had to figure out how to pick up his crutch, balancing on his left leg, while trying not to bend his right. He gritted his teeth as he retrieved the crutch. He hated the feeling of uselessness.

Then the image of Kayla, lying in the hospital bed so pale and serious, crowded out his self-pity. The child would never see her mother again.

He hoped the doc knew what she was

doing and that she was right about Kayla being okay.

As he lay down on his bed for a moment to catch his breath, not bothering to take the scrubs off, it was Jessica he thought of as he drifted into sleep.

JESSICA CHECKED HER WATCH. Over twenty hours had passed since she'd started her shift at Ocean Crest. There was nothing more for her to do at the site. It was time to go home. She'd clean up and get a few hours' sleep, then head back to the hospital. She knew it would be crazy busy there, and not only with the patients they'd sent from the triage site. There were bound to be many more people injured by the earthquake and its aftermath who would've gotten to the hospital by other means.

She glanced at the dog, Scout. Even dirty, he was a very handsome animal. He looked much like a North American German shepherd, but there were slight differences. He was a little larger, his coat darker. His markings were similar to a shepherd's, although there was more black than brown in him. His paws were huge.

He gazed back at her, an assessing look in his chocolate-brown eyes. She imagined that with his darker-than-normal coloring, his nearly black face and his intense eyes, many people would've been intimidated by him. To her, he seemed smart and lovable.

She sensed that Scout was not only highly intelligent but had a great temperament. Although his leash was tied around a post, he'd sat quietly from the time the cop had said goodbye to him, while she checked on the other doctors and gave instructions.

She unwound the leash and gave Scout a heel command, which worked really well. She thought about his handler as she walked to her car. The cop was tall and striking. She couldn't deny that she'd been attracted to him. That had surprised her, since looks weren't the only or even the most essential aspect for her in terms of appeal. He was a perfect example of the old adage that looks were skin-deep. He'd immediately put her off with his bad-tempered attitude, even before she realized he'd be off-limits because he was a patient.

She and Scout reached her car, and she rolled her eyes. She must have been overtired, because she hadn't considered how she'd get Scout in her yellow Miata convertible. A gorgeous but dirty dog, a cranky cop and a little car she loved and kept in pristine condition. Not the best combination.

What had she gotten herself into?

CHAPTER SIX

JESSICA LET SCOUT explore her fenced backyard after she'd brushed most of the dirt off
him and cleaned his paws. Taking him inside, she placed the bag of dog food and toys
she'd bought on the counter, and instructed
Scout to sit-stay until she unhooked his leash,
then released him. Scout made a beeline for
her living room. She laughed as she watched
the dog, with his nose in the air and then to
the ground by turns, doing what she assumed
was a search of her premises. He moved fast
and didn't seem to miss an inch. "No!" she
yelled and rushed over when he effortlessly
leaped up on her cream-colored sofa. "Off,"
she commanded, but it had no effect, since
Scout was intent on digging between the seat
cushions.

"Off," she repeated more emphatically, and
grabbed his collar to guide him to the floor.
He resisted briefly, his head buried between

two cushions. When he hopped back down and sat, he had a small article of clothing in his mouth. Jessica was organized and efficient at work, but had never been particularly neat at home. With her hectic work schedule, she didn't always have time to put things away—and Scout seemed to have found evidence of that.

On closer examination, what he had in his mouth proved to be a sweatband she'd used for playing tennis; she hadn't seen it for quite a while. "I wondered what had happened to that."

She knew enough not to start a potential tug-of-war with a dog, especially a strong-willed one. Instead, she held out her hand and went through a series of commands she thought might get him to drop the sweatband. None of them worked.

"What would the command be to get that out of..." Jessica mused, but she didn't have to speculate for long. Scout dropped the sweatband into her palm. Jessica laughed. "I guess the command is 'Out.'"

She glanced at her formerly spotless sofa, now covered with brown and black fur. "At least your paws were clean," she said with a sigh.

A little more cautiously, she let him familiarize himself with the rest of her house. She'd managed to keep him off the furniture until he tore into the bedroom ahead of her and vaulted up onto her bed. By the time she got to him, he was standing on the middle of her mattress, legs comically spread for balance, her duvet bunched around him, and the sleep shirt she kept under her pillow grasped in his mouth.

He looked so darn adorable she couldn't be mad at him. Besides, her shirt was a practical cotton, wash and wear, so there was no harm done. At least now she knew the commands. A firm "Off" followed by "Out" had the desired effect of getting him to hop down and release her shirt into her hand.

She chuckled at herself for praising him, but she knew he was only doing what he'd been trained to do. She also knew how important positive reinforcement was for animals. She expected that, as a police dog, he was constantly training and retraining with his handler. Which brought to mind a new question. What was she supposed to do with him while she was at work, if the cop hadn't reclaimed him by then?

And that got her thinking about the cop again... She couldn't fault his looks or his height. At her five feet ten inches, few men towered over her, even when she wasn't wearing heels. The cop had. She was sure she'd blushed when he'd first walked up to the triage area without a shirt. Judging by the heat on her cheeks right now, she'd bet she was blushing again.

She was a *doctor*, for heaven's sake, and accustomed to seeing men without their clothes. She'd always maintained a very professional air—a strong code of ethics—and she'd never found herself dwelling on whether a male patient was attractive or not. They were *patients*. But she'd noticed Calen Palmer as a man first, before her professional assessment had overridden that reaction. And what she'd noticed was a very fit, very attractive man. When their eyes met, his had been intense, assessing. Uncomfortably so.

She hadn't even had a chance to examine his injury before the surly attitude came out.

He'd been irritable, bordering on rude. It was off-putting, to say the least.

But he'd gone back into a building to save his canine partner. That said a lot about his loyalty...and compassion. And he seemed to care about the little girl, Kayla, too. Those two aspects of the man appealed to her and were at odds with the manner in which he'd treated her. An enigma, she thought again. And that intrigued her. She didn't have to wonder if she'd see him again, since she had his dog. That made her smile.

The exhaustion finally caught up with her. All she wanted to do was crawl into bed for a few hours and bury her head under her pillow. Her practical side told her to take a shower to wash off all the grime first, have a bite to eat and then get the sleep she craved.

She started with the shower. When she was back downstairs in her kitchen and making a sandwich, her cell phone rang.

"This is Calen Palmer," a deep voice announced when she answered.

The cop. Good thing she'd remembered to write down her cell number before he left in the ambulance.

"I've been released from the hospital," he continued.

"How did things go?"

"As well as could be expected, I suppose." His tone wasn't as antagonistic as it had been earlier. There was more frustration than anger in it. "I'll need to be off work for a couple of weeks."

That didn't surprise her, based on the nature of his injury and the demands of his job. In fact, two weeks was optimistic. She was tempted to ask diagnostic questions. Did they do an X-ray? Was he given a tetanus booster? Did they prescribe the appropriate antibiotics and painkiller? But she stopped herself. She might have triaged him; however, he wasn't her patient anymore. Her responsibility for his care had ended when she'd handed him off to the paramedic. That was the beauty of being a trauma doctor. No long-term attachments to patients. Rapid assessment and immediate treatment. Discharge or transfer to another area, and she was done. Her interest in his well-being was nonclinical. She just wanted to know when she could return Scout to him. "I'm sorry you'll have to be off work," she finally said.

She watched Scout sniff under a wall unit, crouch down and dig under it with his front paws, until he tugged out a sneaker. He sniffed at it for a moment, then picked it up, turned in a tight circle and lay down, one paw draped protectively over his prize. Jessica stifled a laugh.

"I saw the little girl, Kayla, while I was in the hospital," Cal said, interrupting her thoughts. "She seems to be okay."

"Ah..." That threw her off balance. She'd been trying to put Kayla out of her own mind. She'd assumed he'd ask about his dog, not the child. "There are still some tests that need to be done but they're precautionary. If all goes well, there's no real medical reason to keep her..."

"You can't just release her. Where's she going to go?" The belligerence was back and it annoyed her. Who was *he* to tell her what to do with a patient? Even if his sentiment was perfectly in tune with hers. Technically, Kayla was no longer under her care, but she'd called Allison Hartford, head of pediatrics, and discussed Kayla's case with her; she'd been clear about her recommendations concerning the child's care. Knowing Jessica's history, Allison hadn't sounded pleased about her involvement. Jessica had to acknowledge that it wasn't wise, but it was done.

"If you'd let me finish," she said in an emphatic, professional, no-nonsense tone. "There might be no clear medical reason. However, my recommendation was to keep her for observation for a few days regardless. As I said, she should have some tests run. Just to be certain…and because Social Services hasn't been able to locate Kayla's father or any other family so far. Is that acceptable to you?" she added sarcastically.

There was a moment's pause. "I deserved that. Sorry." His voice didn't sound apologetic, but she'd take the words at face value.

"And Scout? Has he given you any trouble?"

Now she did laugh as she watched the dog, his snout stuck in her shoe, one paw still over it. "I wouldn't say trouble. He found a sweatband I'd misplaced months ago. It was lodged between the cushions of my sofa. And now he's found a tennis shoe. I have no idea how it ended up where it was." She thought of her light-colored sofa covered in coarse dark hair. "He did remind me, though, that dark-furred dogs and light-colored furniture aren't an ideal combination."

She heard him chuckle. Unexpected, perhaps, but she liked the sound.

"I'm grateful to you for taking him. Now that I'm done at the hospital, I can pick him up anytime that's convenient for you."

"I don't think so."

"Pardon me?"

"How are you going to get here?"

"I... Good point. I keep forgetting I can't drive. I should've thought of that."

The frustration was back in his voice. "I'll call my brother and ask him to drive me, if you'll give me your address."

Not sure why, she suddenly felt sorry for the tough cop. She doubted he was the type to rely on others very often, but he'd have to get used to it, at least for the next couple of weeks. "No need to bother him. If you're okay waiting a few hours while I get some sleep, I'll drop Scout off. I can do it before I go to work this afternoon."

"Are you sure it's not a problem?"

She sensed she'd been right about his reluctance to accept help, despite having badgered her into looking after Scout for a while. Those had been extraordinary circumstances, though. "Not any more than having him here." She couldn't resist the jab. "Just kidding. No problem at all."

"Thanks. I'd appreciate that." He gave her his address. "Sorry to impose on you," he repeated awkwardly, before he ended the call.

Jessica leaned against her kitchen counter, crossed her arms and watched Scout for a few minutes, then kneeled down in front of him. "Well, pal, it looks like we have a few more hours together." She pulled the sneaker out from beneath his paw, and grinned. "You wouldn't happen to know where the other one is, would you?"

CHAPTER SEVEN

CAL WASN'T HAPPY about the prospect of taking a medical leave of absence from the police department. He'd kept mostly to himself since he'd moved to San Diego, so without work and without his dog, he was bored. According to Jessica, he had four or five hours to kill before she came by.

With nothing else to do, he decided to go in to the police division. Yeah, he'd be starting a medical leave of absence, but he had some paperwork to complete and he wanted to check in with his captain. The problem was—as the doc had aptly reminded him—he couldn't drive. He called a taxi, and figured he'd get one of the other cops to drop him off at home when he was done.

He spent an hour or so in the squad room and took some good-natured ribbing from his colleagues. Just being there made him feel better. He loved what he did, and for the most part got along well with his colleagues.

He kept an eye on the glass-walled office of the K-9 Unit captain, Logan O'Connor. Reflective of Logan's Irish heritage, his short-cropped hair was ink black and he had piercing blue eyes. Even from a distance, Cal saw that those eyes were shooting sparks as Logan spoke to someone on the phone. Cal didn't relish meeting with Logan if the call was putting him in a foul mood. Logan was an exceptional cop, a good friend, but he was known for his temper. It was slow to simmer—and explosive when ignited.

Cal was perched on the side of Sergeant Rick Vasquez's desk in the squad room. Rick, aka Pitbull, was a cop through and through. Cal knew some of Rick's history, although most of it was sketchy. Rick didn't talk about it much, but from the snippets Cal had heard, he gathered that Rick's childhood had been rough. Rick had been born in the drug cartel stronghold of Tijuana. As a kid, he'd fled Mexico after his parents were killed in a cartel-related incident, and pledged to become a police officer to fight drug trafficking. He'd fulfilled his pledge, and his unwavering focus and steely determination had enabled him to rise quickly up the ranks of the San Diego Police Department. He became the youngest sergeant in the history of the SDPD when he was promoted to the K-9 Unit at the age of twenty-seven. Now twenty-nine, he operated with his narcotics canine partner, Sniff. Cal knew he was reputed to be in line for the next lieutenancy.

Of all the K-9 officers, Cal was probably closest to Rick.

The sound of Logan slamming down the phone had them both turning. They watched as Logan, a scowl on his face, gestured angrily for Cal to join him in his office.

"Oh, great," Cal murmured.

"Sucks to be you," Rick said cheerfully. "Hey, maybe he'll take pity on you because you're injured," he added.

"I doubt that very much," Cal retorted as he pushed away from the desk. "I bet he's pissed at me for disobeying Command when I went back into the building to get Scout."

"Yeah, I heard that. If it's any consolation, I'm sure he would've done the same thing for Boomer," Rick said, referring to Logan's explosives-detection canine partner.

"Wish me luck," Cal muttered as he headed off on his crutches.

Logan rose and skirted his desk when Cal entered his office.

"Is this a bad time?" Cal asked, shaking hands with Logan.

"Nah. Brody got himself in another bind and is trying to blame it on Nitro again."

"Nitro's a good dog," Cal said defensively. He felt sorry for the dog, but he couldn't say the same for his handler, Tom Brody.

"Yeah, I think so, too."

Cal knew that was about as far as Logan would go to acknowledge that there were issues with Tom Brody. Not his problem, he reminded himself. He seldom had to work with the guy, but he wondered why Logan kept Brody on. Aside from his bad attitude, he hadn't passed the requisite physical in two years.

"How're you feeling?" Logan asked.

"I'm not quite up for the San Diego marathon, but I'm okay." Cal greeted Logan's canine partner, Boomer, a six-year-old gun-metal-gray Belgian shepherd. Boomer was one of their best dogs, and Logan was a hell of a handler.

"Take a load off," Logan said, indicating one of his guest chairs.

Cal eased himself into the chair and rested his crutches against the adjoining one. He knew he was in for it when he heard the door close behind him, before Logan sat down at his desk.

"What were you thinking?" Logan thundered, now that the pleasantries were out of the way.

Cal had known it was coming, but the swift transition from greeting to reprimand threw him. "C'mon, Logan, I couldn't leave Scout in that building!"

"A direct order is a direct order, Tracker," Logan responded, using Cal's K-9 Unit aka. "Disobeying it almost cost you your life."

"Look me in the eye and tell me you wouldn't have done the same thing if it was Boomer in that building," Cal said. Challenging Logan could backfire on him, but he had to play the card.

Logan exhaled heavily and glanced over Cal's shoulder.

"Right. You would've done the same thing." Cal knew Logan was honest to a fault and wouldn't deny it.

"Yeah," Logan conceded, "but if I did—and this is off the record—I wouldn't have been stupid enough to ask permission first."

"I wasn't the one who asked. It was the firefighter operating the winch," Cal grumbled.

"Really? That's not what I was told."

"Well, he asked first. I just followed up when he had no luck."

"Doesn't matter how it happened. I have to reprimand you for disobeying an order."

"Okay, I'm reprimanded. Can we put it behind us?"

The heat left Logan's voice. "No, Cal. I have to place a written reprimand in your personnel file."

Cal lowered his head. "Aw, c'mon, Jagger…" He used Logan's aka. "Can't we just agree that I've been reprimanded and leave it at that?"

"Unfortunately not. I don't have discretion over the written reprimand. It came from Incident Command. Williams insisted on it."

"So what does that mean? Is my job at risk since I'm still in my probationary period?"

"One reprimand won't cost you your job. Your performance has been exemplary otherwise. Just try to make sure you don't get any more."

It still didn't sit well with Cal, but there wasn't much he could do about it.

"So how's the thigh?" Logan asked, pointedly changing the subject.

"Sore as hell. There's a hairline fracture, up high on my femur, but at least it's not broken. I'll just have to keep the weight off it for a few weeks, and then I'll likely need some physiotherapy."

"And Scout? He's okay?"

"Yeah. He seems to be. I'll take him to the Mission Bay clinic," he said. The veterinary practice was contracted to provide care for the SDPD's canines. "To be on the safe side." Cal smiled. "Scout did a terrific job. He's proving to be as good as we expected."

"Do you want to bring Scout in?"

"For what?"

"With you having to stay off your leg for that period of time, how are you going to take care of Scout and keep up with his training? You know the dogs need constant reinforcement."

Cal hadn't thought about that, but he should have. He'd have to stop taking the painkillers they'd prescribed for him if they were dulling his brain like this. In addition to the ongoing training, one of the criteria for selecting police dogs was high energy, and they required considerable exercise to keep them from acting out. The idea of not having Scout with him troubled Cal. Even more than that, he didn't want the dog spending all that time in one of the concrete kennels at the division. "Any chance one of the guys could take him for a couple of weeks?" he asked.

"I know what you're thinking, but Scout would still have to stay in a kennel when whoever took him was on duty. You know as well as I do that he couldn't be left alone in a strange place."

"No, you're right," he muttered. "I'll manage."

Logan glanced meaningfully at the bandage on Cal's thigh, then at the pair of crutches beside him. "You sure? We can keep him here, see that he gets lots of exercise. It'd be better for him."

"I don't like the idea of leaving him in a kennel. And if I have to be off for more than a couple of weeks? Then what? You've got that guy from Vice who's so keen to get into the unit. He'd jump at the chance to work with Scout. Would I get Scout back?"

Logan jerked a shoulder. "It comes down to how effective a team is. I can't give you any guarantees."

Cal wasn't prepared to take the chance, slight though it might be, that Scout would be reassigned to a new handler. If Scout and the new guy made a good team, there'd be little chance of Cal's getting him back. Despite all the lectures about not treating your K-9 like a pet, it was virtually impossible for a cop not to get close to his dog. Cal had definitely bonded with Scout during the time he'd been with the department. He couldn't imagine being without him.

"No, I don't need Scout to come back in. He's staying with me."

Logan held Cal's gaze. "And how will you give him the exercise and training he needs?"

"My brother. You've met Andrew. He's a teacher, and he's off for the summer. He'll help with Scout." Cal felt a twinge of unease about making the commitment before approaching Drew. But they were brothers. Even if Drew wasn't all that keen on animals, Cal was convinced that Drew wouldn't let him down. "We'll keep up with Scout's training and exercise. You've got my word."

Logan twirled a pen between his fingers. At a soft snore, they both looked at Boomer, who'd rolled over and was sleeping on his back. Logan angled his head.

"Will your brother be able to handle Scout?"

In for a penny, in for a pound, Cal thought. "Oh, yeah. They get along great." Or they seemed to whenever they'd been in each other's company, although they'd never been alone. Come to think of it, Cal couldn't remember Drew giving Scout a single command. "Yeah, no problem. He'll help out for as long as I need him to." When they were kids, Cal was the one to have pets; Drew had been the studious one. Still, they'd make it work.

Logan glanced at the crutches once more. "Will your brother stay at your place? It doesn't look like you can manage even a short walk with Scout right now."

"Drew will stay with me. Or he'll take Scout for the short-term, if necessary."

Logan gave Cal a long, level look, making him want to squirm. "Okay. But if you need help, you let me know."

Cal nodded slowly. "Sure." He reached for his crutches and shuffled out of the office. Then he took the elevator one floor down to the lobby, something he'd never done before. He didn't bother asking any of the guys to drive him; instead he got a cab again.

As soon as Cal was in the taxi, he called his brother. He and Drew were very different people, but with no other family, they were always there for each other. Drew agreed to take Scout for a few days, until Cal was fully mobile again. Cal didn't have the courage to tell Drew that he might need him to do it for a few weeks.

The cab dropped Cal off at his house on Pismo Court. The house backed on to the boardwalk and the beach, and was a short walk to the ocean. He and Scout lived a quiet existence, often going for long runs along the beach. The house suited him and Scout, but at present the beach would be off-limits for him. And with no public transit within easy walking distance, he'd have to figure out how to get around if he wasn't going to depend solely on cabs.

He let himself in, grabbed a quick bite and sat down on his sofa to rest.

He was about to turn on the TV to catch the news when his phone rang. Not recognizing the number immediately he considered ignoring it, then decided to answer. "Calen Palmer."

"Jessica Hansen," was the immediate rejoinder. He detected a note of humor in her voice before she turned serious. "How are you feeling?"

"As if I was hit by a truck…or an I-beam… but I'll live. You get your sleep?"

"Yes."

"How's Scout?"

"Exuberant." He could hear that the smile was back. "Is it okay to drop him off now?"

Cal shifted his weight to try to ease the throbbing in his leg. "Sure," he said through gritted teeth.

Half an hour later, Cal heard a car pull into his driveway. Going by the sound of the engine, he figured it was a sports car. He thought the staid and presumably conservative doctor would've driven a practical sedan. For a few seconds, he wondered if his visitor was someone else.

He hobbled over to the window and squinted through the blinds in time to see the doctor climb out of a spiffy yellow Miata. She managed to do it gracefully despite her height.

As he watched, she noticed his personal car, a classic Porsche 911 Carrera Cabriolet he'd bought on a whim after leaving Lincoln. She tucked her hands in her back pockets and slowly circled it, stopping to peer in through the driver's window before stepping back and giving his car a final appreciative look.

Well, what do you know? The doc likes fast cars.

Jessica Hansen looked much as he remembered her from the quake site. But a cleaned-up version. Seeing her in jeans, low-heeled sandals and a tank top made her seem more... approachable. The thing that struck him most was her hair—long, loose and cascading down her back. It seemed so incongruous with the prim and proper doctor he assumed her to be. Gorgeous hair, clearly intelligent and a fondness for dogs and cars. How could a guy not be captivated?

Turning back to her own vehicle, she opened the passenger door and leaned in to unbuckle the seat belt. Seeing her bent over in the tight jeans caused an uncomfortable ache in his gut, one he hadn't felt for...longer than he'd been divorced. No. He had to ignore it. There was a very good reason he'd steered clear of women in the past year, regardless of how appealing. He would *not* let the doc get under his skin.

With Scout beside her, she raked back that remarkable straw-colored hair. The ache intensified and he tried, once again, to disregard it.

Scout heeled by her side like a well-trained pet, tail wagging, tongue lolling, as they made their way along his walk and up the steps. Leaning heavily on his crutches, he moved into the foyer and opened the door.

Her fist was already raised to knock, and when the door swung open she gasped in surprise. Scout tensed but, seeing Cal, he lunged forward, yanking the leash right out of Jessica's hand and nearly knocking Cal off his one good leg.

Cal laughed and greeted Scout with equal fervor.

Jessica joined in the laughter. "You haven't even been separated for a full day, but you'd think he hasn't seen you in weeks. I wouldn't have expected this sort of reaction from a police dog."

Cal glanced up. "Why? Police dogs are still dogs. They're pack animals, and they bond like any other dog. They just have a job to do. Thanks for cleaning him up."

"No problem." She turned toward her car. "I'll go get his food. And things."

She returned with a plastic container of dog food and a canvas bag, and was about to hand them to him. "Sorry. I forgot you can't carry these with your crutches. Where would you like me to put them?"

"You can leave everything just inside the door there. Thanks for getting food for him. How much do I owe you?"

She shook her head. "Don't worry about it. It was fun having him stay with me."

"Are you sure? You did me a big favor— you shouldn't be out of pocket, too."

"No. Really, it's okay."

"What's in the sack?" he asked.

"Oh, just a couple of things I bought for him while I was at the pet store."

Cal picked up the bag and looked inside. "A couple?" There were five toys and a box of dog treats. Scout must have been so spoiled Cal was surprised he didn't insist on staying at the doc's place. "I should pay you for all this."

"No. That's fine." She bent down to rub Scout's head and dropped a kiss on his snout. The dog leaned against her legs, curved his body and stretched his neck, insisting on more attention.

Cal was amused. Scout generally wasn't a particularly cuddly dog. Suddenly he felt embarrassed at having had the nerve to impose on—or browbeat was probably more accurate—a stranger into taking care of Scout.

"Since you're here, would you like a coffee or something cold to drink?"

"All right. Thanks. But just for a minute. I have to get to work."

When they'd settled in Cal's living room, Cal with a soda and Jessica with a mug of tea, she asked, "How's the leg?"

"Are you asking as a doctor or a…an acquaintance?"

"The latter. Let's say as a…friend." A light danced in her eyes.

Cal shrugged. "It's frustrating. But, as you said, it'll heal and there'll be no permanent impact." He thought of all the people who'd lost their lives in the disaster, a first responder among them. "There are folks dealing with a lot worse as a result of the earthquake."

A shadow passed across Jessica's face, and he remembered the little girl he'd rescued... and her mother. "Any news about Kayla?"

"You mean since the last time you asked me earlier today?" Jessica tugged at a thread on the hem of her shirt. "She's still at the hospital. That's all I really know."

"How's she taking the loss of her mother?" he asked in a subdued voice.

Jessica's eyes glistened as she looked at him. He would've thought that as a trauma doc she'd have to be a little more calloused, but he also knew that most cops never became so tough that tragedies didn't affect them deeply. Seeing the obvious distress on her face, he wanted to reach out to her but held back. He didn't want things to get personal between them.

"From what I understand, she's handling it the way any five-year-old would."

"Kayla told me she didn't have a father. I don't know if that means not at all, as in deceased, or not in her life. Have you heard if there's any news about him?"

One tear spilled over and Jessica brushed at it impatiently. "It's… I don't think Kayla has a father. Like I said, Social Services hasn't been able to find any family, nor could they locate a birth certificate for her."

Cal started to rise, wanting to offer comfort, but the pressure on his leg made him suck in a breath and drop back down on the sofa. All for the best, he thought, once the pain had passed. It was an apt reminder that he should keep his distance. "What'll happen to her if she doesn't have family?"

"She'll stay at the hospital for a few days, anyway. In the meantime, I expect Social Services will try to arrange for a foster home, maybe a group home, until everything's sorted out. Right now it doesn't look like she has any family, so they might need to start the adoption process."

He recalled the brave little girl he'd rescued from the collapsed building. He couldn't help thinking of his own daughter, the same age as Kayla. She was lost to him for the short term—although he refused to give up on the long-term prospects—but at least Haley had her mother. He wondered if Kayla's father was dead or alive, and thought about how sad it would be if both her parents were gone.

Jessica placed her nearly full mug of tea on the coffee table with a slight clatter that jolted him out of his musing.

"I'm sorry. I was just...thinking." There was no point in burdening this virtual stranger—a person he wouldn't see again—with his personal woes.

"It's okay." She rose. "I'd better get to work. Thank you for the tea."

She scratched Scout behind the ears. "Have you made arrangements for his care?"

"Are you offering to help?" Cal had a sudden image of Jessica walking on the beach with them, and that brought with it an odd sensation of longing.

She laughed. "No! Just curious."

"My brother's agreed to give me a hand." He raised his shoulders. "And I'll do what I can. Think of it as physical therapy."

"Don't overdo it. You don't want to slow your recovery or set it back."

"Yes, Doc." Balancing on his crutches, he walked her to the door. "Thanks for your help with Scout. I'm sorry I pestered you into it."

He saw surprise register on her face. "It

was no trouble, really. He's a great dog. Good luck with everything," she said as she opened the door.

As awkward as it had felt to have her in his home, he didn't want her to go. He couldn't think of any logical reason to ask her to stay. And she did say she had to get to work. He watched her walk to her Miata.

"Nice car," he called after her.

She spun around, flipped her hair back in a way that made him want to run his fingers through it and flashed him a smile. "Not as nice as yours, once you get it all fixed up! You should paint it red. It's not a common color for 911s. A car like that…" She ran one hand along the rear quarter panel. "You don't want it to blend in."

"Maybe I *will* paint it red. If I do, would you like to go for a ride?"

"I just might!" she said as she got into her car.

He would never have thought of red, but she had a point. With Scout at his side, he stood in the doorway, leaning against the frame as she backed her car out of his driveway. His parting comment might've been lame, but, somehow, she'd chipped a hole in the wall he'd built around himself after Anna left. And she'd done it in under twenty-four hours.

As she drove off, Cal felt strangely alone.

CHAPTER EIGHT

ANDREW ARRIVED AT Cal's at the agreed-upon time.

"I really appreciate this, Drew." Cal gave his brother a one-armed hug. "I know you're not the biggest fan of four-legged creatures, big or small, but I'm in a bind and I owe you for helping out."

Drew stepped into the hallway. He and Scout eyed each other warily. "Sure. No problem."

"I need another favor, too."

Drew sent Cal a "what now?" look, but said, "Okay. What is it?"

"Before you take Scout home, I need you to drive us to the veterinary clinic. I'll get a cab home from there. Scout has to be checked over, and I told the captain I'd have him looked at." He was already skating on thin ice with Logan. He didn't want to *not* follow through on this commitment, despite Scout's not showing any sign of injury.

"Sure. Okay," Drew repeated. "And don't worry about the taxi. I'll bring you back."

Cal handed Drew a duffel. "I've put everything you'll need for Scout in there."

Drew hoisted the bag. "All this for a couple of days?"

"Just in case," Cal said with a smile as they walked out to Drew's Hyundai Tucson.

"It shouldn't take long," Cal assured his brother as he slid out of the SUV in the parking lot of the Mission Bay Veterinary Clinic. He opened the back hatch and signaled for Scout to hop out and follow him inside.

"How're you doing, Heather?" Cal greeted the receptionist.

She smiled warmly at Cal and walked around the reception counter. "What happened to you?" she asked, glancing at his bandaged thigh with concern as she bent down to say hello to Scout.

"I had an altercation with a reinforced concrete beam. The beam won."

"So it seems. How bad?"

"A piece of exposed rebar tore a chunk out of my leg. Nothing that won't heal."

"The earthquake, huh?"

He nodded.

"Sorry you got hurt. Was Scout with you?"

"Yeah. He seems fine, but I want him checked out, anyway."

"Of course. Madison's running a little behind. She should be with you in a couple of minutes," Heather said as she straightened.

"Madison? What happened to Jane? Did she leave?"

"Jane's still with the practice. It's just that we've grown, and Don and Jane couldn't handle it all. So they brought a new vet, Madison Long, into the practice. She's taken on responsibility for the police dogs, freeing up Jane to specialize with the exotics. You know, iguanas and snakes and things." She wrinkled her nose. "Don't ask me why, but that's her first love."

"Has Madison worked with police dogs before?"

Heather sat down behind the reception counter again. "I'm not sure. She moved here from El Paso. She must have some experience, or they wouldn't have assigned her to be the primary vet for the SDPD. You'd have to ask her."

One of the exam room doors opened behind him.

"And speaking of Madison, here she is now," Cal heard Heather say as he looked over his shoulder.

Escorting an elderly lady holding a very large cat to the reception area was a beautiful woman in a lab coat. She was medium height with long curly red hair. He heard Texas in her sultry voice as she gave the older woman final instructions about her cat.

"Madison, meet your next patient, Scout," Heather announced when the veterinarian was finished with the cat lady. Heather motioned to Cal. "And this is Scout's handler, Officer Calen Palmer, aka Tracker."

Madison glanced at Cal's leg and crutches. She first held out a hand for Scout to scent, then offered it to Cal.

"I'm Madison Long. Nice to meet you," she said before squatting down and ruffling Scout's fur. "He's gorgeous. Is he German or Belgian?"

"Neither," Cal responded. "He's Dutch."

"So this fine fellow came to us from Holland."

He nodded and she stood again.

"Please follow me."

That was no hardship, Cal thought as he watched her sashay into the exam room. He noted Heather's grin and felt a little embarrassed.

"Don't worry about it," she said, laughing. "Madison has that effect on pretty much all the men who come in here."

Watching Madison give Scout a thorough examination, Cal pondered what had happened to him, finding a second woman attractive in such a short span of time, when he'd sworn off women more than a year ago. His unease grew when he realized this *wasn't* the same as with the doc. He could appreciate Madison for what she was—a beautiful and obviously intelligent woman. But there wasn't that disturbing pull he'd felt toward the trauma doctor. With Madison it was more an uninvolved, almost impersonal observation, while with Jessica... Well, it was like a fist squeezing his heart.

Half an hour later, Cal let Scout back inside his brother's SUV and climbed wearily into the passenger's seat.

He rested his head against the seat back and closed his eyes. He hadn't expected a simple task like taking Scout for a checkup to drain him the way it had. "Sorry it took so long, but thanks for waiting," he said to his brother.

"You okay?" Drew asked.

"I've been better," he replied, his eyes still closed.

"How's Scout?"

"He's fine."

They drove in silence for a while. "I need to ask you a favor," Cal said.

"You've already asked me for two, and that's why I drove you to the vet clinic and why I'm going to take your dog home with me."

"How about an adjustment to a favor you've agreed to, then?" Cal opened an eye and watched his brother's profile. "How would you feel about helping out with him until I'm mobile again?"

"I *said* I would."

"No. You said a few days. Now I'm asking if you'll do it until I can walk without crutches."

Drew stared at Cal. "What?"

"You heard me. Could you take care of Scout for a couple of weeks?"

"You're the one who's good with animals. Remember me? I couldn't even take care of a pet rat when we were kids."

Cal chuckled, remembering how his brother had tried to build a maze to train the white rat they'd had as kids, only to have the rat escape and live behind their walls for nearly a week until Cal was finally able to lure him out with some cheese. "You won't need to build a maze this time," he teased his brother. "Scout's trained in agility *and* tracking!" His voice turned serious. "I could really use your help, Drew. I can't let Scout stay in those concrete pens at the division or, worse, risk losing him if someone else starts working with him. Based on how I feel now, after just taking him for a checkup, I know I can't give him the training and exercise he needs."

Drew had a nervous expression on his face. "How long is a couple of weeks? Two?"

"Maybe three. By then I should be healed enough. You're welcome to stay at my place, if that makes it easier for you."

"Nah. I prefer my own space, if that works for you."

Cal shrugged. "No problem with me. Whatever's best for you. We'll need to get his kennel over to your place for the duration, though. You don't want to give him the run of the house when you're not around."

"Yeah. That'll work."

CAL HADN'T REALIZED how much his own company bored him, until he found himself sitting alone on his sofa at home.

He turned on the TV; all he could find were talk shows or game shows. Neither interested him. He could start a book. He loved to read, but with his job he seldom had enough time to get through a novel in less than a month or two. Generally, his reading was so sporadic he lost interest in a book before he was halfway through.

He checked his watch.

Maybe he'd go by the division, give his captain an update on Scout's condition.

He'd go broke on cabs, he mused as he sat in the back of another one, if he didn't figure out how to drive his own car with the use of his left leg alone.

Climbing out of the cab, he saw Tom Brody loading Nitro into his SUV. Brody was the only guy in the unit Cal didn't like. He couldn't put his finger on it, but there was something about Brody that rubbed him the wrong way. He felt sorry for the guy's dog. Nitro was a great dog, but the normal bond between canine and handler didn't seem to exist between them.

"What are you doing here?" Logan asked when he saw Cal standing in the doorway to his office. "I told you not to come back while you're on medical leave."

"I know. I just wanted to give you an update."

"What? Your phone isn't working?"

"Actually…on a related topic, I lost my radio in the collapsed building."

"Requisition another one. I should make you pay for it yourself since you went back in the building against orders," Logan grumbled, distractedly shuffling through the papers on his desk. "So, what did you say brought you here?"

Boredom. But Cal wasn't about to say that. It sounded pathetic even to him. "Like I said, I wanted to update you on Scout's condition. He had his checkup earlier today."

Logan's eyes met his. He had his captain's undivided attention now. "That's why you came in? How bad is it?"

Cal understood why Logan would have

jumped to that conclusion, and he was quick to reassure him. "No. He's fine."

"Good. I've been told they hired a new vet recently. I haven't met her yet, but I should since she'll have primary responsibility for our dogs. Long's her last name. Mandy or Melanie?" He shrugged. "She moved here from Texas, if I remember correctly."

"Yeah. And it's Madison Long." Cal grinned. He thought of Logan's reputation with women. "You *should* make a point of getting over there."

Logan raised his eyebrows. "Something I need to know?"

Cal thought about the gorgeous, curvy red-head with the Texas twang, and his grin widened. "Nothing to worry about. You'll find out soon enough."

Logan seemed about to pursue the cryptic comment, but his phone rang. When he finished the call, he'd obviously forgotten. "So, where were we?"

"I just wanted to let you know Scout's fine."

Logan looked meaningfully at Cal's hand as he rubbed the side of his thigh. "And that's why you came in?"

Realizing he'd been subconsciously trying to ease the pain only made him feel more foolish. "Yeah. Hey, is there any paperwork I can do at home? Anything to keep me busy?"

"Cal, you're on leave." Logan looked exasperated. "I know it must be tough, but I can't let you work, even if I wanted to. You're not cleared for duty. Once you are—for modified duty at least—we can talk about paperwork. For now, go home, rest your leg, heal fast, and catch up on movies and books you've been putting off for lack of time.

"I don't want to see you back here until you're cleared," Logan called after him as he walked out of the office.

IT WAS THE busiest Jessica could remember the hospital being. Understandably, since this was the first time in its history that there'd been an earthquake of this magnitude anywhere in the vicinity.

She took the stairs up to Pediatrics and felt the immediate constriction in her chest as she entered the too-familiar ward.

"What room is Kayla Hernandez in, Nancy?" she asked the nurse at the desk.

Nancy smiled, then turned to her computer screen to check. "Good to see you, Jess. How've you been?"

"Fine. Thanks. And you?" Jessica generally had no problem with small talk, but in this case she felt uncomfortable, despite the fact that she'd always liked Nancy, both professionally and personally.

"Great. My daughter made me a grandmother last week."

Jessica felt the pressure subside and skirted the desk to give Nancy a hug. "That's wonderful. Congratulations!"

"You'll have to come back and I'll show you pictures. Nathan's a real cutie."

"Sure. Of course." But Jessica knew she'd continue to avoid the ward. If not for Kayla, she wouldn't have been there today.

"Kayla's in room 235. Poor kid. She lost her mother in the quake. We don't think she has any family. You remember where the room is?"

Jessica nodded and turned to go.

"We miss you here," Nancy called after her.

Jessica's rubber-soled work shoes squeaked as she walked down the corridor to Kayla's room. When she neared 212, the room she still thought of as Jake's, her heartrate increased. She rushed past without glancing in, and exhaled only when she reached the door to 235.

She remembered it was a four-bed room, but the current demand was such that two extra cots had been moved in. All six spaces were occupied. Jessica tried to block out the other children in the room. She didn't want to think about their injuries and ailments, or wonder if she could help. Still, she couldn't resist a surreptitious glance to make sure they were resting comfortably, that all was in order with the monitors and equipment. She was tempted to check the chart of a young boy, then reminded herself sternly that it wasn't her job. He had excellent care from the doctors on the ward; there was nothing more that she could do.

She placed one foot in front of the other, and focused on the bed in the far corner, by the window. The one occupied by a little girl, her normally olive skin pale, and her long black hair fanned out around her face. Her eyes were closed and she seemed to be sleeping. Jessica walked over, and lifted the chart from the holder at the foot of the bed. She noted the tests her doctor had ordered. "With the bruising that developed, Whitby should've ordered a contrast CT of her chest," she murmured to herself.

"You're the doctor from after the earthquake." Kayla, her head turned, eyes still half-closed, spoke to her. Jessica hadn't meant to wake the child. She'd just wanted to see what her condition was.

"Yes. I'm Dr. Hansen. You can call me Jessica, if you like."

"Is my mommy here?"

Jessica had seen on the chart that Kayla had been told that her mother had passed away and they were still trying to locate her father or other family. Kayla could be in denial or, at her age, might not fully understand that her mother was gone for good. She seemed peaceful now and Jessica didn't want to upset her. "No, she's not, Kayla." She kept her answer honest, if vague.

"And Cal? Is he here?"

Jessica was surprised that the girl would not only remember the cop's name but ask for him. She supposed Kayla needed to find a connection to someone, with her mother gone and no family that they could find. "I'm sorry. He's not here, either."

Kayla's mouth formed a pout and her eyes shone with unshed tears. Before they could spill over, Jessica sat on the side of the bed and took one small hand in her own. She wanted to assure Kayla that everything would be okay, but she knew it wasn't true. "Please don't cry," she said ineffectually as she stroked Kayla's cheek.

"I don't want to be alone," Kayla stated plaintively. "I want my mommy."

"You're not alone, sweetie. I'm right here."

"You'll go away, too! The other man in the white coat said you're not my doctor when I asked."

"Yes, but..." She was about to promise she'd come back, but as Kayla had just pointed out, the girl wasn't her patient and she had no business being in the pediatric ward.

Kayla's tears spilled over, and Jessica gathered her in her arms.

"Hey, don't cry," Jessica repeated as she held the small quivering body against her. She squeezed her eyes shut, feeling the little girl's pain, and wishing she had the power to make everything right in her world. "I'll come back to see you," she vowed, knowing she could give her at least that much. She knew she shouldn't, but she didn't feel she had a choice. This child needed all the love and support she could get.

"Promise?" Kayla asked through muffled sobs.

"I promise."

Jessica stayed with Kayla until the tears subsided and a nurse came to check her vitals. Just before she left, Kayla asked about Cal again.

Jessica considered Calen Palmer as she walked back down the stairs and considered whether it would be appropriate to tell him about Kayla. Kids and dogs had an uncanny ability to see past the superficial and into a person's soul. What did Kayla see in the man that she herself had missed? She was sure he was good at his job and he cared about his dog, but she'd mostly seen attitude and belligerence at the site of the earthquake, directed almost solely at her. She knew she was a natural caretaker, which was both a positive and negative for her as a doctor; perhaps it had been nothing more than her need to help him that had created such antagonism. Until...until she was at his house and she'd seen a warmth, a sense of humor, even a bit of playfulness when she was leaving, that had drawn her.

But those moments, the flicker of humor and warmth, were fleeting. He'd been angry and unpleasant, and that should've been daunting and even a little scary for a child. But not for Kayla. Kayla had obviously seen something more.

She hadn't realized she'd turned down the corridor leading to the hospital's administrative wing until she reached the executive offices. Seeing the hospital's chief of medical staff in his office, she knocked lightly on the doorframe to get his attention. "Do you have a minute, Richard?" she asked when he glanced up from his papers.

"Sure. Come in."

"I have a favor to ask."

"What is it?"

"I'd like to stay primary for one of the patients I triaged at the earthquake site," she explained. She hadn't given herself the chance to think about what she planned to do until she saw Richard. Now that the words were out of her mouth, she wondered if she'd lost her mind. Judging by the look on his face, Richard was probably having the same thought.

"It's…a little unusual but not out of the question. Tell me why you believe it's in the patient's best interests."

She had to give Richard full marks for as always thinking of the patient first. That was her priority, too, of course. "I'm concerned about potential internal trauma."

Richard's expression was skeptical. "We have any number of doctors who can deal with that. Your skills and capabilities are better used in your own area."

"In this case, there are…" She was about to say "complications," but that wasn't accurate. Not in a medical sense. Her assessment remained what it had been at the triage site— Kayla was going to be fine.

"What aren't you telling me, Jess? We've known each other long enough that you can level with me. Are you worried about the competence of another doctor on staff?"

She thought about the attending pediatrician, Michael Whitby, not ordering the contrast CT, but she couldn't say he wasn't competent. "No. It's not that. I'd just like to see this patient through."

"All right. Let's try this. Who's the patient?"

"Kayla Hernandez."

Richard turned to his computer and called up Kayla's file. After a quick perusal, he turned back to Jessica, his face grim. "Are you sure about this?"

Jessica swallowed the lump in her throat. She merely nodded, since she didn't trust herself to speak.

"Jess…she's a *child*."

This time, she managed to find her voice. "I'm well aware of that."

Richard looked at her for so long she wanted to shout that she'd changed her mind.

"Okay," he finally said. "I'll talk to Allison," he said, referring to the head of pediatrics.

"Thank you."

"Jessica, let's make sure neither of us regrets this. If you feel you're not up to it, if you have any reservations, come and see me right away. Understood?"

Jessica only nodded. Her voice seemed to have deserted her again.

CHAPTER NINE

CAL STOOD BESIDE his car trying to figure out if he'd be able to drive with his good leg. When he'd left Lincoln, he'd gone a little crazy and bought the Porsche 911 Carrera Cabriolet. His ex-wife hadn't liked sports cars. In any case, he would never have spent that kind of money on himself while he was married. It had been a rebellion of sorts when his marriage had ended.

He'd been tinkering with the car ever since. It remained a symbol for him, and he refused to get rid of it, no matter how much time and money it was costing him. The car was a work in progress and in need of a paint job, as Jessica had aptly pointed out, but man, it was fast.

He loved the two-seater, convertible sports car, but now he cursed it silently as he tried to get into the driver's seat. With his height and bulk, the car was a tight fit at the best

of times; right now, he was at a distinct dis-
advantage.

He managed to slide in with his injured leg,
and once inside, he realized that it would be
unwise and probably impossible to drive until
he'd completely healed. The manual transmis-
sion only complicated matters. Having shoe-
horned himself into the car with considerable
pain, he was faced with trying to extricate
himself without fainting from the agony.

He'd just made it, and was hunched over,
taking rapid shallow breaths, when he heard
a car approach.

Glancing up, he watched his brother pull
his SUV into the driveway. Cal raised his eyebrows when Drew stepped out. "What happened to you?"

His brother sported a black eye and a jagged scrape across his forehead.

Drew let Scout out of the back of the vehicle and held the leash out to his brother. "*He's*
what happened to me."

Cal's shock must have shown on his face
and he dropped a hand protectively on Scout's
head. "He *attacked* you?"

Drew chuckled awkwardly. "No. That might
be a little less embarrassing."

Cal led his brother up the steps and into the house. "Are you okay if I let Scout off his leash?" he asked cautiously.

"Oh, yeah."

"What happened?"

"Can I have a beer first?"

"Sure." Cal unclipped Scout's leash and turned toward the kitchen.

"No, no." Drew cast an anxious look at Scout. "You go sit down. I'll get it."

Drew returned with two beers and a bag of pretzels, handed one bottle to Cal and sat on a chair.

"So, what happened?" Cal repeated.

"Well, he's a search-and-rescue dog, through and through."

Cal gave his brother a quizzical frown.

Drew took a sip of his beer. "I misplaced my iPhone and couldn't find it. I looked and looked. Scout here—" he gestured to the dog sleeping innocently at Cal's feet "—I let him scent the case and he found the phone, no problem. It must've been in the pocket of my jeans, because he found it in my laundry hamper—after pulling out all my laundry, scattering it over my apartment and chewing a hole in the pocket of my best jeans.

But after he found it, would he give me the phone? *Noooo.*"

Cal worked hard to keep from laughing or even smiling. He could tell his brother wasn't amused, and he didn't want to exacerbate the situation. "Drew, all you had to do was tell him, 'Out.'"

"Do you think I could remember that? The more I tried to get him to *release* the phone, the more he seemed to think it was a game. I chased him…" He raised his hands defensively. "I know. I know. I shouldn't have chased him. But he had my *iPhone.*"

Cal was trying to be compassionate. He really was. After all, Drew was doing him a big favor, but he struggled to control his merriment at the thought of his brother chasing Scout around the apartment, knowing he wouldn't have had a chance of catching him. "And how does that explain the, uh, damage?" he asked with as straight a face as he could manage.

Drew took another drink, then held the cold bottle against his bruised eye. "I tripped on the edge of the carpet, hit my head on the arm of the sofa, and when I tried to break my fall with my left arm, I scratched my forehead with my watch."

"You look…you look like you walked into a wall!" He couldn't hold back the laughter any longer.

"Thanks for the sympathy, Cal. If you think I look bad, you should see my living room."

Andrew acted completely put-upon and Cal tried again to contain his laughter.

Then the humor faded abruptly.

The one night Scout had spent with his brother had obviously been a disaster. His brother was clearly unable to assert his dominance over the strong-minded dog. He doubted Drew would take Scout back, and he already knew Drew wouldn't want to stay with him in his small house. Cal was back to square one.

"Drew, you wouldn't consider…"

"No!" Drew cut him off. "I know what you're going to ask. I wanted to help out. I really did, but look at me! I'm not an animal person to begin with. You knew that going in and we just proved it conclusively. And he…" Drew pointed at Scout, snoring at Cal's feet. "He's not a normal dog. I swear he's smarter than I am. I'm sure he thought it was a game, and I'm convinced he *enjoyed* taunting me."

Cal chuckled again, but knew he had a problem. "Just walk him for me tonight and tomorrow morning. It shouldn't be a great hardship for you to sleep here for one night. I'll buy you dinner, if you're okay with delivery. I'll figure something out by tomorrow."

"Okay," was the resigned answer. "But that's it. One night. I feel bad for you, Cal. If there's anything else I can do, let me know. But I can't help with Scout."

After dinner, Drew took Scout for a long walk and settled down on the sofa for the night. Cal had offered his bedroom but Drew refused it because of Cal's injury.

Cal lay in bed, staring up at the ceiling, trying to decide what to do. Scout didn't like being locked up in the concrete cage at the division, and Cal didn't want to do that to him. He couldn't imagine how Scout would react to being in there for weeks, not just a day. He hoped he wouldn't end up having to leave him there.

He considered hiring a dog walker, but dismissed the thought. Scout required special handling, and it wasn't advisable to walk him with other dogs he wasn't familiar with.

He circled back to the only option he had for Scout. He'd have to take him back to the division. He hated the idea but didn't see a way around it.

Maybe he could manage by himself. He moved slightly without thinking, and reflexively arched his back and grabbed his leg in an effort to ease the pain.

That answers that, he thought ruefully, once the ache had subsided.

He should've been honest with Logan and asked for his help to work something out. He had no choice now. He'd have to talk to Logan, appeal to him. With that resolved in his mind, another thought occurred to him. He worried about Logan's reaction to the fact that he hadn't been entirely truthful. Trust was a key element in their relationship and he'd misrepresented the facts. He'd have to come clean and let Logan know that his brother wasn't capable of taking care of Scout, despite his assurances. The alternative was to make up an excuse, but then he'd only be compounding the lie.

He'd just been written up for insubordination with respect to a direct command, which Logan was angry enough about, and now he'd misrepresented his circumstances to his captain. Yes, misleading him was a minor infraction, but Cal was afraid it would result in a second blot on his record. He worried about the possible impact while he was still in his probationary period. He wondered again if the painkillers were scrambling his mind, since part of him was questioning whether it really was that big a deal. He didn't have an answer.

Yeah, it was all small stuff, and maybe it *was* the pain meds that made him see everything in a negative light, but his worries seemed to be growing.

JESSICA KNEW SHE shouldn't be doing it. Kayla should *not* have been her patient. She'd barely assumed that responsibility and already she was questioning everything she was doing. Whitby hadn't taken it well, and was less than cordial. He'd even made a snide remark under his breath so only she would hear, reminding her about Jake.

Not that Jessica needed the reminder. Jake was the reason Jessica had left pediatric surgery in favor of trauma. She'd voluntarily put herself back in the situation she'd been trying to avoid. She'd broken her own rule with Kayla. She was caring for another child and getting too close to her—getting emotionally involved with her.

Trying to look at it from the positive side, she told herself that maybe this was an opportunity to overcome her phobia. But the negative voice in her head taunted her. What if she messed up again? Kayla would pay the price.

Jessica rubbed her eyelids with her fingertips. This certainly wasn't starting well. She needed to pull herself together; otherwise, she wouldn't be any good for Kayla...and possibly anyone else.

She'd made the decision to keep Kayla in the hospital for a couple of reasons. Social Services' inability to locate family and the time required to find her a foster home was one reason. The mother had reportedly worked a number of odd jobs, cleaning houses mostly, according to Kayla, but anyone who knew her commented on what a nice woman she was. Although obviously a wonderful mother, she'd been a person who kept to herself. Kayla had nowhere else to go.

Jessica had also decided to keep Kayla in for observation. A contrast CT—which Whitby had *not* ordered—revealed fluid on her lung. She didn't want to take any chances with her contracting pneumonia.

Jessica peered into the little girl's room. Kayla looked so small and defenseless, lying in the child-size hospital bed, surrounded by a menagerie of stuffed toys. There were books and games piled on her night table and tray, too. Clearly, Jessica wasn't the only staff member who had a fondness for her. Kayla's eyes were closed, long dark lashes resting over the shadowed circles under her eyes.

Jessica felt the uncertainty, the insecurity, of wondering whether she'd ordered all the correct tests. Whether she was missing something she should've recognized—and in doing so, put Kayla at risk. She shook her head to silence the nagging voices. She'd done all the right things, detected the fluid on Kayla's lungs, and there was nothing else to do but observe and ensure that she didn't get pneumonia. And yet, she couldn't stop herself from fretting.

If she hadn't intervened, it might have cost Kayla her life. Still, Jessica found herself second-guessing everything related to Kayla's care, and that scared her.

Getting permission to be Kayla's doctor might not have been the wisest decision for her, but she hoped it was the right one for Kayla.

She was aware that Richard was watching her like a hawk, which didn't do much to put her at ease. She'd thought about telling him she'd changed her mind, but she knew how that would reflect on her professionally, and she *wanted* to take care of Kayla. In this short time, Jessica had come to care deeply about the little girl.

Jessica was about to back out of the room when Kayla's eyes fluttered open. Rubbing a fist against her eye, she turned to Jessica and a small smile curved her lips. That meant the world to Jessica and helped put her anxieties at rest, if only for the short-term. She moved to Kayla's bedside, adjusted the teddy resting under the girl's arm and tucked the blanket more snugly around her. She brushed back the hair from the girl's brow with gentle fingers. "How are you feeling today, Kayla?"

"'Kay," was Kayla's croaked response, her voice scratchy from too much crying.

Jessica took one small hand in her own, and touched the slight bruise left by the IV needle. "Can you take a couple of deep breaths for me?"

Kayla obliged.

"Does it hurt anywhere?"

Kayla shook her head. "Is Mommy coming to see me today?"

Jessica held the child's hand more tightly in her own. Kayla still hadn't accepted that she wouldn't see her mother again. Jessica caressed the girl's hair with her other hand, then rested it on her forehead. She was checking for fever as much as offering physical comfort.

A knock on the door had them both glancing over. Cal stood in the doorway, balancing on his crutches, a huge stuffed pony under his left arm.

Even on crutches, in loose-fitting shorts, a polo shirt and just a bit disheveled, he looked so attractive that Jessica's heart skipped a few beats.

"Cal," Kayla cried, and tears fell from her eyes.

"Hey, hey! None of that," he exclaimed, and hurried over as fast as he could. He leaned the crutches against the side of the bed and handed her the pony. "See what I brought you?"

She accepted the stuffed toy, nearly as big as her, and buried her face in its plush caramel-colored coat. "Have you found Mommy?" she asked in a hopeful whisper.

Cal glanced at Jessica. "It comes and goes," she said quietly, hoping he'd understand what she meant. She was trying to be circumspect in front of Kayla. She assumed he did when he didn't respond. Instead, he propped a hip against the side of the bed. He bent over and spoke softly in her ear. Kayla slowly calmed down and even managed a watery smile.

Jessica watched, fascinated by the way this big, tough cop could be so gentle and sensitive to the little girl. There certainly seemed to be more to him than first met the eye. She quietly backed out of the room to give them time alone, and went to the nurses' station to do some charting.

Cal found her there nearly ten minutes later.

"Is she okay?" Jessica asked.

"Would you be okay if you'd lost your mother, your only living relative?" Shock must have registered on her face, since he rushed on. "Sorry. I didn't mean to take that out on you. It's just so sad." He spun away, inadvertently putting weight on his right leg. He sucked in a breath and nearly tumbled to the ground, catching himself on the counter.

He had his back to her, but she placed a hand on his arm. "Are you all right?"

"I wish I could've saved her mother. You have no idea how much I wish that," he said.

It wasn't what she'd meant; she was asking about his stumble. But it gave her insight as to what hurt him the most. "Kayla's mother died almost instantly when the building collapsed. It was head trauma that killed her. She was gone before you arrived on the scene. There was nothing you could've done to save her."

He turned back, more cautiously, his troubled eyes meeting hers. "So she didn't bleed out?"

"I read the coroner's report. She…she died when the earthquake hit. Nothing could've saved her after that."

A measure of respite seemed to come over him. "It's hard enough that Kayla lost her mother. I… I couldn't imagine how much pain her mother would've been in, injured as she was, if she died from bleeding out. And to know her little girl was there and trapped with her. Not knowing if she'd be rescued. How could a parent deal with that?"

"Her mother didn't suffer," Jessica assured him. "And she didn't have time to worry about her daughter." Jessica was glad she'd looked into it, not only for herself, but because it now enabled her to offer some consolation to Cal. She thought of the comfort he'd given the little girl.

"Do you mind if I ask what you said to Kayla that stopped her crying?"

Jessica nearly laughed at the sheepish expression that came over his face.

"I told her she might not be able to see her mother, but she should think of her as an angel in heaven, always watching over her."

Jessica thought it was a wonderful thing to say to Kayla. He definitely had a softer side. She found the bond between the cop and the little girl touching. She wondered if he'd come to the hospital just to see Kayla. "What brought you here?" she asked, wanting to change the subject to alleviate his unease.

He tapped his left crutch against the floor. "One of these darn things broke. The handle came right off and the screw hole was stripped, so I couldn't fix it. I had to trade it in for a new one. Since I was here, I thought I'd stop by to sec Kayla."

She glanced at the bandage on his thigh. "How's your wound?"

"Other than nearly falling on my face when the crutch broke, it's healing as well as can be expected. Like you said, it'll be slow but steady. The doctor's cautious about sepsis and wants to keep an eye on it, but all seems to be okay for now." He tapped his crutch against the floor again and made a comical face. "You have no idea how much I hate these, and it's only day two."

Jessica smiled. She wasn't surprised by his comment. She didn't think he'd be patient with his recovery "And Scout? How is he?"

Cal put his weight on his left foot, braced the crutch under his armpit and scratched his hair with his right hand. "Health-wise, he's fine. He got a clean bill from the vet yesterday."

"Then what's wrong?"

"It didn't go well with my brother taking him. They had one night together and Drew got all banged up and brought him back this morning."

"Banged up? Scout *hurt* him?" That didn't make any sense.

"No, no." He laughed. "Drew managed to do that all on his own." He pointed to his once-broken nose, bringing to mind the story he'd told her at the earthquake site about how he'd broken it. "Remember I told you he's a bit of a geek, and not too well coordinated." His smile faded. "My concern is that I've run out of options with Scout. I'll need to take him back to the division today, and he'll have to stay in a cage we have there."

"A cage?" She could understand why he'd be upset about that.

"A kennel, really, but it's all concrete and chain-link fence. We use them if we're at the division and need to do something and we can't take our dogs. That doesn't happen often—department meetings and the like. Scout's not used to it." Cal's lips formed a straight line. "The last time I left him in there, he'd bloodied his snout by incessantly rubbing it against the chain-link."

"Oh, that's terrible! Don't you have any other option? Have him stay with another police officer until you heal?"

"It would be hard to put that responsibility

on another cop, and Scout would still end up in the cage when the cop was on duty."

Even during the short period of time Jessica had spent with Scout, she'd developed a real affection for him. She couldn't believe what she was about to suggest, but she felt for the dog and…if she was honest with herself, the cop. She was starting to see a very different side of him, and she saw how distressed he was at the thought of leaving Scout in a kennel.

As much as Jessica loved dogs, she'd never been able to have one because of the demands of her occupation. If she followed through on what she was contemplating, she'd just have to find a way to deal with all of that for the next couple of weeks.

"Jess, excuse me, but could you look at this for a minute?" a nurse asked, interrupting them. Jessica gave Cal an apologetic smile, took the clipboard from the nurse and perused the chart. "Increase the dosage to five hundred milligrams, please," she said, scribbling the instruction on the chart before handing back the clipboard.

"Sorry," she said to Cal.

He glanced around the busy area. "Can we go somewhere for a coffee?"

Jessica thought about the rounds, the paperwork and the million other things she had to do, especially in the aftermath of the earthquake, and checked her watch. She looked back at Cal, his green eyes so appealing with the slight crinkles—smile lines—at the outer corners. The caring, compassionate person she was glimpsing under the hard shell she'd seen the night of the earthquake intrigued her. She *wanted* to get to know him better. "Okay," she said. "But we have to make it quick, because I have rounds. The cafeteria's on the main floor and quite a distance away. Why don't we use the staff lounge on this floor? Admittedly, the coffee leaves much to be desired, but it's close, and at this time of day it shouldn't be busy."

"Works for me."

Just as they were about to leave, another nurse approached Jessica, and they had a quick conversation.

"Does it ever slow down here?" Cal asked as they sat with their coffee at a small round table in the lounge.

Jessica shook her head. "We're still feeling the aftereffects of the earthquake, but it's a relatively slow day, and this is a ward. Try being in the emergency room after a pileup on the San Diego Freeway."

"I assume it's not unlike being *on* the San Diego Freeway during that pileup, trying to unsnarl it," Cal said with a quick smile.

Jessica returned the smile. "Sorry. I forgot. You're a cop. That can't be easy, either."

Cal shrugged. "We do what we can. Being an emergency room doc can't be any easier."

"Trauma actually," Jessica corrected.

"I'm sorry to sound ignorant, but what's the difference?"

"I'm a trauma surgeon. The emergency department doctors' specialty is emergency medicine. There's a separate trauma unit, and I'm a surgeon on that team." At the confused look on Cal's face, she elaborated. "No matter what you go into the emergency room for, emergency medicine doctors treat it all. The doctors there are trained to handle everything. When there's a major catastrophe, like the earthquake we just experienced, the primary responsibility is that of the trauma team."

He nodded. "What made you choose trauma

as your specialty?" he asked. "I'd expect there were many choices you could've made, especially in the surgical field."

Jessica couldn't help the involuntary cringe. "I... I didn't specialize in trauma right away." She had to shut this conversation down. She purposefully checked her watch again. "I'm sorry, I have to get back to work soon. Before I go, I wanted to talk about Scout." She smiled again. "He's a great dog."

She could see Cal was appraising her as he finished his coffee, but to her relief he didn't pursue the topic of her medical specialty.

"Yeah. Scout's terrific as a dog and also at his job. He and I have only been working together for five months. It might not seem long, but he's more than just my partner. He..." Cal hesitated, seeming to search for words. "He's part of my life. That's why I don't want to take him to the division to stay in a cage."

Jessica softened a little more toward the gruff cop. To her way of thinking, how could anyone *not* care about kids and dogs? But Cal seemed to care more than the average person.

He was a virtual stranger, and she was about to turn her life upside down for him by offering to take Scout. How could she manage to look after a dog—a high-maintenance dog, at that—and keep doing her job with its long hours, odd shifts and unpredictable demands? She reminded herself again why she didn't have a pet, despite her love for animals.

But then she looked at Cal, saw the despondency in his eyes. She *wanted* to help them. She really did. And yet she couldn't deny that one contributing factor was the fact that she'd be able to see Cal...

While Jessica continued to mull over the idea, Cal reached into his shirt pocket and pulled out something that resembled a baseball card. He smiled as he placed it on the table and slid it toward Jessica.

She glanced down. It *was* a baseball card. Scout's card! It had his picture on it, head slightly tilted, his eyes expressive and alert. His name was printed in large letters on the top right. The San Diego city seal in the top left corner, with the words *America's Finest* above the seal and *To Protect and Serve* below. She smiled, picked up the card and turned it over. Scout's name, a smaller version of his photo, the seal and police department motto were also on the back, but this side of the card listed Scout's "statistics"—his breed, when he was born, his handler's name. There was also a short paragraph on his history. Scout was born in Holland and brought to the United States to become a police service dog in March four years ago. It listed Scout's specialized training in search and rescue, and handler protection.

She flipped the card over again and stared at Scout's picture before raising her eyes to meet Cal's. The card had done it; it had tipped the scales. "You really have no other option? Not a friend or another police officer?"

He shook his head. "No." He sounded sincere.

She exhaled. "Okay, I'll do it."

"Do what?" He seemed confused.

"Take Scout until you're able to care for him again."

Cal gagged on the coffee he'd just sipped. His face red, he started coughing.

She sprang up to help. "Are you okay?"

He waved her away, but coughed a few more times. "I'm okay," he choked out, his face still flushed.

"You'd do that?" he asked when he could. His expression was comical, a mixture of incredulity and elation. "I thought with what you said about your work commitments and all, it would be a huge imposition."

Jessica took a deep breath and hoped she wouldn't regret what she was about to do. She nodded. "It won't be easy, but I'll take Scout on two conditions," she said. "First, you have to do everything your doctor tells you to do and you have to follow through with the physiotherapy that'll be recommended." She held up a hand when he was about to interrupt. "This is essential. I want you to heal as fast as possible, and I don't want any setbacks that would prolong your convalescence because you did something…" She paused. She was about to say "stupid" but softened it to, "Ill advised. Okay?"

Cal nodded with a grin. "What makes you think I'd do something like that?"

Jessica simply raised a brow. "Second, you have to promise me that you'll keep looking for another solution. I'll take Scout, but I'll have to reduce my hours and ask some of my colleagues to cover for me. So I need you to see if there's anything else that would work."

"Okay." He looked relieved. "You have no

idea what this means to me. I really appreciate it. A couple of weeks at the most, right?"

"That should do it. You might not be back at work by then, but you should be mobile enough to take care of Scout."

"I know this is a lot to ask, especially of a stranger."

Cal was so earnest and genuinely grateful. That, combined with the way he was with Kayla, made it hard for Jessica to remember how he'd acted during their first meeting. Watching him now, she found it hard to remember his harsh, hostile demeanor that night. She felt a flutter in her chest—and an "uh-oh" sounded in her brain.

She was falling for the cop. She smiled as she took stock with a fresh perspective. The tall athletic build, the thick short-cropped hair, the touch of five-o'clock shadow, the crooked nose, strong mouth and chin and those expressive eyes. Physically, he was a near-perfect specimen and that was not a clinical assessment. Contrary to what she'd initially thought, he seemed to have a kind, generous disposition, too.

"Everything okay?" Cal asked.

Jessica felt her cheeks flame. "Oh, sure. Is Scout at your house now?"

"Yes, he is."

"Why don't I pick him up on my way home after work?"

"That would be great. What time will you be done?"

"My shift is scheduled to end at four, but I hardly ever get out on time. I'll give you a call when I'm ready to leave."

"No need to call. Just come by when you're done."

She finished her coffee, rose and took both their mugs to the dishwasher. "I have to get back to work now, but we'll need to talk about logistics. Scout's schedule. What I should do while I'm at work, and so forth."

Cal got up awkwardly and she opened the door for him.

"I still have your address," she said. "I'll see you after work."

"We'll be there," Cal assured her. "I don't have anywhere else to go." He held out his hand to shake hers and, in a serious tone, added, "Like I said, I really appreciate this. We both do." As they walked toward the nurses' station, he said, "If it's not too much trouble, would you mind keeping me informed of how Kayla's doing?"

"I can do that. We're watching for pneumonia, but I expect she'll be fine. I'll do everything I can for her."

Just as she said it, another doctor walked by them and must have overheard. "Well, whatever the kid's ailment, she's got the best darn pediatric surgeon in the city and likely the state."

Jessica was embarrassed and shook off the statement, but Cal was curious.

"What did he mean by pediatric surgeon? You're a trauma doc."

"Yes. Yes, I am," she said curtly, and hurried off to do her rounds.

CHAPTER TEN

THE DOC WAS LATE. It was nearing six and Jessica still hadn't shown up. Cal fed Scout and let him out in the back, watching him from the deck. Hardly the exercise he needed, but at least he was able to perform his basic bodily functions. Cal was confident she *would* show—reasonably confident, anyway. He trusted the doc, even if she hadn't called. But he was the one who'd told her not to bother.

What was it about her that seemed to reduce his IQ to that of a Neanderthal?

Scout might've had dinner already, but Cal hadn't and the grumbling of his stomach reminded him. He thought about calling Jessica at the hospital, just to make sure she hadn't changed her mind or forgotten, but lack of trust wasn't a good way to begin whatever kind of relationship they were going to have over the next couple of weeks. He might as well eat, he decided, since he had no idea when she'd show up.

Cal had just marinated a steak and already had potatoes on his barbecue when he heard a car pull into his driveway. Looking out the window, he saw Jessica's yellow Miata. He glanced at his watch. Almost seven.

He opened the door before she could knock.

"Smells wonderful," she said as she bent down to greet Scout. "I'm sorry I'm late. We had an emergency surgery. Occupational hazard."

"Not a problem. I lost track of time, too. So much to occupy me," he joked, making her smile. He motioned for her to follow him into the kitchen. "I was just starting dinner. If you don't have plans, why don't you stay and we can discuss Scout while we eat. Hopefully it'll taste as good as it smells."

Jessica's cheeks turned pink. "I really shouldn't. I'm sure you have things to do and I should get home. Get Scout settled. I don't want to put you to any trouble."

"It's no trouble." Cal couldn't remember the last time he'd seen a grown woman blush. Anna certainly never had. He found it unreasonably sweet. There was something vulnerable and shy about her right then that appealed to him. "I'd like you to stay," he added to his own amazement. He wondered if he'd hoped for it all along, since the steak he was marinating was large enough for two healthy appetites. "All I have on my agenda is cooking dinner. We do need to discuss Scout. And in the meantime, you might as well experience my world-famous Jack Daniels–marinated steak."

Jessica's color remained high and she gave him a timid smile. "If you're sure…"

"Absolutely. I'm barbecuing, anyway. This steak is too large for me to finish in one meal. Since you're here, you can help with some of the preparation, which will make it easier for me with my bad leg."

"Ah, the sympathy ploy!" she teased, and glanced down as Scout sat next to her. She rested her hand on his head in what appeared to be a reflexive action. "All right," she said as she walked toward the kitchen counter. "What can I do to help?"

"You can pour us some wine." He gestured toward the bottle of red he'd left breathing on the counter. "The glasses are in the cupboard beside the fridge."

She stepped over, walking with an easy grace, and reached up to get the glasses.

He was startled by how much he liked seeing her move around his kitchen...his space. After she handed him a glass filled with the rich red cabernet, she tasted the wine in her own glass. "Very nice. What next?"

"Tell me how you like your steak, then take a seat and enjoy the wine."

"Medium rare," she said as she settled on one of the stools by his kitchen counter.

"Okay. I'll be right back."

She put her glass down and rushed over when she saw him trying to juggle the plate with the steak on it. "Here, let me take that out for you."

He handed her the plate gratefully. "I said you'd be a help." He grinned as they went out on the back deck and he placed the steak next to the foil-wrapped potatoes already on the grill.

"As I said when I got here, the aroma's delicious. But world-famous?"

"Well, at least in my own mind. Seriously, I've had lots of favorable comments about my marinade." He smiled again. "And it's one of the few meals I know how to make."

By the time he brought the steak back in—medium rare—she'd made a salad and set his kitchen table.

Cal instructed Scout to lie on his bed as they sat down to eat.

"Tell me about Scout and how this is going to work," Jessica said as she took her first bite of the steak. "Mmm...this *is* delicious!"

"Didn't I tell you? As for Scout, whatever works best for you. I'll need to spend some time with him on his training. We can do that anywhere. At the division, here on the beach or at your place. Training in different environments helps the dogs. When you go to work, if it's not inconvenient, you can drop him off here. Leave him for the occasional night, if you have plans. My biggest challenge is giving him the exercise he needs. Running with him, playing with him or just taking him to a park would be very much appreciated."

Cal went over all the basic commands with her. She took another bite of her steak, closed her eyes and made a satisfied face. That gave Cal a moment to observe her, and he took full advantage. He liked what he saw. Yes, he thought she was beautiful, but her beauty wasn't traditional. And it wasn't skin-deep.

She was smart and generous, and she liked dogs and sports cars. Neither of which had found favor with his ex-wife.

Jessica was tall and Anna had been short. Jessica was sinewy and Anna curvy. Jessica... What was he doing making comparisons to his ex-wife? But that got him thinking of Anna and why he'd had no interest in women since his marriage ended. It was a good reminder, because he could see himself falling for the beautiful doctor. But that was definitely *not* in the cards. He needed a *lot* more time to get over what had happened.

When Jessica opened her eyes and stared straight into his, he felt an uncomfortable sensation in his chest, and wondered if all his assertions about not being ready for a relationship had just fallen by the wayside. He turned the conversation back to Scout, to keep things impersonal.

Scout, as if sensing that they were discussing him, sauntered over and sat down between them. Cal reached down to stroke Scout an instant after Jessica did. His hand landed on the back of hers.

His immediate impulse was to draw his hand back, but he made himself keep it there a moment longer. He liked the feel of her hand beneath his. Then he thought of Anna again…

When they'd finished their meal, he rose to clear the plates.

Jessica stood, too. "Please let me do that. You've been on your leg too long already."

"I can do it." He could tell that his voice sounded churlish, and he knew it wasn't Jessica who'd caused his change in attitude. Thinking of Anna and how things had ended between them still upset him, despite the intervening time and distance.

"Doctor's orders," she said. The humor in her voice helped lighten his mood again.

"Okay, but I'll get the coffee. Would you like some?"

"That'd be nice," she replied, loading the dishwasher.

As Cal prepared the coffee, he thought back to what a colleague of Jessica's had said while he was at the hospital. "When we spoke earlier, you said you didn't start out specializing in trauma medicine, and that doctor said you were the best pediatric surgeon in the city…state," he corrected himself. "Is that true? That you were in pediatrics?"

Jessica hesitated as she was about to turn

on the machine. "Well...yes." She straightened and faced him.

"How did the change come about?"

Jessica shifted her gaze away from him. "A personal choice," she said after a while.

Cal shook his head, not understanding. "You're marvelous with Kayla. So natural. Working with children must be one of the most rewarding areas of medicine. You must've made a huge difference to the kids. I'd think that would be very gratifying. Why did you leave it?"

Jessica was suddenly preoccupied with stirring sugar and milk into her coffee. Lines furrowed her brow, and she was silent for so long Cal was about to interject. Then she murmured, "I needed a change. It was the best thing for me to do," she added.

"But was it the best thing for the kids? I bet you were doing a lot of good."

"No," she whispered. "I really wasn't."

Cal didn't know what to say, but the question was there, circling around in his mind. He decided to approach it indirectly. "You're taking care of Kayla, though."

"Yes," was Jessica's barely audible answer. She looked as though she was going to say something more, but didn't. This was obviously not something she wanted to talk about.

"Okay." He let it slide. He didn't want to pry or make her feel uncomfortable. Not any more than he already had. "Still no luck finding Kayla's family?"

"No. At this point we've resigned ourselves to the fact that she doesn't have any. At least not in the state. Social Services is looking for a foster home for the time being, but they're having trouble. The earthquake's made everything more difficult. Some families who would've fostered are trying to rebuild and can't take in any more children until they do. Health issues have also arisen in some cases."

"Then what'll happen to her?"

Jessica exhaled. "They're trying to find a family as fast as they can. In the meantime, as I said, I'm keeping her at Ocean Crest for observation."

"If there's no risk and no complications, you can't do that indefinitely, can you?"

"No. It would be a stretch, keeping her once her lung has cleared." She raised her eyes, now dark and stormy gray. "If we discharge her before a foster family is found, she'll have to go into a group home. I wish that wasn't the case."

"The people who run those group homes do the best they can for the children," he said, trying to reassure her, but he lacked sincerity. He knew that cops from his division had been called out to homes like that too many times—for drug-related issues, or drunk and disorderlies. He thought of his daughter, Haley, and the prospect of her ever having to live in a facility like that, and a cold chill snaked up his spine. And if he wouldn't want Haley to endure a place like that, how could he wish it on Kayla? He didn't want to think about it. "Why don't you take our coffee into the living room?" he said abruptly. "I'll get Scout's things together and join you in a minute."

JESSICA PUT THEIR mugs of coffee on the table in front of the sofa and wandered around the room. She took a silver-framed photograph from the mantel, and examined the picture of the beautiful blonde child, maybe a year younger than Kayla.

When Cal entered the room, she turned, picture in hand.

The look on his face had her hurriedly replacing the frame. "I'm sorry," she murmured, not sure why she was apologizing.

Cal rubbed his hands across his hair. "You have nothing to apologize for." He moved over to stand beside her and straightened the frame.

"I just thought... You seemed so..."

"*I* need to apologize. You didn't do anything wrong."

Curiosity was getting the better of her. "Do you mind if I ask who she is?"

He shrugged. "If I don't want people to ask, I shouldn't have the picture out. That's Haley." He straightened the frame a touch further, stared at the photograph. "My daughter."

"Oh..." Why hadn't it occurred to her that he had a child? Or that he'd been married? She supposed that because he spoke so readily about Kayla, she would've assumed he'd speak just as freely about a daughter, if he had one. "She's very beautiful." Jessica took a closer look. She could see the resemblance now. In the eyes, the shape of the mouth. "She's about four?"

Cal glanced at the photograph again before

limping over to the sofa to take the weight off his leg. "Yeah. In that picture she'd just turned four. That was taken over a year ago."

Jessica had a horrible thought that would've explained his reaction to seeing her holding his daughter's photograph. She couldn't imagine losing a child. She believed in the old saying that parents should never outlive their children. She didn't even know how to broach such a terrible subject. "Is she…" she started hesitantly.

"She's five now."

Jessica felt relief, both because the little girl was alive and because Cal hadn't picked up on what she'd been thinking. "The same age as Kayla," Jessica murmured, for no reason other than to move away from what had been on her mind.

"Yes, she is."

Jessica joined Cal on the sofa and took a sip of her coffee. She could see that there was something very painful here. His body language, his curt speech and the tormented look on his face all attested to it. She brushed a hand soothingly over his good knee. "Do you want to talk about it?"

Cal took a drink of his coffee and stared

at the spot her hand had touched. "It's…" He hesitated. "I'd rather not."

His demeanor was polite but impersonal as they finished their coffee—a distinct contrast to the friendly banter they'd enjoyed over dinner—but Jessica had glimpsed the hurt beneath the veneer, and wondered about it. It had to do with his daughter, and she sensed that it cut deep.

Jessica thought about Cal all the way home. Spending a lot of time in the emergency department, with cops coming and going, she'd become accustomed to their habitual flirtatious behavior. But Cal showed no such tendency. Just the opposite. He seemed to be detached and disinterested, especially after they'd spoken about his daughter. Yet, along with the pain, there was a depth of emotion he'd tried to conceal. She might not have known the cause, but her heart went out to him.

Scout adjusted his position in the passenger's seat, drawing Jessica's eyes to him.

Thanks to Scout, she'd certainly have more occasions to see Cal…which could give her a chance to figure out exactly how she felt about him.

CAL SAT BACK on the sofa after Jessica had left with Scout. His leg throbbed unbearably, but he didn't want to succumb to taking a pain-killer. He hated what they did to his mind and spirits; he'd rather deal with the pain. He rested his head on the cushion and closed his eyes. He was a mess, and he wasn't just refer-ring to his physical state.

He let the evening replay in his mind. He'd enjoyed Jessica's company. She was warm, in-telligent, and he was undeniably attracted to her. He'd liked seeing her in his home, moving around in his space, making herself comfort-able. It made him feel a…a what? A yearn-ing? For a relationship? To be able to share his home with someone again? Do something as basic as preparing dinner together?

He'd been thinking of asking her out. Not because of Scout or because she was helping him. But because he liked her and wanted to spend more time with her to see if there could be something…personal between them. He wasn't sure what he would've suggested with his limited mobility—maybe dinner and a movie—and he'd been mulling that over in his mind before he'd entered the living room and found her holding the picture of Haley.

He'd had two immediate and conflicting reactions to seeing her looking at Haley's photograph. The first was a sense of how terrific she'd be with his little girl. The second and more dominant was the usual amalgam of hurt, anger, betrayal and grief that he'd been living with since Anna had torn Haley away from him. He'd thought those feelings had dulled over the past year, that he'd learned to live with them. But tonight they'd returned with a vengeance, prompted by the simple fact that he'd seen a woman he was attracted to looking at a picture of the daughter he had no contact with.

If those emotions could still consume him, he wasn't ready for dating, let alone anything more serious.

CHAPTER ELEVEN

CAL WAS PLEASED and not a little relieved that
the arrangements he and Jessica had come to
were working out. The added benefit from
Jessica's perspective, she had explained to
him over the telephone, was that Scout had
found her other tennis shoe, as well as a long-
lost pair of sunglasses and a wooden mixing
spoon from the kitchen. She'd admitted with a
laugh that the sunglasses weren't usable anymore, thanks to Scout's needle-sharp teeth.

Cal and Jessica spent snippets of time together to do basic training work with Scout,
but despite that and the long runs Jessica took
him on, morning and night, Scout was starting to show the effects of his reduced level
of exercise.

With the hospital operating over capacity
due to the earthquake, it was nearly a week
before Jessica had a full day off. Cal suggested they take Scout to the SDPD's canine

training yard to let him get some exercise but also work on his agility. Jessica agreed without hesitation. The challenge became how to get the three of them to the yard, considering that both his and Jessica's cars were two-seaters.

Cal cajoled Drew into swapping vehicles with him for the day. He laughed at how nervous and excited Drew was about taking the Porsche—it reminded him of a kid with a shiny new toy on Christmas morning. Except his car was far from shiny, since it was still in need of that paint job. He resolved to get that done as soon as he was back on his feet, so to speak.

He winced when he heard the car's gears grind as Drew drove the Porsche out of his driveway, but because of the enjoyment his car seemed to give Drew, he decided to let him borrow it whenever he wanted.

When Jessica arrived, they loaded Scout in the back of the Hyundai, and Jessica drove them to the division. Cal signed her in at the front counter, took some ribbing about his crutches from a couple of cops, and they headed to the training yard.

The yard was a large, fenced-in grassy area

that almost resembled a children's playground. There were wooden climbing structures erected in locations throughout, including a tall structure with narrow open stairs leading to a horizontal plank and a ramp on the other end. Several hurdles, each at least three feet high, a steep plywood wall about seven feet in height and various other obstacles completed the yard's training equipment.

An exercise was under way when they arrived. Cal and Jessica stood outside the fence and she watched the dogs and their handlers go through their drills. Most dogs were working on agility, although one was doing some form of detection. He could see her smiling at the enthusiasm the dogs exhibited. The dogs loved what they did. He was glad she could see that, too.

When the group was finished, Cal spoke briefly to the other handlers as they exited, making introductions, before they entered the yard.

Scout's eagerness was obvious, and Cal asked Jessica to unclip his leash. He'd brought Scout's Kong with them and, leaning a crutch against the fence, he threw the toy for Scout to let him burn off some energy.

Cal was now faced with a challenge. Generally when he worked with Scout on agility, he would run alongside him, instructing him on which obstacles to scale, correcting him if he missed one. That was definitely not going to happen today with his injury. He could direct Scout from a distance to climb the first couple, but he wouldn't be able to take him through the whole course.

He glanced down at Jessica's practical sneakers—the ones Scout had found for her, she'd explained. "How do you feel about getting some exercise?"

She looked at him with a startled expression. "You're not serious?"

He laughed when he realized she thought he wanted her to *climb* the obstacles. "Not the way you think I meant." He told her she'd have to jog alongside Scout and indicate with a hand gesture the obstructions she wanted him to scale.

"Sure," she agreed. "Sounds like fun."

"He'll be fast. You set the pace, but remember he has to maintain a minimum speed to climb the steep inclines or jump over the hurdles and barricades." He sent Scout off to clear the first obstacle to show Jessica what to expect. Jessica grinned as she signaled for Scout to follow her. She jogged toward the first climbing platform. Scout loped along beside her, but when she gestured at the platform, he simply streaked around and beyond it, and ran the whole circuit, avoiding every barricade, and sprinted back to Cal.

Jessica burst out laughing and turned to face Cal. "Either your dog needs *a lot* of refresher training or I'm not cut out to be a handler!"

Cal chuckled. "Probably a combination of both." He moved to the first obstacle and instructed Scout to climb it again. When the dog did it effortlessly, Cal called him back. "What he did—ignoring you—isn't surprising," he told Jessica. "Scout's smart. Would *you* want to go through all that work if you didn't have to?"

"I suppose not. So what should I do now?"

"If he goes around an obstacle, stop, call him back and indicate it again, until he clears it. As I said, he's smart. After the first few times, he'll know there's no getting out of it."

Cal stood back and watched Jessica try three times to get Scout to scale the first obstacle. When he finally did it on the fourth go, she hooted and clapped. When her eyes met his, her delight so clearly evident, Cal felt a jolt that was nearly physical in its intensity.

"Good. That's great," he encouraged. "Okay," he added, trying to get his brain to function again. "Now start with the first one again, because he now knows what you expect of him, then lead him through the course. Remember, if he avoids an obstacle, call him back and signal him again."

Scout did well on the first two obstacles. When he sailed effortlessly over the first of the two hurdles that came next, it was Jessica who broke stride. She looked over at Cal. "Wow! Did you see that?" She laughed at herself. "Of course you saw it and you've seen it many times before, but Scout cleared that hurdle so *easily*. It looked like he was flying." She called him back. Signaled for him to do it again, then took him to the second one and repeated the command. She stopped again. "He's so fast and agile! He just jumps up and over, but it shouldn't be so easy at that height."

Cal watched Jessica, her face alight with excitement, and that odd little jolt hit him again. This time it persisted.

He sat on a wooden box and watched Jessica work with Scout. They ran the course four times, the final one flawless and quicker than the preceding three. She was…mesmerizing. He had no idea where that word had come from, but it was apt. She was as sleek and agile as the dog. Finally she plopped down on the grass and, calling Scout to her, rewarded him with lavish affection. She got up, gave Scout the heel command and they ran over to Cal.

"That was terrific!" she said. She squatted down to ruffle Scout's fur and praise him again for his performance.

Cal had a strong urge to touch her. Simply stroke her cheek. And when she smiled up at him, he couldn't seem to take his eyes off her.

"I understand the agility training now, but how do you train the dogs to do their jobs?"

He shook his head. He was glad she'd snapped him back into reality. He'd actually been wondering what it would be like to kiss her laughing mouth, and that was definitely out of the question. "It's all based on positive reinforcement."

"You mean treats?"

"Not necessarily. We train our dogs with nothing more than a toy and lots of praise.

You saw how excited Scout was to be in the yard and do what you asked him to—once he realized you weren't letting him off the hook. It's as simple as that, but it takes practice and repetition."

"Can you show me how you teach him to track?"

"We do the tracking exercises mostly outside the yard. We set up a three-mile course. The subject will walk it, leaving two to three objects hidden along the way. Things like a credit card, a handkerchief, a phone. He or she will wander through the area, whether it's a residential community or undeveloped space. The dog has to find not only the subject at the end of the trail, but the items that were discarded."

"It's incredible that a dog can track over such a large distance and after the passage of time. How do you train dogs for other duties, such as narcotics or explosives detection?"

"Let me show you."

Cal led Jessica back into the building and signaled Scout to go into his kennel. He unlatched another one. A gunmetal-gray dog, the size and shape of a German shepherd, bounded out. In addition to his spectacular coloring, he had gold-amber eyes; the near-black coat and gleaming golden eyes were an unusual combination and made for an extraordinarily beautiful dog. The dog greeted Cal exuberantly, then turned his attention to Jessica.

He sniffed her hands, handbag, and did a quick circle around her.

Jessica grinned. "Am I cleared of drugs, then?"

"Explosives in this case. Boomer, meet Jessica. Jessica, meet explosives-detection dog Boomer."

"Boomer? Really?"

"Really. You don't like his name?"

"Yes," she said, chuckling. "I do."

"Good. The dogs don't care, and we need to have a sense of humor about it all," he said. "Boomer, into the yard," he instructed. And the dog shot off.

Cal moved to a locked cabinet. He extracted a cylindrical container, and secured the cabinet again.

"What's in the container?" she asked.

"Explosives residue."

She took an involuntary step back and eyed the container warily.

"No need for concern. It's a trace amount, about what people would have on their hands if they'd set a bomb. The residue itself is not explosive."

"Do you work with Boomer, too?"

"No. But we do training exercises together sometimes. Boomer is Jagger's dog."

"Jagger?"

"Yeah. That's our captain Logan O'Connor's aka. Boomer is his K-9 partner. Ready?"

"Sure." Jessica carried the cylinder for him and they started toward the yard.

"Why do you call your captain Jagger?"

Cal turned to her. "Do you know the Rolling Stones?"

"Yes. Of course," she responded, sounding perplexed.

"Well, suffice it to say that our captain has some moves."

"You're talking about the song, 'Moves Like Jagger'? Your captain dances?"

Cal burst into laughter. "I'm not sure, but that's not how he got his alias. He has moves with the ladies. Much like Mick Jagger."

"Oh." Jessica smiled, looking a little embarrassed. "Got it."

They followed Boomer out to the training

yard. Cal asked her to keep Boomer with her and distract him while he set up the exercise.

He lifted a precut section of turf and hid the cylinder in a box buried under the surface, before returning to Jessica.

He alerted Boomer that he was now on the job and directed him to search for explosives. They watched as the dog executed what appeared to be a well-planned search of the area, clearing section by section as he made his way toward the location of the planted cylinder. As soon as he detected the scent of the explosive residue, he sat and stared intently at the spot where Cal had placed it.

Jessica nodded slowly. "He's found it. What's he doing now?"

"That's called passive indication. The dogs are trained to sit and indicate the location of what they find. Dogs used to be trained for active indication, which means they'd scratch or dig in the area where they detected the scent. We generally don't use active indication anymore since it can cause damage to property, and the department could be liable. Passive indication is just as effective but without the potential for damage." He got up, and she followed him over to where Boomer was sitting.

Cal praised Boomer and removed the cylinder, handed it to Jessica to carry, and they headed back to the building, Boomer leaping around him.

Jessica drove them to Cal's house. As she was about to let Scout into the passenger's seat of her car, Cal had a hurried argument with himself. "Jessica?" he called. When she turned to him, he adjusted the crutch under his right arm, shifted more of his weight onto his left foot. "I was thinking. Why don't you leave Scout here this afternoon?"

She released her door handle and straightened, watching him.

He shuffled a bit more. "You could come back around six or seven. That would give you some time to yourself, do errands or whatever. And when you come back…" He paused. Debated once more the wisdom of what he was about to do. In the end, his heart seemed to outweigh his head. "When you come back, say around six, would you like to have dinner with me? Maybe go see a movie after that?"

A smile curved her lips. She closed the

distance between them. The smile was reflected in her eyes, too. "I'd like that." She handed Scout's leash to Cal and rubbed the dog's head before turning back to her car. "See you at six."

CHAPTER TWELVE

ALL AFTERNOON, CAL debated the wisdom of having asked Jessica out to dinner. He was attracted to the beautiful doctor, no doubt about that, but he knew the wounds he carried weren't just the ones that were visible. Part of him was terrified of falling for someone, and risking more pain.

He almost picked up the telephone a few times to call her with some excuse to cancel—his leg was acting up or he was too tired from the exertion at the training yard that morning. Once he even started dialing her number before changing his mind again.

As the afternoon passed, he grew increasingly irritated with himself. What was wrong with him? It was just dinner and a movie. He should look at it as a simple thank-you for her help with Scout. It didn't have to be anything more.

But the more he thought about it, the more he worried that he might *want* it to be more.

He fed Scout, let him out back, then they went back inside so he could shower. Showering was a little easier now that he could change the bandage himself, but getting dressed still posed a problem. Something like a pair of jeans was still too difficult to put on. Other than the pair of scrubs he'd worn home from the hospital, he'd been wearing shorts. He couldn't wear shorts tonight, since that would limit their restaurant choices considerably.

He settled on a loose-fitting pair of khakis and a pale blue dress shirt. At ten to six, he thought about sitting on the front porch to wait for her, but decided that would make him look foolishly eager. Which made him realize he was, in fact, that eager. Darned if he'd show it, though.

He sat in the living room by the window and knew exactly when she turned into his drive.

Jess drove, of course, but they took his Porsche, ostensibly because it offered more leg room. Cal was a bit anxious as to how well she'd handle his car, since hers was an automatic, but he needn't have worried. She drove it like a pro. She obviously appreciated the car and knew how to get top performance out of it. He couldn't prevent his gaze from drifting back to her time and again. He loved seeing the joy on her face as she tested the performance of his car.

He'd made a reservation at the Waterfront Grill on Pier 32 Marina. They were seated at a corner table that allowed him to prop his crutches against the wall and out of the way. Soon after that, they ordered their meals and selected a bottle of white wine.

They kept things light as they finished their appetizers. While the waiter cleared their plates and topped up their wine, Cal scanned the room—and couldn't help frowning at what he saw. He glanced at Jessica and noted her eyes had followed his to a family being seated at a nearby table, father, mother and a child of five or six in a frilly white dress, with long blonde curls. She reminded Cal too much of Haley.

"I can't begin to understand what it's like not to be able to see your daughter," Jessica said quietly.

"Excruciating." Cal felt his mouth twist as he spoke.

"You haven't seen her at all since you left Lincoln?" she asked.

"No, and it's torture. Just watching a family like that…" His voice trailed off and he shook his head.

"If you'd prefer not to talk about her…"

"No, it's fine. It's there whether I talk about it or not."

Her eyes were compassionate. "Is there any chance for you to visit her?"

"I've tried, believe me. When I've called to talk to Haley, and Anna—my ex-wife—tried to get her to come to the phone…" He inhaled deeply, took a sip of his wine. "I could hear Haley in the background. She was, at best, reluctant to talk to me…at worst, crying. I didn't force it, figuring it would only make things even harder. I hoped and I *still* hope that—as clichéd as it sounds—time will heal, and at some point I'll have a chance to reestablish a relationship with my daughter."

"How did it happen? If you don't mind me asking."

"It started with the breakdown of my marriage." He paused while the waiter served their main course. That gave Cal the opportunity to decide whether he should change the subject. But if he had any expectation that there might be something between him and the doc, she should be aware of his baggage. So when the waiter left again, he continued. "I have to be receptive to tells and nuances in my job." He shrugged ruefully. "You'd think I would've realized my marriage was unraveling before my eyes. But I didn't have a clue. I came home from work one day. I had a bunch of flowers for Anna and brought dinner home, wanting to surprise her. We'd had a…situation at our house that was very stressful for Anna. For all of us. I wanted to make it up to her. To surprise her." He snorted.

"Anna's the one who surprised me. She was distracted over dinner, and as soon as Haley was in bed, she dropped the bomb on me. She said she could no longer tolerate being the wife of a cop. She said it wasn't anything *personal*." He laughed bitterly, and took a long drink. "How much more personal can it get than a wife telling her husband that the marriage he'd thought was solid and happy was over?"

Cal hung his head. The sense of loss burned

through him, as bright and sharp as it ever had. He felt Jessica's touch on his shoulder, and she ran her hand along his arm. The re-assurance she offered disconcerted him. He wanted to take her hand in his and hold tight. Instead, he linked his own fingers.

"What triggered it?" she asked.

"She said her decision was prompted by a break-in at our house. The situation I men-tioned."

"How would a break-in have caused it?"

"It wasn't a random act. It was targeted. Our home was vandalized by an associate of a drug dealer whose arrest I'd been involved in." He sighed. "I was on the drug squad then. Thank God Haley and Anna weren't home at the time, but Anna said it was the tipping point for her. She said she'd been thinking about it for a while, and that was the last straw." He rubbed his forehead, then the back of his neck. "I don't want to imagine what could've happened if they'd been home." And that was something he'd had to live with since the break-in, and it was why he didn't com-pletely blame Anna.

"She wanted out of the marriage. I suppose it was my fault."

"How could that have been your fault?" Jessica sounded outraged on his behalf, and the knot in his gut loosened slightly. Her eyes were a tempestuous, stormy gray.

He shrugged again. "If she'd been thinking about it for a while, there must have been something very wrong between us, if she chose not to discuss it with me, and for me not to have seen any signs. How could that have happened if I was a good husband?"

"You're being too hard on yourself."

"Maybe." He didn't believe it, but it helped to hear her say it. He accepted the hand she held out, took comfort in it and stroked his thumb over her knuckles. How could those strong, competent hands feel so smooth?

"And your daughter? That doesn't explain what's going on with Haley."

Cal thought back to the day his world came crashing down on him over a year ago. His ex-wife's declaration that she wanted out of the marriage, the internal police investigation of his conduct and the alienation of his daughter.

He didn't want to ruin their dinner, but he'd probably accomplished that already. He couldn't believe how much he'd opened up about his personal struggles to a near-stranger. "I'd rather not get into it," he said. "It's complicated and not a pleasant topic."

"I have good ears. And a soft shoulder, if it's needed," she murmured.

Her words gave him pause; she seemed genuinely interested. He'd gone this far; he might as well finish it.

"The short version is that Anna was determined to move back to Cedar City, Utah, to be with her family. Of course I pay support for Haley, but Anna felt it would be easier for her financially if she moved home. That way she could also get her mother's help with Haley. She's now living with a guy she dated in college, and I'm not sure how much that had to do with her desire to move back to Utah. It really doesn't matter at this point.

"She was determined to move to Cedar City and take Haley with her. Apart from any problems we might have been having in our marriage, she'd never come to accept Lincoln as her home. I suppose it was just another unresolved issue between us."

He moistened his dry throat with the wine.

"Not surprisingly," he went on, "I wasn't willing to let Haley leave the state. I insisted on joint custody, but that would've prevented her from moving. She claimed it was to protect Haley from what she perceived as the dangers of my job. She demanded sole custody."

"That's terrible," Jessica exclaimed.

He sighed. "Be that as it may, Anna had made up her mind and, as I discovered, she'd do whatever she had to in order to get her way. Regardless of how unscrupulous or unethical it might've been. It was highly unlikely that she would've gotten what she wanted—so she accused me of substance abuse."

Jessica looked horrified.

"Oh, it gets better," he said sarcastically. "She accused me not only of drug use, but of…" His voice trailed off and he struggled with what came next. "Psychological abuse of her and of Haley."

"That's unconscionable! I can't believe she'd do that to you. To the father of her child."

Cal had always worried that anyone who knew about Anna's allegations might judge him or wonder if there was any truth to her claims. Jessica seemed incensed, but he didn't see the least bit of doubt on her face. He felt immensely relieved—and consoled—to know she believed him and was in his corner. He hadn't considered how much that would mean to him. The constricting knot in his gut eased some more.

"She was devious," he continued. "It wasn't a spur of the moment thing. She must've been planning it for a while, because she had what she presented as evidence. Things like emails supposedly sent from my account to hers."

Now he saw a flash of uncertainty in Jessica's eyes.

"I know, you're wondering if I did those things."

"No! I'm just curious about how she managed to set you up."

"Getting into my personal email account was easy. She knew my password. Perhaps unwise of me, but I used the same password for everything. Anyway, she used fake emails to substantiate her accusations.

"Even though I maintained my innocence, there was an internal police investigation. That was hard. Domestic violence, and spousal and child abuse are things cops hate, and I was judged by my peers before I had a chance to be proven innocent. In the end, it wasn't hard to prove that I couldn't have sent those messages, since I was on shift or on calls with no access to email."

Jessica nodded, her expression sympathetic.

"Worst of all, Anna used the circumstances to bias Haley against me. She made me out to be a monster. Haley was a young and impressionable kid, and with me out of contact with her during the investigation, thanks to a temporary restraining order..." He had to pause again to gather himself as the resentment built. "Well, the police investigation found no evidence of drug use or anything to substantiate her other allegations. I was exonerated, but the process took *three* months." His voice cracked and he spread his hands. "Can you imagine how long that is to a four-year-old child? All that time without seeing her father? And the harm a mother can do if she's so inclined?"

Jessica shook her head mutely.

"After three months, my daughter would set eyes on me and burst into tears. Do you have *any idea* how that made me feel? I was cleared of everything, but there was no undoing the damage. Within the police department, my reputation, which had been as good as gold, was brought into question. Other cops looked at me differently. And Anna's lies caused Haley to fear me.

"Even though the allegations were found to be entirely without merit, by the time the custody case went to court, the judge couldn't ignore Haley's reaction to me—her tears and obvious distress. So Anna was granted sole custody and given permission to move Haley out of state. I had to comply with the order."

"But that was a year ago, correct? Isn't there anything you can do to overturn the ruling now?"

Cal sighed. "My lawyer suggested that. That we appeal to have the judgment overturned, but what matters most is how Haley feels about me. She's lost to me for now. I can see that clearly. I was afraid that any action I took to hold Anna accountable would've resulted in a rehash of everything. My first priority was and is my daughter. Whatever Anna's faults or misguided motivations, she loves Haley… I know what you're going to say. How can she love Haley and do what she did? I struggled with that, too. But other than that, she *is* a good mother. I didn't want to do anything that would cause further harm or compromise an opportunity in the future to get my daughter back in my life." His voice faltered as he said the last words, and he looked away quickly, out the window and over the dark expanse of water.

CHAPTER THIRTEEN

"I'M SORRY ABOUT last night," Cal said to Jessica when he called her at the hospital the next morning.

"Why are you sorry?"

"Getting into all that personal history. It was heavy stuff for a first date."

"Is that what it was?" He could hear the smile in her voice. "A first date?"

"Well…yes. I suppose." He felt flustered, but didn't mind. She was teasing him and he was enjoying it.

"I thought you'd want to know that I'm going to have to discharge Kayla."

He was immediately concerned about Kayla. "Where will she go? Has there been any progress finding relatives?"

"Social Services concluded that Kayla's mother probably entered San Diego illegally from Mexico, which would explain why

Kayla has no family on record nor does she have a legitimate US birth certificate."

Cal switched the phone to his other ear. He didn't realize what was on his mind until the words tumbled out of his mouth. "Can she live with me? Either as a foster—or, better yet, can I adopt her?"

Jessica's laugh was awkward. "Did you just say what I think you said? Are you serious?"

Was he serious? Had he considered the huge impact that would have on his social life? He wanted to laugh. What social life? Even if he had one, weigh that against what he could do for Kayla. "Yes." He thought about what adoption could mean for Kayla and for him. "You heard me correctly. Do you think it's possible?"

Jessica's voice was hesitant. "I don't know. What you're suggesting is wonderful, but think it through carefully. It'll change your life. And it'll be even harder for you since you're single."

"Kayla's mother was a single parent and by all accounts a very good one."

"If you're sure, I can put you in contact with the people you'll need to talk to," Jessica offered.

Before they hung up, Jessica gave Cal the contact information for the person at Social Services who was handling Kayla's case, but he didn't pursue it. It wasn't something he wanted to jump into without thinking it through carefully.

Over the next few days, Cal and Jessica spoke often, mostly about Scout and his care. She'd told him Kayla had been moved to a group home. That made him think again about the possibility of adopting her. It had been on his mind, but he hadn't come to any decision.

Soon a week had passed, a week since he'd last seen Jessica, and he was surprised and at times annoyed by how much he wanted to see her. His follow-up hospital appointment was scheduled that afternoon, and he had every intention of stopping in to visit Jessica when he was done. He considered calling her first, but didn't want to risk her saying she was too busy. He'd take the chance that she'd be available, even if it meant waiting.

His doctor cleared Cal to go back to work, although with modified duties. He was thrilled at the prospect. He no longer had to use the crutches, but was given a cane. He thanked the doctor and made his way to the trauma unit.

As it turned out, Jessica was in her office, working on her computer. Cal propped his hands on either side of her doorway and leaned in. She had all that thick straw-colored hair piled on top of her head in some messy arrangement. He hadn't realized how long and...*graceful* was the word that came to mind...her neck was. Or how perfect her posture. She sat at her desk, her legs crossed at the ankles, scrolling through images—possibly X-rays from what he could see—on her screen.

She jumped at his greeting, and swiveled around on her stool, one hand at her throat.

"You startled me," she said, stating the obvious.

"Sorry. I didn't mean to. I had my checkup and thought I'd let you know the good news. I'm cleared to return to work. Modified duties for a while, but I can go back."

Jess rose. "That's terrific! For both you and Scout."

"Yeah. Scout'll be happy, too. Do you have time for a coffee?"

"I'd love to, but I'm sorry, no." She gestured toward the computer behind her. "I have surgery in a little while and I was just reviewing the X-rays."

Cal straightened. "No problem. I happened to be here, so I thought I'd ask. Would you like to come by after work with Scout?"

"Oh, I'm sorry again, but I'm on evenings this week."

"What about tomorrow before work?"

"Sure. That'll work."

"See you then, and good luck with the surgery."

JESSICA ARRIVED AT Cal's house midmorning. He met her on the front porch as she was getting out of her car.

"How's the leg feeling?" she asked, unhooking Scout's leash to let him run and greet Cal.

Cal bent down—squatting was still beyond him—to ruffle Scout's fur. "Better." He took a few steps, turned and held his arms out to the side. "Ta-da! No crutches!"

"Do that again," Jessica instructed. Cal took a few more steps as she watched him with a critical eye. "You still have a limp, not surprisingly, but you're doing very well. How does it feel when you put weight on the leg?"

"Tolerable. The doctor said I should be using it as much as I can to prevent atrophy. In fact, you'll be pleased to know that I think I can handle Scout on my own now. We might not be able to go for runs on the beach just yet, but walking, with or without a cane, isn't a problem." Cal wondered if it was regret he saw in Jessica's eyes as she crouched down to give Scout attention. "You're going to miss him, huh?"

She glanced up. Nodded.

"Do you have time to go for a walk with us?"

"I don't have to be at the hospital until this afternoon, although I did want to stop by to see Kayla at the group home on my way in. But a walk would be nice."

They strolled along the boardwalk, Scout heeling between them.

Wispy, gauzy clouds drifted lazily across the blindingly bright sky. A playful breeze sent tendrils of Jessica's hair dancing. Their progress was leisurely out of respect for Cal's healing leg as much as to enjoy the beauty of the day.

Scout became progressively more impatient with their slow pace. Cal knew he associated the beach with fast runs and diving in the surf. Scout needed exercise. Despite Jessica's best efforts, he hadn't received the level of activity he was accustomed to. When Cal pulled Scout's favorite Kong toy out of his pouch, the dog's entire body quivered with anticipation and he barked excitedly. Cal sent the toy winging through the air and into the water. Scout streaked after it in a blur of motion and cloud of sand.

They stopped to watch him dive into the shallow surf and resurface with the toy in his mouth. Taking a few steps out of the water, he stopped on the wet sand to shake himself off before sprinting back to Cal and Jessica.

"How does he do that?" Jessica asked with a laugh.

Cal shrugged. "I'm not sure. I don't think he'd be able to see in the foaming surf. Maybe he can still scent the toy despite the water. It's unerring. He always knows just where it is."

After numerous repetitions of that routine, they started walking again. Nose to the ground, Scout ran in a haphazard fashion along the beach.

"See that?" Cal pointed to the dog. "He's tracking."

Jessica watched with amusement. "But you didn't tell him to."

"I didn't have to. It's a game to him. Tracking is so deeply ingrained, he picks a scent and follows it."

"Looks like he's having fun."

"Police dogs are working dogs. They might have dangerous jobs—the most dangerous on the force—but they love what they do. It's a game to them."

"Why do you say their jobs are the most dangerous? I would've thought it'd be the tactical team or Vice."

Cal whistled to Scout to call him back, not wanting him to get too far ahead. "Tactical is a perfect example. The tactical team is dispatched to high-risk situations, but think about what they do, how they do it and how they're equipped. They have full-body armor, are heavily armed and they minimize risk with every move they make. The K-9 Unit works with the tactical team quite often. For example, we get involved if there's a dangerous suspect or potential explosives in a building, or a suspect's escaped and they need to track him. In those situations, we *lead* the tactical team.

"Say it's a case of a dangerous suspect escaping. Scout and I get called in." Scout was off chasing a scent again and Cal pointed to him. "See what he's doing there? Nose to the ground, basically at a slow run?"

Jessica nodded.

"That's ideal tracking, when the suspect is ahead of us by some time and distance. If the trail is too fresh, the dog will have his head up, scenting the air. He has a wide swath to cover, maybe twelve to twenty feet in width, because the scent hasn't settled yet. With time, say, thirty to sixty minutes, and distance, the trail is narrowed and he tracks with his nose to the ground and at a much quicker pace." He called Scout back again.

"He can track a single scent an hour later?"

Cal grinned. "That's what he's trained to do. And he can pick it out along a busy sidewalk."

"But why is it so dangerous?"

"Let's say we're chasing a suspect, and he's hiding instead of running. With the pace Scout needs to maintain, the suspect could see us coming from a distance, and we could be running right at him without knowing it. It's easy to get shot that way."

Cal called Scout back again as a little girl and her mother approached from the opposite direction. The girl pulled her hand free of her mother's and ran toward them, giggling. Her mother called and ran after her but not fast enough; the little girl had already reached them and crouched down in front of Scout.

Cal instructed Scout to stay while she petted and hugged him. The mother caught up to them. "I'm so sorry," she said breathlessly, and obviously relieved that her daughter hadn't been attacked by the unknown dog. "I always tell Cindy not to play with strange dogs, but it doesn't do any good. She loves animals too much."

"No need to worry. Scout won't harm her," Cal said.

"He's a police dog," Jessica added for the benefit of the obviously nervous young mother.

With the woman relaxing, Cal couldn't resist showing off a bit. He instructed Scout to do a few of his cuter tricks. The girl was in hysterics, and the mother was laughing, too, until she finally said they had to go.

"Bye-bye, Scout," Cindy said repeatedly, blowing kisses to the dog as her mother took her hand and led her off.

Scout had had enough excitement and exercise, and Cal thought he might have overdone it for his first day without crutches. His thigh ached as if a dagger was being twisted in it as they headed back to his house, but no way was he going to let the doc know.

Jessica was unusually quiet, too.

"Everything okay?" Cal asked.

"Oh…yes. I was just thinking… I've been concerned about Kayla…"

Cal stopped abruptly and placed a restraining hand on Jessica's arm. "What's wrong with her? You said she was fine."

"Health-wise, yes. My concern has to do with her mental state. She's withdrawn and becoming progressively more so since she went into the group home."

They started walking again, slowly.

Without thinking, Cal took Jessica's hand. It seemed so natural to him, and he liked the feel of her hand in his. Cal was thankful for the distraction, too, since his thigh was aching almost unbearably.

He recalled the past couple of times he'd

seen Kayla at the hospital. She'd always struck him as a serious child, especially for her age. But it occurred to him now that she'd seemed even quieter during his last visit. "Doesn't Social Services have counselors for, you know, posttraumatic stress?"

"They do, yes. And they've been working with her. But it doesn't seem to be helping. Which brings me back to what I was thinking. Just an idea..."

They'd reached Cal's house. He couldn't prevent the groan of pain as he started up his back steps. Jessica immediately placed a hand under his right elbow. "You overexerted yourself, didn't you?"

There was no point in denying it. "I suppose." They reached his deck and he paused to suck in a few deep breaths. Seeing the concern on her face, he was quick to reassure her. "I'm okay. Just a twinge." He forced a smile. "But back to Kayla. What's your idea?"

"Why don't we sit down so you can rest, and I'll explain." They sat on the chairs on his back deck, while Scout drank from his bowl and settled down to gnaw on his Kong.

Jessica rested her elbows on her knees and leaned down to stroke Scout. "Seeing how that little girl, Cindy, reacted to Scout, how happy and excited she got, I was wondering if a therapy dog might lift Kayla's spirits. I've seen those dogs do wonders with patients of all ages. In fact, we just had a new one register at the hospital. He's an Alaskan malamute. I'm sure that dog weighs more than me, but he's as gentle as a teddy bear. The owner moved to San Diego not too long ago, and she's really interested in working with our patients on a volunteer basis.

"Maybe I'll see if she thinks she could work with Kayla. My only concern is his size. I'd worry the dog might be too intimidating for Kayla because she's so small."

Cal grimaced as he stretched out his right leg and made a mental note to take it a little slower from now on. "Would I be able to bring Scout to the home she's in?"

Jessica looked confused. "Since he's a police dog, I would think so."

He shook his head. "No, not as a police dog exactly."

"Sorry?"

"As sort of a therapy dog—for Kayla. Or better yet, can we arrange to take Kayla to a park? She seemed comfortable with Scout at the earthquake site. It was Scout, actually, who pulled her out of the cavity she and her mother were trapped in. We could reintroduce her to Scout, and have him show her some of his tricks." He gave Scout a quick succession of commands. Scout obliged, and Jessica laughed.

"Yes, I believe we could make arrangements to take Kayla out with us."

"Great. Let me know when we can do it."

CAL WAS HAPPY to be getting back to work, even though it meant modified duties for the short-term. He was using the cane occasionally, but the pain was more bearable and a mere echo of what it had been. It felt good to walk into the division.

"Hey, Tracker! Nice to have you back." Rick Vasquez greeted him with a smile and a firm handshake. He rubbed Scout's head. "You had a nice holiday, I trust?"

"If only," Cal responded.

"Doesn't look like you'll be chasing down bad guys for a while," he said, indicating Cal's limp as they walked along.

"Unfortunately not. It's better than sitting

at home, but I've never considered desk duty one of my favorite things to do."

Rick laughed. "Who has? But the rest of us will be happy. We'll be able to dump all our paperwork on you."

Cal chuckled. "Why am I absolutely certain that you're *not* joking?"

Cal spent some time with the captain, took Scout out into the exercise yard, worked on agility training and called it a day at the end of his shift, something that had rarely happened in the past.

Still, by the time he got home, he was exhausted. Being off for a couple of weeks and dealing with his injury had depleted his strength and endurance. He'd have to get back to the gym and start running on the beach again as soon as he could, he thought glumly.

His phone rang shortly after he got home. It was Jessica. She'd arranged a visit with Kayla for him and Scout. The prospect of seeing the little girl restored his mood. And thinking of seeing Jessica again brightened it even more.

CHAPTER FOURTEEN

CAL AND SCOUT waited on a bench in Balboa Park, not far from the group home Kayla was living in. Scout wore his official police collar and Cal had attached the dog's police badge, as well. They were generally worn only for ceremonial purposes, but Cal could swear that Scout sat up straighter, held his head higher, whenever the badge was fastened to his collar. Cal remembered he used to do much the same when he'd first earned his badge as a rookie. He ruffled Scout's fur and then his hand stilled.

Jessica was walking toward him, Kayla's hand in hers.

The tall, lithe blonde with her hair pulled back in a ponytail, the ends dancing on the wind, smiling. The girl, in contrast, was tiny and fragile especially since she'd lost weight. Her long dark hair was loose and curling around her shoulders. The doc wore jeans and a T-shirt; the little girl a simple pink romper.

As Cal watched the woman and child walking toward him, hand in hand, emotion clogged his throat. He coughed brusquely, blinked a few times and rose from the bench.

He knew the instant Kayla noticed him. "Cal!" she cried. Tugging her hand free, she ran toward him. He grinned and bent down awkwardly to hug her as she threw herself in his arms. Wanting to join in the excitement, Scout scampered around them. Kayla stumbled back, and Cal grabbed her hand to steady her.

"Hey, Doc," he greeted Jessica as she joined them. He gave Kayla's hand an encouraging squeeze before letting go, and instructed Scout to stay in his sitting position. "Kayla, do you remember my partner, Scout?"

The girl clasped her hands behind her back, swayed from side to side and took a hesitant step toward the dog. "He got me out of the hole Mommy and I were in?" she asked, looking up at Cal.

"Yes. He did."

"He's your doggy?"

"He's more than my dog. He works with me. He's a police officer, too."

Kayla giggled. "Dogs can't be police!"

"They sure can!" Despite the pain that seared his leg, he squatted down and showed her Scout's badge. "See. He has his own police badge and everything."

She touched the badge, but pulled her hand back quickly when Scout tried to sniff it.

"It's okay, Kayla. He won't hurt you. I promise," he added. When she still looked hesitant, Cal took her hand again, raised their joined hands and let Scout sniff hers. She chortled when Scout's cool, wet nose touched her. Obviously more comfortable, she reached out for his badge and tried to read it.

"San Diego..." She glanced up at Cal. "What does the rest say?"

Cal read the words to Kayla. "San Diego Police Department. And down here..." He pointed to the metal portion below the crest. "It says PSD Scout."

She traced the letters with a forefinger. "What does PSD mean?"

"It's short for 'police service dog.'"

Nodding, she stroked Scout's head. "He really is the police?"

"Yes. Scout, say hello to Kayla."

Scout gave a short, happy bark, sat back on his haunches and extended a paw.

Laughing, Kayla shook the offered paw. "Can I play with him?" she asked.

"Sure." Cal smiled at Jessica and pulled the Kong out of his pouch. Scout was immediately alert, but on Cal's command held back. "Grab it by the rope. That's good. Now throw it for him to fetch."

Her first attempt had the Kong landing only a couple feet away. Scout pounced on it, brought it back, dropped it at her feet and sat down with an expectant look on his face.

"That was great." Cal handed her the Kong. "Try it again and see if you can throw it a little farther."

"'Kay," she said. This time the Kong went flying about ten feet. Scout immediately whizzed after it.

Kayla bounced and clapped excitedly.

Cal and Jessica exchanged a warm look over her head.

"Can I do it again?" she asked when Scout had deposited the toy near the toes of her sneakers.

"Go ahead. As many times as you like."

Cal and Jessica sat on a bench, and watched as Kayla got more and more proficient at throwing the toy. Her delight at having Scout chase and retrieve it didn't diminish with the number of times they played their game.

"You're good with her. Really good," Jessica observed.

"Thank you." He took her hand briefly in his. It meant a lot to him that she thought so, especially after everything that had happened with Haley. "Scout likes kids. Most of the police dogs do some community work. Pitbull, for instance, works with inner-city youth, counseling them about the dangers of drug use."

Jessica turned to him, surprise evident on her face. "The San Diego Police Department uses pit bulls as police dogs?"

Cal threw his head back and laughed. "Sorry. I can see how that would be confusing. Pitbull is Sergeant Rick Vasquez's alias. He and his narcotics canine partner, Sniff, a yellow Labrador retriever, work with the kids."

"Oh, I get it. We see a lot of young victims of drug-related crimes in the emergency room. It's tragic. Not all of them make it. That's an important job, uh, Pitbull has."

"He does it on the side, as a volunteer." Cal thought about Rick's childhood in the midst of the drug cartels in Mexico, and knew exactly why Rick did the volunteer work. "He cares about the kids. Their official job, his and Sniff's, is to patrol the San Ysidro border between San Diego and Tijuana, Mexico. Their mission is to thwart the cartel-related drug trafficking that takes place across that section of the border."

Jessica knew enough about drug smuggling to understand how dangerous the San Ysidro border was. She'd treated too many young people who were the victims of shootings, knife fights or drug overdoses. "You really do have the most dangerous jobs in policing, don't you?"

Cal watched Kayla fling the Kong again. He shrugged. "It's what we do. The risk is part of the job. We try to be careful, but it's there."

When it became obvious that the child had tired herself out, Jessica called her. Kayla ran back to them, Scout pacing himself to stay at her side. Out of breath and with a huge smile on her face, she rested her hands on Cal's knees and gazed up at him. "Can we do that again sometime? Please?"

Cal forced himself not to show the pain the

simple act of her leaning on his leg caused. "Sure."

Jessica rose and took Kayla's hand. "We'll let Cal get back to what he needs to do, okay?"

"Okay, but I have to say bye to Scout." Kayla threw her small arms around Scout and hugged him tight.

When Cal stood, she threw her arms around his legs, too. Cal winced, and Jessica threw him an apologetic look, obviously appreciating his discomfort.

"Thanks, Cal," she said as Jessica took her hand. "That was fun!"

"Thank you," Jessica mouthed over her shoulder and gave him a thumbs-up as she took Kayla back to the home.

CAL PHONED JESSICA the day after their visit with Kayla to tell her he'd retained a lawyer to pursue the adoption procedure.

He said he'd made his mind up after spending time with Kayla again. Cal had raised the possibility a number of times, but it was a huge commitment and Jessica had to admit that on some level she hadn't believed he'd follow through. But there was no denying it now. He wanted to adopt Kayla.

Yes, he was wonderful with children. She'd seen it with Kayla and she'd seen it with the young girl on the beach. But for a single man in his prime, with no significant relationship, to adopt a young child? Had he truly considered the significance of that responsibility? What it would do to his personal life? And how would he manage it with the long and unpredictable hours associated with his job?

He must have reflected on all of that, she told herself. It would've been foolish not to, and Cal was not a foolish man. But he was willing to take on such a life-changing obligation, which meant he was a very *special* man.

Caring about Kayla as much as she did, Jessica had discussed the process with Social Services. Since Cal was single, with a demanding job, it was a long shot at best.

The social worker had considered the appropriateness of the potential adoption from Kayla's perspective. What it would mean for the little girl. Not having a mother figure, at least not until—or if—Cal had a serious relationship or got married. Having to rely on care providers other than Cal when he was at work. The social worker had also brought up the possibility that Cal might've been trying to replace Haley, but had satisfied herself that it didn't seem to be the case. Even so, there were a slew of deterrents.

On the plus side, Cal was highly responsible and reliable. He could support the child financially. And the man and child had developed a strong bond. If love wasn't already a factor on both sides, they were well on their way toward it.

And, to Jessica, that was the most important thing of all.

As she'd told the social worker assigned to Kayla's case, if there was anything she could do to support Cal's application, she would.

With all that thinking about Cal… Jessica decided she'd call and perhaps *she'd* ask *him* on a date! She'd see when their schedules would next allow it.

CAL HAD BEEN pleasantly surprised when Jessica invited him to get together. She'd suggested a number of possibilities. He'd opted to invite her over for a couple of reasons. He still tired easily, especially after a day at work, and he liked more and more seeing her in his space. In his home. After dinner, he'd brought her out to his back deck and watched her crouch down to play with Scout. Her laughter was light and spontaneous when the dog rose up and placed a front paw on each of her shoulders.

He found the laugh lines at the corners of her lips irresistible. He chuckled with her.

Had he ever been able to laugh so freely? Maybe before his divorce? Before his estrangement from his daughter?

He didn't have an answer.

Cal was fighting his feelings for Jessica. He had been for a while now. It seemed to be a losing battle.

The air was warm despite the lateness of the hour, with a gentle breeze carrying the scent of salt from the ocean, and a light floral aroma that must have been Jessica's perfume. He heard the notes of a mournful blues song from a neighbor's open window.

He tried to remind himself of what Anna had done. Her deceit and manipulation. And why he wasn't prepared to have another relationship. He ticked off all the reasons he *shouldn't* get involved with Jessica.

She laughed again, tossing back her head, when Scout licked her face.

None of his reasons mattered. The battle was lost.

"Jess," he whispered.

She glanced over at him. He simply held out his hand, trusting she'd take it.

The corners of her mouth relaxed, and her eyes were questioning, but without a word she placed her hand in his.

He drew her to her feet, tempted to move closer to her. He wondered if she'd come to him. With the slightest pressure, he drew their joined hands toward him, hoping for the best, preparing for worst.

And she stepped forward.

Slowly, he raised their hands, kissed the back of hers, then released it, placing it on his chest. When she kept it there, he slid his arms loosely around her waist.

He felt something all-consuming, something that soared through him, when her arms wound around his neck and she closed the distance between them.

The need to kiss her was overwhelming. But there was some undefinable force within him that wanted to take it slow. They would never again have a first kiss. Her eyes were a luminous silver-gray in the moonlight. Glowing. Inviting. She was so tall her eyes were nearly at the level of his.

Her lips curved upward again, giving rise to those irresistible laugh lines.

He lowered his head and watched her eyes flutter closed. He brushed his lips across one eyelid. Then the other. He heard a soft moan. Saw her eyes open, surprise registered in their depths.

It made him smile. "You're stunningly beautiful, Jessica," he said so quietly that he didn't know if he'd actually spoken the words out loud.

But the crinkles appeared at the corners of her eyes, and he knew she'd heard him.

His willpower to resist her was exhausted. He lowered his head again. She closed her eyes again, and her sigh feathered against his lips.

When they drew apart, he was breathless. He felt more spent than after a five-mile search-and-rescue exercise. And all he wanted to do was dive right in again.

Instead, he slid a hand down her arm, took her hand in his. "Walk with me."

It wasn't a question, but she nodded and he led her down the stairs to the soft sand beach.

Jessica paused to pull off her sandals so she could walk barefoot.

He felt he should do the same and slipped off his shoes. He took Jess's sandals from her, left them with his shoes on the bottom step and linked his fingers with hers.

The moon had risen above the horizon but it was still low enough to cast its light in a gilded path across the iridescent black surface of the water. The sand was cool, coarse and faintly moist beneath their feet. He caught a whiff of her floral scent again, and inhaled.

Scout understood that this wasn't training, exercise or play, and walked sedately beside them.

Cal tried to remember if he'd ever felt so attracted to a woman and yet at ease with her at the same time. Not to his recollection. He slowed and she turned to him. With the stars bright overhead, when his lips lowered to hers, he, too, closed his eyes and savored the moment.

THE NEXT MORNING, Cal rolled over in bed but resisted opening his eyes. He preferred to sleep with the blinds and at times even the patio door open, to allow the night sky and fresh ocean-scented air to drift into the room. He'd situated his bed so he could see the water. He had no worries about intruders. Not with Scout sleeping on his own bed by the door and Cal's police-issue handgun in the locked compartment of his nightstand.

Having lived most of his life in Lincoln, he never tired of waking to the sun cresting the horizon and the soothing sounds of the waves rolling in. This morning he kept his eyes closed, wanting to preserve the images and sensations from the night before.

He was falling for the doc. He loved the feel of her in his arms, her hands in his or on his shoulders. Beautiful, yes, but it was the beauty inside that astounded him. She was smart, funny and had dedicated her life to helping people. Oh, yes, he was falling for her.

He gradually opened his eyes, and gazed through the doors at the surf pounding the sand with its early-morning ferocity.

Scout knew when Cal woke, and he scrabbled up to sit at the side of the bed, waiting for his morning run, followed by breakfast.

In the bright light of day, the contentment Cal had felt during the night faded. He sat up abruptly, dragged a hand over his hair and wondered what had gotten into him the night before. He'd kissed Jessica. She'd kissed him back.

But what now? He wasn't relationship material. He didn't trust in love and happily-ever-after. It wasn't fair to get into a relationship with all the baggage he was dragging around.

Maybe he should avoid her altogether, if he couldn't control his feelings. But that wasn't right or fair, either. He couldn't hide from things, or run away like Anna had.

He pulled on a pair of gym shorts and a T-shirt. He scooped kibble into Scout's dish for when they got back. Then he went into the bathroom, splashed cold water on his face and brushed his teeth.

He hoped a good, hard run would clear his head of all that foolishness about pursuing a relationship with Jessica.

Even if he *had* fallen for her.

CHAPTER FIFTEEN

CAL AVOIDED JESSICA for a few days. He came up with excuse after excuse, but felt miserable about it. He missed her. He missed simply *talking* to her. When she left a message telling him how much his and Scout's visits meant to Kayla, the difference they were making in her outlook and asking if they'd be available for another visit soon, he couldn't ignore it.

Seeing Jessica again during the hourlong visit with Kayla reminded him of all the reasons he was attracted to her. When she suggested they have coffee afterward on an outdoor patio that allowed dogs, he didn't have the resolve or the desire to say no.

As much as he wanted to simply reach out and touch her, just hold her hand, he wouldn't allow himself the luxury. He sensed, from the sadness in her eyes, that Jessica was unsure of where things stood between them. He respected her for not putting him on the spot.

They discussed Kayla mostly, until Jessica took another sip of her coffee and looked at him pensively. "I have an idea…" she began.

"About what?"

"Your daughter. Haley."

Cal's tone was cool when he spoke. "What about her?"

"I realize this is a sensitive subject, but hear me out, please."

Cal's only response was to raise an eyebrow.

"Have you tried to get in touch with Haley recently?"

His immediate inclination was to retort that it was none of her business, but he knew she was only trying to help. "I have, once or twice, but what's the point?" Scout rose from beneath the table, ambled over to Cal, and tried to rest both front paws on Cal's lap. Although it was something Scout did often, Cal blocked him because of his injury, and Scout accepted it without complaint.

Watching the interplay between them, Jessica's face lit up. "See, here's my idea. How does Haley feel about dogs?"

"She loves them. She'd always wanted one but Anna wouldn't hear of it. They're too messy and too much trouble." He hadn't intended to mimic his ex-wife's voice, but it just came out that way, and he was appalled. "Sorry," he mumbled.

"Don't worry about it. I'd probably be a lot less kind."

Cal ran a hand along Scout's back. The dog lay down and rested his head between his paws.

Jessica looked thoughtfully at Scout. "Have you considered using Scout to make a connection with Haley?"

"What do you mean?"

"Think about how Scout's helped Kayla. How your visits with her have made such a difference in dealing with her loss." She gestured at the dog. "Remember how happy and excited that little girl on the boardwalk was? Cindy? She couldn't get enough of Scout. She was blowing kisses to him the whole time her mother was dragging her away. Why not see if you can establish a bond with Haley through Scout?"

"Haley won't see me. She won't have anything to do with me." His pain and exasperation broke through. "If I try to set up a visit, I'm told it upsets her."

"But what if the visit wasn't just you? What if you made it clear, and it was communicated to Haley, that you'd like her to meet your dog?"

Cal weighed her words. He'd do anything to have a relationship with his daughter. "You really think it would work?"

"It can't hurt to try. That's for sure. I'm optimistic, but if it doesn't work, there's no downside, so why not?"

"What do you suggest?"

"Take Scout to Utah with you. Introduce him to Haley. Kids respond well to animals. We see it at the hospital with therapy dogs all the time. I'm sure Scout would be a natural. Maybe with his assistance, you can start to rebuild your relationship with your daughter."

"According to the court order, my visits with Haley have to be supervised." That stung. The implication that he could be a threat to his own daughter rankled him to his core. He watched Jessica carefully, fearing she'd think he was a monster to have warranted such an order. All he saw was curiosity and concern.

"The couple of times I tried to see her, even under those circumstances, she cried almost the entire hour. Do you have *any* idea how that made me feel? I couldn't stand to see her like that, and haven't scheduled another."

The judgment Cal feared from Jessica was nonexistent. Her look remained open and enthusiastic.

"Don't let it bother you that there'll be someone else there. Especially if having a caseworker supervise makes it more comfortable for Haley. The objective is for her to see you and to see how wonderful you are with Scout. Maybe then she can start to trust you again. Take things one step at a time. Get to see Haley even if it has to be supervised. Let Scout take the lead until Haley's comfortable with both of you."

Cal was skeptical. Why would Haley be less afraid of him because he had a dog? But Jessica was an intelligent, intuitive person who worked with physically and emotionally shattered people every day. If *she* thought there was a chance... Well, maybe... Haley was older now, and with the passage of time whatever lies his ex had told her might not be as sharp in her memory. He was willing to try anything for Haley. He nodded slowly. "I'll see if I can set up something. Thank you," he said. "Thank you for wanting to help."

When he returned home he put the wheels in motion. Jessica's warmth and genuine concern—what she was trying to do for him and his daughter—nearly overwhelmed him. He knew he wanted to see her again, and chastised himself for trying to drive her away. He hoped they could pick up where they were the night they'd walked on a moonlit beach.

CAL WAS WORKING with Scout on basic detection exercises in the division training yard. When his phone rang, he picked it up without glancing at the display. A pleasant voice with a hint of the South in it greeted him. "My name is Melody Ashworth. I'm the caseworker assigned to your daughter."

"My daughter?" Cal was having trouble breathing. He released Scout to play and lowered himself onto a wooden storage box located near the entrance.

"Haley's a charming, sweet young girl."

"Yes, she is." From what he could remember. "Thank you. You're calling about my request for a visitation?" Stupid question, he thought. Why else would she be calling? But he couldn't think straight. He was preoccupied with the possibility of seeing his little girl again.

"Yes, that's correct."

"And?"

There was a heavy sigh on the other end of the line. "Your case is…complicated, Mr. Palmer."

No kidding, he thought, resting an elbow on his left knee and his forehead in his hand.

"Your ex-wife was somewhat hesitant, but you have every right to see your daughter. I went to see Anna in person, to understand her reservations, but also to explain your legal rights."

This was not going well. Cal realized he'd set his hopes too high as he felt the sharp edges of despair slicing through him.

"Mr. Palmer? Are you still there?"

He tried to keep the disappointment from his voice. "Yes. Yes, I'm listening." When Scout ran over and leaned against him, Cal took some comfort in the physical contact with his dog.

"My concern, Mr. Palmer," the woman continued, "is that Haley's reluctant…dare I say, somewhat fearful…of seeing you."

Cal hadn't thought the agony could be any worse than what he'd already been through. He was wrong.

"I reviewed your files and couldn't find anything that would help me understand why that is."

He made a scoffing noise as he thought of how his ex-wife had poisoned his daughter against him. "If you come to understand it, please let me know." He groaned. "Sorry. I didn't mean that to come out the way it did." He paused. "Do you have any kids?"

"Yes, I do. A boy and a girl." There was a reserve in her voice.

"Then I hope you can understand my frustration. I just want a relationship with Haley." He felt a glimmer of hope. "What about Scout? Did you say I'd bring Scout with me?"

"Yes. The mention of the dog captured her interest." She paused. "I can go ahead and arrange the visitation…" Her voice trailed off.

Cal dropped his head into his palm again. "Yeah, but it would have to be forced. My daughter is afraid of her own father."

"I'm sorry…"

She did sound apologetic, and yet there was no point in pressing it. What would that accomplish? It was why he hadn't insisted on visitation in the past year. He'd hoped that, with time, her feelings would change. Obviously not enough time had passed. "No. The last thing I want is to cause distress for Haley."

"HAVE YOU HEARD back about Haley yet?" Jessica asked a few days later as they sat on his back deck, watching Scout play in the sand. There'd been an odd blip in their relationship, but they seemed to be on track again. She respected his need to take it slow and she was willing to give him the time he needed. Still, she felt a little thrill when he reached for her hand and held it in both of his.

"Yes."

The news couldn't have been good, if he hadn't offered it up, but she wanted to know what the outcome was. "And?"

"It didn't make a difference. Haley's still afraid of me, and I'm not going to push it."

"I'm so sorry." Jessica's disappointment was palpable. She really felt for Cal and had truly believed her idea would work. She sensed he wanted her to drop the subject, but here was her problem of getting too involved again. She just couldn't let it go. "So she had no interest in meeting Scout?"

He exhaled. "The caseworker said she seemed interested. Obviously not interested enough."

"How about if…"

He applied pressure to her hand. "Jess, I appreciate what you're trying to do, but it's not going to make any difference."

"Wait. Just let me explain my idea. Wait," she said again when he started to cut her off. "You said she was interested in Scout. Let's start with that. I remember you showing me Scout's baseball card. I loved it! How could anyone not love it? So send Haley a couple of baseball cards, along with some other pictures of Scout. Include a couple of you with Scout. You know, the one in your living room, with you on one knee and your arm around him?" Jessica rushed on, not giving Cal a chance to interrupt. "She'll love the pictures of Scout. And seeing you with him might help her feel more comfortable…" She finally ran out of steam and paused.

The silence pleased her, since it meant Cal must have been considering what she'd said. At least he hadn't shut down the idea immediately; it wasn't an outright no. She bit her lower lip, waiting.

"It's futile," he said with finality. "It's not going to work."

"But if you'd just…"

"No." He released her hand. "It's getting late. We should call it a night."

IT WAS A crazy idea, he thought as he watched Jessica's Miata pull out of his driveway. He'd already tried setting up a visitation with Haley, one that included bringing Scout along. It hadn't worked. He hadn't realized how high his hopes had been until he was told by Melody Ashworth that nothing had changed. Sending a few pictures wouldn't have any effect—because of the way Haley felt about him. Why set himself up for more disappointment?

Cal reached into the top drawer of his desk and took out one of Scout's baseball cards. He stared at it for a long moment. Maybe, just maybe…

Then he took out a couple more, flipped through some photos on his computer, sent five to print and composed a short letter to Melody, sending it to print, as well.

Putting everything in a letter-size envelope, he stuck a few stamps on it, and whistled for Scout.

This was a crazy idea, but not entirely without merit. No matter how much it would hurt if she rejected him again, he had to try. Otherwise, he'd just keep wondering.

He put the envelope next to his keys, and he and Scout headed to his bedroom.

THINKING ABOUT HALEY made him think more about Kayla, too. And the more Cal thought about her, the more determined he was to adopt her. He followed up with the contacts Jessica had provided, as well as the lawyer he'd retained. The lawyer wasn't encouraging when he phoned her.

"Unfortunately, the circumstances associated with the custody case for Haley raise red flags with the authorities," Stephanie advised.

"But all the allegations were proven false!" Cal objected.

"Okay. Let's say a yellow flag, then. They shouldn't consider it, but human nature being what it is, it's on record and it'll make them think twice. The authorities are risk-averse about endangering children. I'm sure you can appreciate that."

"Of course." Cal wanted to hurl the coffee mug he held against a wall. With slow, careful movements, he placed it on the counter instead and took a deep breath. "So I don't have a chance?"

"I didn't say that. *However*, your chances aren't good. In addition to the point we just discussed, qualifying for fostering or adoption will be more difficult because of your marital status."

Cal felt the sharp sting of disappointment when he hung up. He wasn't a bad person. Why was it that *nothing* seemed to be going right for him? The things that seemed to matter most were all beyond his reach. But then he thought about Jessica. *She* was something positive in his life.

CHAPTER SIXTEEN

CAL WAS TINKERING with his Porsche, trying to locate the source of an annoying rattle, when he received a call from Logan, rather than from Dispatch. He knew it had to be important if the captain was calling him directly. As they spoke, he quickly realized that time was critical.

A seven-year-old boy was missing. It was unknown whether the boy had wandered off or if he'd been abducted. All the boy's mother knew was that he'd been in their fenced backyard playing, and she'd gone inside to answer the phone. It was a wrong number, so she'd only been gone a moment. When she'd come back out, her son was gone and the back gate, leading to a neighborhood park, was swinging open on its hinges.

The mother had been hysterical and the father not much better when he arrived home. That might have been a problem for the other cops trying to get statements from the parents, but Cal and Scout had gotten what they needed—the T-shirt the boy had worn earlier that day. Scout had the scent and was following it at a rapid pace. Cal's thigh was aching and he wondered fleetingly if the pain would ever go away entirely. He favored his right leg with a slight limp as he did his best to keep up with Scout and not slow him down. He didn't want to break Scout's concentration. If he did, he could have trouble reestablishing the trail.

Cal knew when Scout was closing in as he burst forth with even greater speed. They weren't that far from the house, just approaching a service yard for the park. Scout circled and scented a service hatch left partially open, before sitting next to it and whining softly. It was the passive indication that he'd found the boy.

Cal pushed the hatch open all the way and shone his flashlight into the opening. The boy was there! He could see him at the bottom of the pit. He radioed in for assistance.

He called down to the boy. There was no response. Cal had no way of knowing if he was still alive and unconscious, or…

He couldn't get to him. Not on his own.

Thankfully, an SDPD cruiser pulled into the service yard and screeched to a halt. Two officers ran toward him. Since the boy was still unresponsive, they decided to lower the smallest of them, a female officer, into the cavity. Scant seconds later, they were hauling her out again, the young boy cradled in her arms.

Cal, the best trained in first aid, checked the boy for vitals. Both his heartbeat and breathing were dangerously slow and shallow. His right arm was at an abnormal angle, and Cal was positive he had a closed fracture.

"How long before the ambulance gets here?" he asked the other officer.

"Dispatch didn't have an ETA. There was a collision on Highway 163 near Park Boulevard, involving a school bus and a transport. Numerous kids were injured and all available units were dispatched. They'll be here as soon as they can," he responded.

When kids were involved, everyone acted with that much more alacrity, but caution, too. Those units would be tied up for a while, but he had a kid here, too. Ocean Crest Hospital was less than a ten-minute drive from where they were. He used a sling from his vehicle's first aid kit to immobilize the boy's arm and lifted him carefully. "You're driving," he said to the male cop. "You're taking us to Ocean Crest."

The cop raised his hands. "You've been on the job long enough. You know it's not procedure."

"Would you rather see the kid die?" Cal hissed. "The ambulance will take fifteen to twenty minutes, minimum, just to get here. You heard that. The kid's barely hanging on. With the fracture in his arm, he might have internal bleeding. If he has cracked ribs, his lung could be collapsed. And if he hit his head, he might have a concussion. Do you need me to continue? You're worried about *what*? Being written up for not following procedure?" Cal was nearly shouting now. "I'll drive, if one of you holds the kid."

"I'll drive," the female cop said. She glanced at her partner, who shook his head. "I'll drive," she repeated, this time holding Cal's gaze. "You coming?" she asked her partner.

He debated for only a moment. "Yeah," he grumbled, and climbed in the back of the cruiser, taking Scout with him.

They'd called it in. The boy's parents had

been notified, and they were on their way to the hospital, too. The female cop was a more than competent driver. They were at Ocean Crest in under seven minutes, and the kid was still alive.

The other cop agreed to stay in the cruiser with Scout, while Cal and the female cop took the boy in.

Cal was headed at a quick pace for triage, the female cop next to him, when he spotted Jessica.

"Go to triage. Tell them what we've got, while I see if I can get him looked at sooner."

Cal called Jessica's name, just as she was about to disappear behind a set of sliding doors. When she turned, he rushed over, ignoring the pain in his leg, the boy still in his arms. "I need your help."

She looked at the boy, then at him with alarm. "What happened?"

"He wandered away from his house and fell down a service shaft. I'm worried about his heart rate and respiration."

Jessica motioned for Cal to follow her into the emergency area. She checked a couple of curtained cubicles until she found an empty one and waved for him to place the boy on the bed. She checked his vitals; her hand shook as she brought the stethoscope to his chest. Her eyes were wide and round when she spoke. "He's going to need surgery for the arm. It's badly broken. I think he's got a collapsed lung, too, and likely needs a chest tube. He…has to have help, and quickly," she said before hastening out of the cubicle.

"Where're you going?" Cal yelled. He wanted to run after her, but the boy's breathing was getting worse by the minute and he didn't want to leave him.

Where on earth was she going? She'd confirmed that the kid needed help fast—*and then she just takes off?*

He stuck his head out of the cubicle. "I need assistance here!" he bellowed down the corridor. "I'm a police officer. I have a boy here who needs aid *now.*"

Before he could decide what else he should do, a tall, slim man in hospital scrubs and a lab coat, with a stethoscope hanging around his neck, trotted toward him. "Are you the cop with the injured boy?"

"Yes, but…" He scanned the corridor for Jessica.

"Then let's have a look at him," the doctor said briskly.

Cal stepped outside the cubicle to make room for the doctor, and did one final scan of the emergency room area for Jessica. She was nowhere to be seen. The female cop, however, was jogging toward him.

"I take it you bypassed the triage altogether," she said when she reached him.

"He needed help right away."

She nodded. "I get that. I gave them the particulars so they could open a chart on him."

"Yeah. Thanks." He couldn't stop wondering what had happened to Jessica. If she went to get another doctor, why hadn't she come back? Couldn't she see the rough shape the boy was in? He could've used her expertise in both trauma and pediatric surgery. But Jessica still was nowhere in sight.

The male doctor did a quick assessment, and a flurry of activity ensued.

The boy was under their care now. Cal and the other cop had done all they could here and they should head out, but he was still confused about Jessica. Where was she? What if her desertion of the young boy had cost him his life?

"Officer Palmer, did you hear me?"

"Sorry. What?"

"I asked if you'd be able to put in a good word for me with my sergeant. Collins, that's the other cop, he's pissed big-time about us transporting the boy in the cruiser. He's going to want his pound of flesh from me for going against the rules."

"Yeah. Sure." Hearing noises, Cal turned back to the cubicle where the kid was. The doctor, aided by two nurses, was pushing the gurney rapidly down the hallway. Cal knew enough about the configuration of the hospital to realize they were taking him to the surgical suite.

And, he wondered again, where Jessica was, if she was the best?

CHAPTER SEVENTEEN

JESSICA HAD TROUBLE breathing and her head was pounding. She'd left the emergency room and run to a staff washroom, locking herself inside. She leaned back against the door, closed her eyes and waited for her heart rate to settle.

She'd nearly fallen apart. What was she thinking? She *had* fallen apart. The little boy, barely breathing, had reminded her so much of Jake—the boy whose death she still felt responsible for. She was terrified to provide care or make any decisions about his well-being. She was petrified that her actions could have been fatal for him. In that panicky moment, she hadn't considered that with the boy's life hanging by a thread, her inaction could have done the same thing.

The look Cal had given her when she'd glanced back as she was rushing away was a combination of fury and disbelief. And the last thing she'd seen as she turned to run was disappointment. Still, his reaction couldn't come close to the self-loathing she felt. As a doctor, hadn't she sworn to treat the ill to the best of her ability?

Over the past few weeks, she'd learned enough about Cal to know that he'd expect an explanation from her.

How was she going to explain her failure to Cal, to Richard? She never spoke about Jake anymore, and she didn't want to talk to Cal about him, either.

And most importantly, how was she going to live with herself—especially if the boy didn't make it?

After splashing cold water on her face, Jessica left the staff washroom. First she went to the emergency room nurses' station to check on the boy's condition, then made her way up the stairs and to her office.

She was furious with herself. She hadn't even had a chance to become emotionally involved with the boy and she still couldn't cope. Despite the age difference, he reminded her so much of Jake. Not just his overall appearance and coloring, but the fact that there was a serious arm injury. She remembered

Jake had a sling on his arm, too, when the ambulance had first brought him in.

Her running away could have been a matter of life or death for the boy. She'd learned that he'd gotten a chest tube and been taken to surgery. She'd been right about the need for both, but being right meant nothing if she couldn't help him.

Thank God he was getting the care he needed. Morris was an excellent doctor and a competent surgeon. At the moment, she couldn't say the same about herself. The boy would be okay, she tried to assure herself. That was what mattered most.

She skirted the trauma unit nurses' station, not wanting to talk to anyone. She let herself into her office, closing and locking the door behind her before anyone realized she was there.

The potential consequences of what she'd done appalled her.

She sat down and rubbed her temples. She had to wonder if she'd made the right decision by staying in medicine.

She'd have to tell Richard what had happened. If she didn't, she suspected he'd hear about it from someone else. She didn't think she could remain at the hospital.

But maybe there was another option. She'd decided against it in the aftermath of losing Jake. Maybe now she needed to rethink things...

She had a department meeting in half an hour that she couldn't miss. She hoped she could pull herself together by then, but it gave her some time. She turned on her computer and entered the key words— "organizations providing doctors to developing countries." The search engine quickly produced "about 123,000,000 results in 0.83 seconds."

She groaned. Narrowing her search down to South and Central America produced "about 44,700,000 results."

Scrolling through a few pages showed her that there was no shortage of need for doctors across the globe.

If there was one thing she understood about herself, it was her own inability to remain emotionally detached. Years ago, she'd kicked around the idea of working overseas; that was when she was first grappling with the feelings of guilt and inadequacy following Jake's death. She'd considered joining one of the organizations that sent doctors to developing countries around the world to provide much-needed essential care. She hadn't thought about it since she'd switched to trauma, but now that it seemed her decision paralysis had resurfaced and might have put a patient at risk, her options might well have narrowed down to reconsidering overseas work—or leaving medicine altogether.

She thought of Kayla and how the possibility of inadvertently hurting her had scared her to death. And now, with what had just happened with the boy Cal had brought in... She couldn't risk having that occur again, not to Kayla or to any other patient, young or old.

Working overseas, she'd be providing basic first aid—vaccinations, health education, stitches, helping with routine births. Nothing life-threatening that she couldn't handle from an emotional perspective. She would travel around, visit remote villages that didn't have access to health care. That kind of assignment would be ideal.

She stared at the daunting results of her search. If she was genuinely serious about exploring this, where should she start? And how would she know if an organization was reputable and credible?

She did another search for international aid organizations with headquarters in California, if for no other reason than to keep her mind off everything that was haunting her.

With a little more effort, she came across one organization, Care Across Continents, that had its corporate office in San Diego. Care Across Continents was an organization similar to Doctors Without Borders. It interested her, and after some more digging, she discovered that one of its board members was a former university professor of hers. She'd always liked Harold Massey. What better way to learn about the organization, to find out whether she'd be a good fit, than to meet with a long-standing director?

She chewed on the tip of her pen while she waited for the phone to be answered. When an elderly sounding lady picked up the phone, Jessica asked for Dr. Massey. She was told he wasn't in the office. Jessica explained why she was calling, and she was given an appointment to see him the following Monday.

When Jessica hung up, she felt excited and panicked at the same time. She'd initiated the process, and she knew it was the right thing for her. She wouldn't let anyone—not her parents, her friends or Cal—talk her out of doing this.

She rubbed her temples with her fingertips, but the headache that had been raging there was now only a dull ache.

If all went well during her meeting with Dr. Massey, she'd submit her application for a foreign assignment with Care Across Continents right there and then.

And at least temporarily, she'd managed to get her mind off the incident earlier that day.

AT THE END of his shift, Cal swung by the hospital. Learning that Jessica had left, he drove directly to her home. The kid he'd rescued was going to be okay. He was assured of that while he was at the hospital. But it was no thanks to Jessica. He needed to understand what had happened there.

He thought about leaving Scout in the back of his truck with the cooling system on, but decided to bring him along instead.

He knocked on Jessica's door.

After knocking a few more times, he went back to her driveway and looked through a small decorative window in her garage door. Unless she'd gone out for a run or a walk, she was home since her car was in the garage.

This time he used more force, banged on the door, and didn't stop until she finally opened it.

"What the…" he started, but the words died in his throat when he saw her. Her hair was still tied back, but it was disheveled, with strands sticking up all over. Her eyes were red-rimmed, and he suspected she'd been crying, but what concerned him the most was her color.

Her normally tanned skin was pale as alabaster.

"Hey!" He reached out for her, cupped her elbow with his hand and led her back inside. "You okay?"

She nodded listlessly, which did nothing to reassure him. "Here." He guided her to the sofa. "Sit down and I'll make you a cup of tea."

"No, thanks. I'm fine. Really," she said in a reedy voice.

His burning anger over what she'd done at the hospital was doused by his concern for her. She must be sick, he speculated, and that was why she'd rushed off and left the boy the way she had. "Are you ill?"

She shook her head.

It wasn't making sense to him. "If you're not ill, then what? What happened at the hospital today?"

She lowered her head into her palms.

Cal patted her back reassuringly. "Tell me what's wrong," he coaxed. "What happened today?" he asked again.

"I can't…"

"Can't what?"

"I… I can't talk about it. The only people who know are my parents, some of my colleagues and the hospital administration. In all the years since I made the switch, I hadn't confided in anyone else."

"The switch?" He was trying to keep up with her. "You mean this has something to do with leaving pediatrics and moving to trauma?"

Her eyes filled with tears as she nodded.

"Help me understand," he coaxed, as he passed her a box of tissues from the side table.

She was silent for a long moment but finally whispered, "Maybe it's time I talked about it." She paused, and gulped audibly. "I lost a patient," she said so softly Cal had to lean in to hear her.

"I'm sorry, Jess." He reached for her hand and held it. "Not too many people outside your profession would understand how that must feel, but as cops we have to face that sad reality sometimes, as well. Not being there in time to save someone. Unfortunately, it happens, despite our best efforts. We can't save everyone."

JESSICA UNDERSTOOD THAT he was trying to help, to make her feel better, but his comment cut deep. She felt her muscles tense. In her case it had been just the opposite. It wasn't that she couldn't save Jake. She was *responsible* for his death.

She tried to tug her hand back, but he held tight. "You don't understand…"

She couldn't continue. She lowered her head again and squeezed her eyes shut.

"I lost a friend once." Cal filled the silence. "Todd was a good cop. He got called out to a domestic disturbance. Usually we don't respond to domestics on our own. They're often… problematic. But the 9-1-1 caller sounded desperate. Todd was closest and arrived in a few minutes. I was maybe twenty minutes away, normal driving time. I made it there in less than fifteen.

"It was too late. When Todd attempted to restrain and arrest the husband, the wife— the 9-1-1 caller—stabbed Todd in the back with a kitchen knife. Her aim was deadly." Cal shook his head. "The wife had the crap kicked out of her by the husband, and she still tried to protect him."

Jessica raised her head, and her eyes met his. She swallowed the lump in her throat. She understood the psychology of abused women. She knew a little about it from her classes in university, seen it firsthand with some of the patients in the emergency department. She covered their joined hands with her other hand, and it was her turn to momentarily give comfort. "I'm so sorry…"

"It was a long time ago. I've…well, I haven't accepted it. I doubt that you can ever accept something like that. But I've learned to live with it. I just wanted you to know that if anyone can understand, I do."

Jessica shook her head sadly. "No. I don't think you can."

She saw the flicker of hurt in his eyes. He'd

shared an obviously painful memory with her, trying to make her feel better. Maybe, as she'd said earlier, it would help if she talked about it.

"It isn't the same," she began. "You couldn't have done anything other than what you did. As tragic as it is, you didn't have a chance to save him because you weren't there." She paused, willed herself not to let the tears fall.

"My situation was different. I *could* have saved the boy. *Should* have!" There was vehemence, anger, pain—she could hear it all jumbled together in her voice. She broke eye contact. It would be easier to tell him without looking at him, not seeing the judgment or censure that was sure to come.

"I was performing a procedure on a young patient and it went horribly wrong." Now she did pull her hands back. She clasped them together, scraped at one thumbnail with the other. "Jake was under my care. He was a vivacious, athletic, previously healthy thirteen-year-old boy who sustained a deep-tissue infection in his arm. The infection was a rapidly spreading strep necrotizing fasciitis." Realizing he might not know what that meant, she glanced up briefly. "He was playing football and tried to catch the ball in the end zone. He caught it high in the air, but landed hard on his side and past the end zone. There was a rusty, old survey stake in the ground and it tore through the fleshy part of his upper arm. He got strep—an infection— as a consequence."

She rose and moved away from him to stare out the window. "With the spread of the infection, the hospital's chief of surgery suggested it would be advisable to amputate the limb. Jake's parents—*Jake himself*—begged me to save his arm. They thought he was good enough at sports and loved it enough to go pro. I couldn't help caring about this bright, engaging young boy." She turned to face Cal, and her vision blurred. "How could I not?"

In order to continue, she had to turn away again.

"The decision as to whether the arm should be amputated was ultimately mine, once I assessed the extent of the infection during the surgical procedure. I had to decide whether I could get all the infection out and save the boy *and* his arm. Or if the infection was too advanced, I'd have to amputate the arm to save Jake's life."

She pressed her lips together. She could remember standing in the bright glare of the operating room lights as she debated that very question for interminable minutes with her surgical team standing by. She could see Jake's face—the mop of bright red hair, light smattering of freckles visible across his cheeks and the bridge of his nose above the oxygen mask. The image was so real, as it always was whenever it came to her, awake or in dreams, she could almost count the freckles. She wrapped her arms around her torso to fight off a terrible chill.

"I… I decided to save the limb. The procedure was successful. Jake and his parents were elated. They were grateful…so grateful. They sent me a huge fruit basket that I shared with the team. All of them loved Jake. It was impossible not to."

She paused. She knew Cal was listening even though she couldn't see him. She wondered if he'd say anything. Spare her from having to finish it. But he remained silent. Scout rolled over in his sleep, and his paw must have connected with the wall. She could hear the scraping sound before he started snoring again.

"Overnight Jake's blood pressure plummeted and he died of sepsis."

She heard Cal push his chair back, heard him approach. He was behind her, wrapping his arms around her, resting his chin on her shoulder, his face next to hers. "You can't blame yourself for that. You made the best decision you could under the circumstances. We're all human. None of us is perfect. None of us makes the right decision one hundred percent of the time. Also, you couldn't ignore his parents' wishes. With Todd and me, I tortured myself for a long time. What if I'd taken Carnegie Avenue instead of La Salle Boulevard? Would I have gotten all green lights and not had to slow down to clear those intersections on La Salle? Could I have been in time, if only I'd had the guts to drive even faster?" He paused.

She felt his warm breath on her cheek and inhaled the fresh, clean scent of his soap.

"It's not your fault," he repeated. "You can't blame yourself."

She exhaled heavily and shook her head. "I can and I do…*every day*. And I'm not the only one. Jake's parents blamed me, too. They accused me of malpractice."

He gently turned her to face him. "They were grieving, distraught. Under the circumstances, it's understandable, but that doesn't make them right."

"Yeah. People told me that, too. My parents. Colleagues. But I was struggling with my own grief and self-recrimination, and I was too preoccupied to notice the change in people's attitudes. I was found guilty by my peers before the investigation even began. I had no collegial support. The hospital was sued, too."

"What were the findings of the investigation?"

She lifted a shoulder, let it drop again. "I was cleared of malpractice. All my actions and decisions were deemed defensible and consistent with best practices. I got to keep my job. There was a settlement with Jake's family, not on the basis of fault, but to avoid a lengthy court battle that could have reflected negatively on the hospital."

Cal thought about his own circumstances after Anna's allegations, and the parallels did not escape him. "So you did what you considered best for the boy and you were vindicated by the investigation."

"The investigation might have found in my favor, but I… I couldn't…*not to this day*… overcome my own feelings of guilt…of culpability. I seriously thought about giving up medicine altogether."

He tightened his hold on her, and she turned to face him. "What made you change your mind?"

"My parents. They've always believed in me. They've always been my rock." She laughed. "They even played their trump card. They'd put me through university—not easy with their income. How could I throw all that away, they asked. In the end, I let them convince me."

"And you changed your field of specialization."

"Yes. I knew that by allowing myself to get close to Jake, get emotionally connected with him, I'd lost my perspective…"

"That's ridiculous!" Cal cut in. "How could you think such a thing. If you didn't care, you'd be a lousy doctor. Don't confuse caring with losing perspective."

She huffed out a breath. "All right, I believed and still believe that becoming too close to a patient can cloud my judgment, can make me potentially incapable of unbiased decisions. Please let me finish," she urged as he was about to interrupt again. "In hindsight, I've asked myself over and over, if I'd been strictly analytical, scientific, removed my feelings from the equation, would I have amputated the limb to save Jake? My entire career I've struggled to maintain the 'detached concern' that was a basic tenet they tried to drill into us in medical school. I don't know how other doctors achieve it. We're dealing with people's *lives*, not manufacturing widgets here. Well, with me, the 'detached concern' tenet never took, and I feel my inability might have cost Jake his life."

"So…not wanting to risk getting emotionally involved with a patient again, you left pediatrics in favor of trauma medicine?"

"Yes." She was comforted that he seemed to understand her rationale. Her parents had been relieved about her compromise, but never understood it. "I felt that with trauma, I wouldn't spend enough time with a single patient to establish a connection. Right or wrong, it's also easier for me to maintain my…detachment with adults. In trauma, I see fewer children."

"That's the decision you made, and I respect it, but is it really a solution?"

"I felt—feel—it was the only one I could make at the time, short of leaving medicine."

Cal stepped back and his gaze held hers. "What about Kayla?"

Jessica felt the blood drain from her face. "Kayla's your patient. You kept her as your patient."

She nodded mutely.

He placed his hands gently on her shoulder. "So, you've broken your own rule with Kayla, by caring deeply about her and choosing to be her primary care physician."

"Yes." The word was more of a breath than a whisper. Tears clouded her vision again, and she could feel her panic building. "Thank God she wasn't badly injured, because I struggled with it nearly every day, wondering if I was doing the right thing for her, ordering the right tests, not missing anything I should've seen. None of those decisions meant life or death in her case, and I was still a mess."

"And you found the fluid on her lung that the other doctor would've been oblivious to because he didn't order the CT. That alone could have saved her life."

She sighed. "Today, I saw that boy, so similar to Jake, and I couldn't deal with it." The tears were stinging her eyes, and when she looked up at Cal again, she braced herself for the reprimand.

Instead, Cal gathered her in his arms, cradling her head against his shoulder. "In a world that's been very cruel to Kayla, she was fortunate to have you watching out for her."

"And today...?" She gazed at him, wanting his understanding, not willing to hope for absolution.

"Today couldn't be helped."

Jessica slid her arms around him and let the tears flow.

CHAPTER EIGHTEEN

MONDAY AFTER WORK, Scout and Cal walked out of the division and toward his car. With each passing day, Cal felt stronger, and not quite as drained. He was hoping they'd clear him for regular duty soon, as opposed to this joke of modified police work, which essentially amounted to administrative tasks.

He'd wanted to call Jessica, but the day had gotten away from him. He'd been worried about her ever since she'd confided in him the week before. He couldn't begin to understand the demons she was trying to overcome, but he wanted her to know he was there for her, to support her, whatever she needed. The incident had somehow made him care even more about her; perhaps it was her vulnerability.

He realized he wanted to both protect her and cherish her. He knew she was working nights this week, and he wouldn't be able to spend the evenings with her.

Near the parking lot, he heard heated voices in the training yard and walked over to the fence. He saw Vasquez and Brody and Brody's dog, Nitro, and words were definitely being exchanged. Curious, he stopped to watch.

Brody yanked Nitro's leash, and they exited the yard through the far gate, while Rick headed back in Cal's direction. Rick called his dog, Sniff, who'd been lying quietly in the corner of the yard, not far from him and Scout.

Rick's face was flushed and Cal could see the tension in his stride and deportment as he left the yard through the gate closest to Cal.

Cal fell in step beside Rick as Scout and Sniff exchanged greetings. "What was that all about?"

Rick shook his head. "Don't get me going about that moron. He's lucky I didn't clock him."

"The guy's a jerk," Cal agreed.

"If that's all it was, I could let it go." Rick stopped, shoved his hands in his pockets and stared down at the ground. "I'm worried about Nitro. He's an exceptional dog, but he's still young and impressionable. I think that moron is going to ruin him."

"I wish I could disagree with you, but… I can't." Cal thought back for a moment. "In fact, I told Jagger the very same thing the day I came in after the earthquake."

"Frankly, I don't know why Logan keeps Brody on. Brody's a disgrace to our unit."

"Yeah, I can't argue with that, either. Want to grab a beer? I'll buy."

Rick patted Cal on the back. "Thanks for the offer. I'll take a rain check. Right now I want to blow off some steam with Jagger and then go for a workout. You should get home, anyway. I know the days are still wearing on you." Rick whistled to Sniff, but called out to Cal before he entered the building. "I won't forget about the rain check, though. You owe me!"

When Cal got home, he took a Coke Zero and a couple of frozen burgers from his refrigerator, and noticed the message light flashing on his phone. Taking a long drink from the can, he put his voice mail on speaker.

"This is Melody Ashworth, the caseworker for your daughter." The voice with the Southern accent drifted through the room.

Cal lowered the can slowly and moved

closer to the phone. His heart was thundering and his palms were suddenly damp.

"I'm pleased to let you know that the visitation with your daughter, Haley, has been arranged, as you requested. The pictures of Scout did the trick. Thank you for sending them to me."

The message went on to give him the proposed date and time. "The visit will be supervised by me," she added. "Your request to introduce Haley to your service dog has also been authorized. To facilitate this, I recommend the visit be at Cedar City's municipal offices. There's a small private courtyard at the back of the building. If that's acceptable to you, we can meet there." She explained that her role was to ensure Haley's well-being. If his daughter seemed distressed or at risk in any way, she'd end the visit immediately. Although her comments got his back up, his focus remained on the fact that he'd be seeing Haley.

Cal jotted down the particulars Melody provided, saved the message and, with a loud, "Huh," dropped into his easy chair in the living room. Gradually he let a smile spread across his face until he was grinning. He let out a hoot so loud he startled Scout. Calming him, Cal shook his head slowly. "Well, what do you know? It worked!"

He was going to see his little girl.

He sprang up, startling Scout again. After assuring him once more that all was well, he went back to the phone.

First, he called Melody Ashworth to confirm the meeting and, pushing the offensive cautionary words out of his mind, he thanked her profusely for making it possible.

Next, he called the number for Ocean Crest Hospital and entered Jessica's extension. He knew she was working, but when the call went to voice mail, he decided against leaving a message. This was not the type of appreciation you expressed through voice mail.

The welcome news must have given him his second wind; he no longer felt the least bit tired. He grabbed a light jacket and headed back out the door.

He stopped at a market on his way to the hospital and bought the largest bouquet of flowers they had.

At Ocean Crest he went directly to Jessica's office, but found her door locked. Glancing around, he recognized one of the trauma nurses at the unit station. Her name was Marian...or Marcia. He remembered her from the triage area at the earthquake site.

"What lovely flowers!" she said when he approached her. "Are they for a patient? Lucky person, whoever it is."

Cal surreptitiously read the name on the tag pinned to her lab coat. "It's nice to see you again, Marcia. No, they're not for a patient. These are for Jessica. Is she around?"

"Oh, I remember you from the earthquake triage site. Sorry, but Jessica stepped out for a couple of hours."

The disappointment must have shown on his face, as Marcia—preoccupied though she seemed to be—checked her watch and hurried on. "She had a meeting or something. Or an interview. I can't remember exactly what she said. Anyway, she only went a few blocks away and should be back anytime. You're welcome to wait. Or I can take the flowers for you and put them in water."

"Thanks. An interview?" He remembered Jessica telling him she'd considered getting out of medicine altogether after the tragic incident with the young boy. He hoped that wasn't the case. "She's not planning to leave medicine, is she?" He was mildly annoyed that if she had an interview she hadn't mentioned it to him.

Marcia laughed. "Oh, definitely not! No. It's... Let me think. It's with an organization. What was it called?" The telephone rang; she picked it up and spoke for a few minutes, then turned back to Cal. "Now, where were we?"

"You were telling me where Jessica is."

"Oh, right. She's meeting with..."

A doctor came over then and had a brief discussion with Marcia. She made some notes on her computer.

"Now, can I take those flowers for you, or would you like to wait?"

"Where did you say she went?" Cal was feeling distinctly uncomfortable with what he was hearing.

"Oh, right. She's meeting with someone from..." She snapped her fingers. "That's it! The Care Across Continents organization. You must've heard of them. Who can blame them for being interested in Jessica with her experience and credentials?"

Marcia's face showed pride, almost as if

it was her daughter she was talking about. But Cal's mood had soured. "I didn't realize they were looking for doctors to work here," he said cautiously.

"They're not, no. It's an assignment out of the country."

"Oh. Thank you." Cal didn't know what else to say. He didn't know what this meant or why she hadn't told him.

He didn't bother passing the flowers to Marcia, nor was he inclined to wait.

He retraced his steps to the entrance but he felt dejected. He'd thought there was something between him and Jessica. He'd let his guard down. He'd confided some of his most personal feelings to her—about his work, his marriage and Haley—and she didn't even tell him she was planning to *leave* San Diego. Leave the continent, for that matter.

Just as he was beginning to fall in love with her… Love? Was that what he was feeling? He'd have to think about that later. But they unquestionably had *some* kind of relationship, some kind of bond. He'd trusted her, and the fact that she'd withheld such crucial information troubled him. He hadn't thought she'd be deceitful, but it seemed he'd misjudged.

His ex-wife, Anna, came to mind. How long had *she* kept critical information about their marriage from him before she dropped the bomb—telling him it was over?

Was Jessica doing the same thing now?

Maybe it was him. Maybe *all* the women in his life were destined to be devious and untrustworthy. Although he'd been finding it harder and harder to resist the beautiful doctor, his resolve to avoid romantic entanglement had just resurfaced full force.

He saw a waste container outside the main entrance doors and tossed in the flowers.

JESSICA SAT BEHIND her desk after returning to the hospital from her meeting with Dr. Harold Massey. She stared out the window but her mind wasn't on what was going on outside.

The meeting had gone well. Harold had introduced her to Raymond Goulding, the executive director of Care Across Continents, and she'd left her résumé with him. He promised he'd look it over and, if all seemed to be in order, he'd give her a call in a few days to set up an interview.

Jessica thought about Kayla and the other

important things she'd have to deal with if she left the country.

Kayla would be fine. She was confident about that. The child was doing so much better in her group home, thanks to Cal and Scout and their visits. She contemplated Cal's desire to adopt Kayla, and she hoped his efforts would come to fruition. But she reminded herself again that there was nothing she could do about it. As her father was prone to saying, she couldn't save the world, wish as she might.

But even if the adoption didn't work out, Jessica had to trust that the system would take care of Kayla. She'd done everything she could, and she had to shut it down now. Kayla's health was fine, and the child was no longer her responsibility, not since she'd been discharged.

That was for the best, Jessica reminded herself. Although Kayla's injuries hadn't been too serious, Jessica had found herself questioning virtually all her decisions related to the girl's care. The memory of Jake, the boy who'd lost his life because of her, continued to make her doubt herself every step of the way.

Then her thoughts turned to the boy Cal had brought into emergency and what she'd done. She'd panicked and run away. She couldn't keep doing that. She couldn't.

But if she left California...

She thought about Cal, and the constriction in her chest made her gasp. Had she acted too rashly? How could she leave Cal, considering how she felt about him?

But if she stayed...and someone died because she didn't provide the proper care...

She'd wondered whether it would be different with Care Across Continents, and she'd concluded it would be. She'd see a patient once—usually for basic things—and that would be that. There'd be no opportunity for emotional attachment.

But what about the boy in emergency? No. That was an aberration. That wouldn't happen again. It was the emotional entanglement she had to avoid.

She heaved a huge sigh. Of relief?

She was torn between Cal and pursuing the job opportunity with Care Across Continents. A headache was starting to pound behind her temples.

In the end, she knew she'd have to go with her heart. The opportunities for a lifelong love were too few and far between. She'd stay in San Diego to be with Cal—and then figure out the rest.

CHAPTER NINETEEN

RAYMOND GOULDING, THE executive director for Care Across Continents, called Jessica a week later. He said he was very impressed with her credentials, and he wanted to see her for an interview. It was more of a formality, he stated. Just to be sure she had all the information she needed to make an informed decision.

It was on the tip of her tongue to thank him but decline gracefully. Then she thought about her reason for doing that. The reason was Cal. But Cal had changed. He'd been cold and distant for a week or more. Her attempts to contact him had been unsuccessful or politely rebuffed.

Hurting from what she saw as his rejection, she decided to go ahead with the interview. At least she wouldn't be closing the door prematurely. She'd know what her options were with Care Across Continents, and she'd have to confront Cal, understand what the possibilities were for them.

The following Monday, with still no word from Cal, Jessica met with Raymond Goulding. He was middle-aged, brilliant and obviously very committed to the work of the organization. She and Raymond hit it off and she knew she'd be comfortable working for him. He gave her every indication that the position was hers if she was interested, and if her references checked out. The mention of references brought Jake to mind, but there was nothing negative on her file, since all her actions and decisions had been found to be appropriate.

If she accepted the job, she wouldn't have many dealings with Raymond. He was based in San Diego and responsible for administration and fundraising. Rather, she'd be reporting to the country's chief doctor, wherever she was assigned, and working with the care team there. It was good to know that the organization was well-run and if she had any questions or problems she could always contact Raymond.

She was almost certain that they'd offer her the position; Raymond had as good as said so. And she wasn't just running away from her problems; the organization and their work interested and invigorated her. She'd wanted to join their team.

She realized she'd just thought of it in the past tense. And now? Was she still enthusiastic? And if not, why? The indecisiveness she'd struggled with seemed to be invading other areas of her life.

But the answer was simple. Calen Palmer. Whether she liked it or not, she'd been falling in love with Cal. He'd become her priority. But did he want her? And if she abandoned her plans to work with Care Across Continents, what would she do here? How would she deal with her continued tendency to care too deeply about her patients? Trauma might have reduced the frequency of these occurrences, but didn't completely solve the problem.

And on the subject of Cal, she couldn't ignore the change in their relationship. Why couldn't he be consistent?

She'd barely seen him in the past couple of weeks. Yet, for the first time in years, she'd been thinking about the possibility of a long-term relationship. She'd grown not just to love him but also to respect him. He always seemed to be on her mind, and when she wasn't with him, she longed to be.

She'd tried to figure out what had prompted the change in him. The only thing she could come up with was the fact that Cal had gone back to work. Nothing else had changed. Maybe it hadn't happened right away, but that was all she could think of.

A chill ran down her spine. Was it possible that she'd been no more than a convenience for Cal? Someone to help out with Scout and alleviate some of his boredom while he was off work? And now that he was back at work, he no longer needed her?

No. That couldn't be it. Cal wasn't like that. He was a warm, caring, *honest* person. He wouldn't treat her in such an insensitive manner. But then what was it? Nothing else came to mind. The hurt was immediate and intense.

The right and necessary thing for her to do was accept the job that Care Across Continents was going to offer her.

She got up from her desk, went to the ward's kitchenette to pour herself a cup of coffee and returned to her office. Her resolve to take the job had solidified. There was no point in trying to discuss it with Cal. He was hardly speaking to her now, anyway.

CAL WAS EARLY. *Very* early, and he knew it. He couldn't help it. He was too excited and anxious to see his daughter after nearly a year.

He hadn't wanted to be late, but he hadn't counted on being over half an hour early, either. He got up to pace the small, confined courtyard behind Cedar City's municipal offices. He tossed the Kong for Scout a few more times. The dog just gave him a frustrated look. Running the short distance from one end of the yard to the other didn't give him much to do.

He could see the nervous energy building in the dog. It shouldn't have surprised him, with the limited exercise Scout had been getting.

Great! All he needed was for Scout *not* to be on his best behavior with Haley, and the whole opportunity could backfire.

If Haley was scared of Scout, his chance would be shot. He called the dog, and recognized that his tone was uncharacteristically harsh. It wasn't Scout's fault; he hadn't done anything wrong. It was his own nerves and

Scout was picking up on it. "Sorry, pal." He offered Scout a dog biscuit.

This meeting was so important to him, and it *had* to go well. He felt guilty as he suddenly remembered that he hadn't thanked Jessica for making it possible.

His leg was starting to ache, so he sat back down on the bench and checked his watch for the hundredth time. He shot up when he heard the door from the building open.

Standing there, holding the hand of a full-figured woman, was his own beautiful Haley.

His little girl was right there in front of him and so beautiful. He just wanted to rush over and hold her, but he knew he couldn't.

Instead, he walked slowly toward the pair and introduced himself to Melody Ashworth, then focused all his attention on his daughter.

She'd grown! By his estimation, she had to be another two or three inches taller. Her blonde hair was longer, too, but still curling wildly as it always had. And her eyes—those striking china-blue eyes—were round as saucers and staring at him.

Taking a few slow steps forward, ignoring the throbbing in his thigh, he crouched down to be at eye level with her. "Hi, Haley, sweetheart." Her mouth formed a pout and her lower lip trembled. He could see her small hand clench the woman's.

He knew her well enough that he could tell she was about to burst into tears; he couldn't let that happen. If it did…this would all be a wasted effort.

He sent Scout a couple of quick hand signals. Scout edged over to him, dropped down, straight as a bullet, front paws extended, and placed his head on the grass between his paws.

It was one of Scout's most engaging, least threatening poses, and Haley's gaze was immediately drawn to the dog. Her lips relaxed as did her grip on the woman's hand.

"Haley, I'd like you to meet Scout. Scout is a police dog. Scout, say hello to Haley."

Scout lifted his head just enough to emit a happy bark.

Haley giggled, and Cal's heart swelled at the sound he'd longed to hear for far too long.

Cal sent Scout another hand signal and the dog covered his snout with his paws. "Scout's shy, Haley," Cal explained. "He needs you to make friends with him. Are you okay with that?"

Haley glanced up at Melody. The woman

nodded encouragingly, and released Haley's hand. The little girl stepped closer.

"Why don't you say hi to Scout?"

She gave Cal a timid look, and smiled at the dog. "Hi, Scout."

The dog shifted his paws to the ground.

"See? He's not so shy anymore. Would you like him to sit up and shake your hand?"

"Uh-huh." She nodded, blonde curls bouncing around her face.

"Then ask him to sit and shake a paw."

She did, and although she took a hurried step back when Scout abruptly rose, she accepted the paw he extended, then broke into peals of laughter.

Cal was elated. He looked up at Melody with a smile, and was gratified to see that she was smiling, too. She nodded again and wordlessly backed away to sit at a patio set positioned under a large tree.

Haley was charmed by Scout; Cal needn't have worried. Scout was at his most endearing. For the first time since Cal and Anna had separated, Haley exhibited an openness and a lack of unease with him. When their hour was up, Haley gave Scout a big hug, and felt comfortable enough to embrace Cal, too.

Holding his daughter loosely in his arms, Cal felt his eyes burn. He squeezed them shut and delighted in the feel of holding Haley, the fragrance of a soft floral shampoo in his nostrils.

After Melody had escorted Haley out of the courtyard, Cal collapsed on the bench, leaned back with his eyes closed and blew out a breath. Scout nudged his hand, then rested his head in Cal's lap.

They sat that way for several minutes, with Cal embracing the sensation of seeing his daughter again.

"Mr. Palmer?"

Cal nearly jumped out of his skin. He sat up hastily and saw Melody Ashworth standing before him. He wasn't sure why, but he felt a pang of apprehension "Yes?"

"Could I talk to you for a moment?"

He stood up. "Of course." The pang intensified. "Is something wrong?"

She smiled gently, dispelling much of his unease. "No. On the contrary. Why don't we sit down?"

She led him to the patio set. "I watched you and your daughter carefully this afternoon," she began.

His anxiety was back. Then he reminded himself that she'd said there wasn't anything wrong. He held his breath and waited for her to continue.

"I thought you might like to know before you leave here today that, based on my assessment and best judgment, I'm going to recommend regular visitations. There's no question in my mind that you love your daughter. I saw absolutely no indication that you're a threat to her in any way. I'm going to suggest a couple more supervised visits. If nothing changes, you'll have my recommendation for regular unsupervised visitation rights."

Cal was speechless. To have his visit with Haley go better than he'd imagined, and now have this caseworker say what she just had—it exceeded his wildest dreams. "But my ex-wife…"

"Leave her to me. I'll talk to her. We'll see how it goes."

Cal rose and extended a hand to Melody. She stood, too, and they shook.

"I don't know how to thank you," he said as he and Scout walked through the back gate. He was surprised he'd been able to get the words out, he felt so overcome by emotion.

He took a few moments to gather himself before pulling out of the parking lot.

The drive along I-15 S back to San Diego went quickly and he drove as far as the California border before stopping for a few hours' sleep in a motel. He was up early the next morning to finish the trip, arriving at his house shortly before eight. He felt energized despite the seven-hour, five-hundred-mile drive.

He was due at the division by 9:00 a.m., and he had just enough time for a shower, change of clothes and a quick breakfast before he and Scout were on their way again.

"You're looking good this morning," Logan commented when Cal walked into the unit room.

"I'm feeling good, Jagger," Cal responded.

"I'm tempted to take you off modified duties."

Cal felt the spring in his step and grinned at Logan. "I'd love it. Convince the human resources department, will you?"

"Phone for you, Tracker," a female officer called out to Cal. "You *are* looking good today," she said with a sassy grin as she handed him the phone.

"Thanks, Shannon," he said to the officer, then he spoke into the phone. "Palmer here."

"This is Melody Ashworth," the voice on the line announced.

He hesitated and felt his blood run cold. "Ms. Ashworth. How are you?"

"I'm fine, thank you."

"Why are you calling the division?" he wondered.

She chuckled. "Because I've been trying your cell but it keeps going to voice mail."

Cal yanked his phone out of its holster. The battery was dead. Of course it was. He'd been so preoccupied with seeing Haley that he hadn't bothered to charge his phone on the way to Utah or back again. "Sorry," he murmured.

"Don't worry about it. I have news for you."

Cal's heart was racing again. It was too soon for her to call with good news about his visitations, wasn't it? "Yes?" He couldn't think of anything else to say.

"As we discussed, I've arranged two more supervised visits with Haley. If all goes as I expect, you'll have unsupervised visitation rights after that."

Cal's legs gave out and he sank into the

chair by the desk. He thanked Melody profusely before hanging up.

"You okay, Cal?" Shannon asked.

"Okay? Are you kidding! I'm better than okay." He whooped loudly. With all eyes on him, he grabbed Shannon's hand, and with his other arm around her waist, he did as graceful a jig as he could manage with his healing leg.

The day flew by, and before he knew it he was letting himself and Scout into his house. Not that he wanted to look a gift horse in the mouth, so to speak, but he continued to mull over what had led to his good fortune. The only thing that made sense was that Anna—having accomplished what she'd set out to do and acknowledging that Cal's current job didn't pose a threat to Haley— had relented.

Whatever the reason, Cal was overjoyed. He didn't mind making the seven-hour drive to and from Cedar City on a regular basis, if it meant spending time with Haley.

The developments of the day were certainly cause for celebration. He didn't feel like being alone. He immediately thought of Jessica—but pushed that thought aside. He still hadn't gotten over Jessica's not telling him about her plans to leave the country. It was all too similar to what Anna had done. Not confiding, holding back salient facts that affected both of them profoundly. Although Anna had gone on to do a lot worse.

Cal popped the cap on a cold beer and called his brother, inviting him over for dinner. And why not Jessica? Whatever was—or wasn't—between them, she'd made his reconciliation with Haley possible. He still harbored resentment toward her, but she *was* the person responsible for today's news.

He should invite her over and thank her.

With Andrew there, it was a safe bet that they wouldn't get into anything personal. He could thank her, and keep it all nice and light.

Yeah. That made sense.

He scooped kibble into Scout's dish, and called her. Jessica sounded reserved but agreed to dinner.

Drew got there first, and was overjoyed to learn the news. He gave Cal a bear hug, and thumped him on the back several times, eliciting a deep-throated growl from Scout.

"Sorry…" He held his hands out and backed away. "I wasn't hurting him," he tried to assure the dog. Scout's eyes remained intent on Drew. "Tell him, will you please?" he appealed to his brother. "Tell him we're good before he gnaws my arm off."

Cal took a sip of his beer and chuckled. "Scout, settle," he ordered.

Drew wiped at his brow.

"You weren't seriously worried, were you?"

Drew cast a cautious glance at Scout. "Nah. Not really...but he does have very large teeth."

Cal laughed as the doorbell rang.

He moved to answer it, but Drew protested quickly. "You've got a bad leg. I'll get it."

Cal chuckled again. "You just don't want to be alone with Scout."

"Yeah, well. That, too."

Cal leaned a shoulder against the kitchen doorframe and took another sip from the bottle as he watched Drew open the front door.

He expected to feel anger—or disappointment—when he saw Jessica. Instead, he felt... he felt that tight knot form in his gut.

She was wearing a girlie, flowing dress with flowers on a yellow background, made from some clingy material that accentuated her curves. She had on a pair of strappy sandals with thin high heels; they left her shapely feet next to bare. Her toenails were painted a bright red that for some reason he found very sexy. The colors of the dress set off the light tan of her skin and contrasted with her blonde hair—which she'd left loose, the way he liked it best.

Since most of the time they'd spent together had been either at the hospital or with Scout, he hadn't seen her in a dress and with her hair down at the same time. She was quite a vision.

He continued to watch as Drew made a spectacle of introducing himself. When Jessica noticed him and their eyes met, she angled her head slightly. Questioningly.

Keeping his expression inscrutable, he nodded to her before going back to the kitchen to check on their dinner.

Cal made sure the conversation between him and Jessica remained light and casual. He made sure they were never alone.

The evening was a pleasant one and it allowed him to express his gratitude to Jessica, but Drew's presence kept everything friendly and impersonal. If the angry green jaws of jealously weren't nipping at him, he might've been amused by Drew's obvious attempts to flirt with Jessica.

Shortly after dinner, Jessica rose, explaining she had an early start at the hospital the next morning. She thanked Cal for dinner, shook hands with Andrew and assured them both that she didn't need to be walked out to her car.

JESSICA BACKED HER Miata out of Cal's driveway and headed home. She caught herself tapping her fingers on the steering wheel and forced herself to stop.

Now she was really confused. She'd come over assuming that Cal wanted to make amends for the change in his behavior. That he'd explain whatever had been bothering him. As it turned out, that had been wishful thinking on her part. He'd been pleasant enough. Certainly appreciative of her part in getting him back together with Haley—and she was thrilled for him. But other than showing his appreciation, he'd been nothing more than a cordial and pleasant host. There'd been no personal connection, not the slightest indication that he was interested in her. And there'd been nothing of the sort for more than three weeks now.

In fact, if she hadn't known better, she would've guessed that Cal was encouraging his brother to…to what? Be interested in *her*? Was that what tonight was all about? To set her up with his brother?

Andrew was a sweet guy, but that was *not* happening.

She'd been seriously thinking about abandoning her plan to leave the country and work with Care Across Continents. So seriously that she'd been struggling with what she'd do in San Diego if not provide patient care.

But now she wondered if she'd misinterpreted all along the signals she'd been receiving from Cal. She thought back and tried to pinpoint again when and what had caused the apparent change in Cal. Even now, the only thing she could come up with was his return to work. Tonight had made it abundantly clear; she felt his withdrawal. He was not interested in her in a romantic way.

Turning the matter over and over in her mind on the drive home, she kept coming back to the conclusion that she'd just been a convenience to Cal while he was recuperating.

Jessica let herself into her house and slipped out of her sandals in the hallway. Unaccustomed to wearing high heels, she rubbed one sore foot, then the other.

She couldn't hold back a sound of frustration, almost a muffled scream.

The only decision she could come to was that Cal didn't reciprocate her feelings. And if she was wrong?

Before she made any drastic decisions, she had to confront Cal—initiate a discussion between just the two of them—to make sure. The opportunity hadn't presented itself that evening. But if she was correct that he really *didn't* care about her, at least not in the way she craved, she was better off away from him.

And that eliminated the one obstacle that would keep her from following through with an assignment for Care Across Continents.

By the time she'd drifted off to sleep, she'd decided to accept the job.

CHAPTER TWENTY

CAL WAS VERY grateful to Jessica for her idea and for the encouragement that made his reconciliation with Haley possible. He had his daughter back in his life. Maybe he'd received a less than hopeful response to his adoption application for Kayla, but he hadn't given up on that. Drew, for one, had assumed that with his relationship with Haley reestablished, he would abandon his adoption efforts.

It annoyed Cal that his brother didn't know him well enough to realize that his desire to adopt Kayla wasn't simply to fill the void left by Haley's absence in his life. Nothing and no one could ever have done that. Nor did he consider Drew's assumption to be respectful enough of Kayla—whom he'd never met—and how Cal felt about her. She was a remarkable child dealing with unimaginable circumstances and she deserved a loving home.

And Cal could provide it. The girl had no one. She knew him and felt comfortable with him. As outgoing as she was with him, he'd seen how she reacted to hospital and group home staff she was unfamiliar with. There was a shyness, a definite reserve. Putting a timid little girl in an entirely unknown domestic situation had to be hard on her. Of course, the family who'd eventually foster her would be caring and well-screened by the agency. In due course, Kayla would warm up to them. But in the meantime?

He was more than willing to adopt her; he *wanted* to do it.

He'd even broached the subject with Anna. Now that he was seeing Haley, and he and Anna were on speaking terms, he felt it would be best if he asked for her support. He knew Social Services would be calling Anna as part of the background check, and he didn't want her to be surprised by the call. Or worse, be unpredictable in her statements.

Their conversation went remarkably well. She sounded incredulous at first, but when he explained his rationale and outlined Kayla's circumstances, Anna relented. Cal wondered if her encouraging attitude had anything to do with the fact that she'd recently become engaged to the guy she'd been living with. Whatever the reason, the only thing that mattered to him was that she'd be an important ally in his efforts to get the adoption granted.

With both Jessica and Anna supporting his efforts to adopt, making Kayla his daughter could be a real possibility.

JESSICA WAS IN her office, sitting in front of her computer. She was staring at the screen but oblivious to the figures in the spreadsheet before her.

She'd received the offer the day before. The job was exactly as Raymond had outlined— except for one thing. They wanted her to head up their team in Honduras. It was a professional honor.

She'd taken the letter home. She weighed the pros and cons all evening.

Eventually, she decided she couldn't pass up the opportunity. There was too much at stake, and there were too many reasons in favor of accepting, including the fact that she wanted to make a real difference in a country that desperately needed it. But she'd also finally resolved that she wasn't cut out for the kind of medicine she'd been practicing. Her emotions invariably got wrapped up with each patient she spent any appreciable time with, not just children. It was just more pronounced with them. She didn't trust her decision-making under those circumstances.

Working for Care Across Continents made it unlikely that she'd develop any attachments, and her work would predominantly involve more routine, non-life-threatening treatments. The *one* reason she would have stayed in San Diego...well, it was a moot point.

She'd come to accept that she'd developed strong feelings for Cal, but she couldn't ignore the emotional distance he'd put between them ever since he'd returned to work.

If things had been different with Cal, would she have made a different decision? *Yes.* She answered her own question. If she'd felt there could be a future for her with Cal, she wouldn't have considered leaving San Diego.

Moot point, she thought again, and signed her name to the agreement, slipped the document back in the envelope and placed it in her bag to mail on her way home.

Now that she was accepting the Care Across

Continents offer, she had to tell Cal that she'd be leaving San Diego. No matter what the current circumstances were between them, she had to be honest.

"I HOPE I'M not disturbing you." Jessica jumped and pressed a hand to her heart as she swiveled toward the doorway at the familiar sound of the deep male voice.

"Oh, not really. I was just…" What *had* she been doing? Other than thinking about him.

She glanced at her screen. "I was reviewing the month's report on patient outcomes." She felt a threatening sting behind her eyes and a constriction in her throat. Anyone who saw Cal standing in her doorway right now would never know he'd been injured. He looked healthy, vital and so very handsome.

She wanted to go to him. To hold him and be held by him. But if she did, she knew she'd fall apart, and probably reconsider the decision she'd already made.

There was no point. She'd only get hurt again.

"I won't keep you. I was here for my final checkup. I just wanted to let you know in person that with your support and Anna's, my lawyer thinks I have a reasonable chance of adopting Kayla."

Jessica's mouth was dry and she struggled with what to say. "That's wonderful news," she finally managed. "I'm very happy for both of you. I hope it goes through smoothly." She was astonished that her voice sounded so normal, when everything inside her was so tumultuous.

His eyes narrowed and he stared at her, unsmiling. "Well, I just wanted to say thanks. I'd better get to work now."

As he turned to leave, he almost bumped right into Marcia. He reflexively steadied her and murmured an apology before he headed off.

"Here are the files you wanted." Marcia walked into the office and handed them to Jessica. "Wasn't he the one who brought you those flowers a couple of weeks ago? Good-looking guy."

Jess glanced up. "Flowers?"

"Yes. A huge bouquet. You don't remember? He came to see you and had all those flowers. I asked if he wanted me to take them for you, but then something seemed to distract him and he left."

"When was that?"

"Oh…wait…it was the Monday before last! I remember because you were at your interview for Care Across Continents."

"It wasn't an interview," she murmured. "It was just an exploratory meeting then."

Marcia waved that away with one hand. "Well, whatever, but I'm sure that was the day, because I told him you'd be back shortly and he could wait for you if he wanted."

"And he just left?"

"Yes. He seemed to be very cheerful when he arrived. But, like I said, something seemed to bother him because he didn't seem too happy when he left."

"Did you tell him where I was?" Jessica was getting an uneasy feeling.

"I don't think so. Why would I?" Marcia frowned. "It was such a hectic day. I was trying to juggle at least a dozen things when he showed up. But he seemed very nice and he had that huge bunch of flowers for you. Maybe I did say something." She looked contrite. "Shouldn't I have? You haven't made a secret of it around here. I'm sorry, I don't remember…"

"I CAN'T BELIEVE we've hit another snag," Cal complained to his lawyer. "You'd think Social Services was trying to *prevent* kids from finding happy homes rather than facilitating it."

He could hear the frustration in Stephanie Lindquist's voice over the phone. "It's complex," his lawyer began. "And not made any easier by you being single and…well, let's acknowledge the elephant in the room…male. And a male with an allegation of…"

"That allegation was frivolous and vexatious, to use your legal jargon." His anger boiled over. "It was cleared up. Dismissed. My ex-wife—the person who made the allegation to begin with—is acting as a reference for me in the adoption proceedings. I thought we'd been through all this already."

"Take it easy, Cal," Stephanie said. "We have to face reality. Even with the support of Dr. Jessica Hansen *and* your ex-wife, the authorities feel that Kayla would be best placed in a two-parent home. She's never had that stability in her life, and she's never had a father figure."

Cal rubbed his forehead. "Isn't that all the more reason for her to have one now?"

"I made that argument."

He sat down on his sofa and rested his head against the back. "What do we do now?"

"There's nothing more we can do at this stage. It's in their hands. We wait and see what they come back with."

Cal's response was a long, drawn-out sigh.

"We've done everything we can," Stephanie told him. "Let's hope for the best and trust that the system will work as it should."

But Cal wasn't optimistic.

After the depressing discussion with his lawyer, Cal wasn't in the mood for company, but Jessica had called and asked to see him. When he'd tried to make excuses, she said it was important and assured him she wouldn't take up too much of his time. She'd sounded remote and perfunctory on the phone. It would be easier to resist her this way, but he couldn't help missing the warm and vivacious doctor he'd fallen for.

Well, of course, he had something to do with her demeanor. *He'd* been keeping *her* at arm's length for a couple of weeks now. He couldn't blame her if she'd withdrawn. It was for the best, anyway, if she was leaving.

There wouldn't be any long, heart-wrenching goodbyes.

His feelings for Jessica weren't diminishing, but the undercurrent of resentment remained. It was a major decision affecting them both and—just like Anna—she'd never given him the opportunity to weigh in on it, or to set right whatever wasn't working for them.

Cal had to admit that his emotional wounds were deep and her action had rubbed them raw again. He might have *married* her, given the chance.

And although that shocked him, it had likely been simmering under the surface for some time.

But he'd misjudged her and it was out of the question now. Thank God he'd never raised the possibility with her. He didn't have to deal with the rejection; he didn't know if he could have.

Yes, he was renewing his relationship with Haley and he was still determined to adopt Kayla, but if Jessica had leveled with him about her desire to work overseas—if the job was so important to her—he might have figured out a way to accompany her.

Good grief! He didn't realize that had even been lurking in his mind. He had no idea how it would have worked, since he had to consider Haley, Kayla and, of course, Scout.

They were two mature, intelligent adults. They should've been able to come up with a solution that suited all of them. But the opportunity hadn't been presented.

He groaned.

He might be old-fashioned, but he'd always seen himself as the kind of guy who married once, for life. That hadn't worked out so well for him. Yet, now he seemed willing to make the commitment again—with Jessica—and that was a sobering thought.

But even if she'd given him the choice, could he have left Haley and Scout and, if all went well, Kayla?

Impossible questions. No good answers.

Forget marriage. With Jessica, with anyone.

If he had love to give, it would all have to be directed at Haley and, hopefully, Kayla. He'd be the best father he could.

But he missed Jessica and the way they'd been together. He pictured her moving about his home and remembered how he'd liked having her there.

No, he wasn't going to cancel seeing her. Besides, it might help to see her and get his frustrations out, instead of keeping them penned up. If *she* didn't broach the subject, *he* would.

He showered, changed, fed Scout and took him for a short walk. He was ready just before she was due to arrive.

Jessica showed up on time, as she usually did when it wasn't directly after work. Seeing her gave him that little jolt he'd come to expect. She was wearing a white shirt and jeans, her hair straight and loose, one side tucked behind her ear. She had on some faint shimmery lip gloss that made her lips shine, but her mouth was unsmiling when he opened the door.

He brushed his lips across her cheek. He couldn't resist. He offered her a drink as they walked into the living room; she asked for a soda.

No, he couldn't deny his feelings for Jessica, sitting here with her, when all he wanted to do was take her in his arms. Cal realized how much he missed the relationship they'd been forging. When Jessica finally said something about the hospital, it opened the door for Cal to prod her about what was bothering him most.

"How are things at work?"

His comment coaxed a smile out of her. "As well as can be expected."

He forced a smile. "So it's still a good place to work?"

Jessica raised her eyebrows. "Our patient outcomes are among the best. And I have tremendous respect for my colleagues and the hospital administration."

He'd done enough interrogations as a police officer to know the signs to watch for. Not that he was *interrogating* Jessica, but he'd been scrutinizing her reaction and he saw the slight narrowing of her eyes at his question. "So you're happy there?"

"Yes."

This time he didn't have to watch for subtle clues. Anyone would've been able to read her. She threw up her hands and frustration was written all over her face. "What's this about, Cal?"

He'd been hoping she'd confide in him. That clearly wasn't going to happen. Should he evade or barrel through? He'd been dancing around it since the day he went to see her at the hospital and learned of her plans from that nurse.

If he expected *her* to be direct, maybe it was time for him to do the same. "I understand you're considering a job that would require you to leave San Diego."

She'd been lifting her glass to her lips, but her hand stilled and her face paled. Ice rattled in her glass as she replaced it on the coaster. With a slow, deliberate motion she linked her fingers together, resting them on her lap. "I'm not just considering," she said emphatically. "I've accepted the job and I'll be leaving San Diego."

CHAPTER TWENTY-ONE

CAL FELT AS if he'd been sucker-punched, even though he expected it. "When are you leaving?" he asked.

Jessica looked at him, wide-eyed. "Sometime in the next couple of months. But that's all you have to say?"

"Because I already knew. Well, suspected. I didn't know you'd made the decision."

"How did you…?" Then she remembered the discussion she'd had with Marcia about the flowers, and how Marcia couldn't remember what she'd told Cal. "Marcia? The trauma nurse?" she clarified.

Cal nodded. He kept his expression inscrutable, what he thought of as his cop look. But his voice was hard. "It's not the way I would've hoped to learn about something this important. I've been…" He was going to say *falling in love with you*, but stopped himself. Darned if he'd make an even bigger fool of himself. Instead, he went on the offensive. "Can you understand how I feel? That you didn't think you needed to share something this important with me?" He waited, so she'd know it wasn't a rhetorical question. While he did, Scout came over to lie by his feet.

"I… I'm sorry. I can imagine…" she finally said.

The words sounded feeble. Inadequate.

"Can you? I feel…betrayed." His anger erupted. "I opened up to you, confided my most personal ordeals—about Haley and my ex. And you didn't feel we were close enough to take me into *your* confidence? To tell me that you were thinking of leaving the country? Worse, it's not even that big a secret, since your colleagues at Ocean Crest obviously know." He paused again, struggling with his own feelings. "You should have told me."

"I'm sorry…" she whispered. "I told you now."

"It's a little too late. It's also after the fact. You've already accepted. It's a done deal." He got up to pace. He had to work off his anger in some way. "Would you have told me even tonight, if I hadn't prodded you into it?"

He knew he sounded harsh, but other than having Haley back, his life was in shambles. "One morning I would simply have found you gone. Is that the way it would've been?" The thought of not seeing her again pained him more than he'd expected.

"I would have told you. I *was* going to tell you. Tonight."

His laugh was bitter. "Yeah. Right. I'm supposed to believe that? This didn't just come out of the blue. Did they approach you or did you go to them?"

"I went to them," she admitted softly.

"So, you must've started the application process a while back. Then, *today*, of all days, you decided you were going to tell me?"

"Yes…because I sent back the contract today…"

He looked at her grimly; he felt as if every muscle in his body was stretched to the limit. "It's done, then?"

She nodded.

The finality of it weighed heavily on him. He realized he'd held out some hope that there'd been a misunderstanding, or that she hadn't actually accepted the offer. That she wouldn't actually *go*. "As I said, a little after the fact." He rose. It was time to bring the evening to an end.

After he closed the door behind Jessica, he stood at the side of his living room window, where he could watch her but she was unlikely to see him. He accepted that this would probably be the last time he saw her.

Her shoulders were hunched; her gait lacked its usual spring as she walked to her car. She swatted impatiently at some bug that must have flitted by. Her body language told him she wasn't happy.

Well, so be it. Neither was he.

DRIVING HOME, JESSICA mulled over the evening. Now she understood why Cal had seemed emotionally withdrawn from her lately. It wasn't related to his starting work again and no longer needing her. It was *her* fault. She'd hurt him by not being honest with him. Just like his ex-wife. She could see the parallel.

She'd always thought of herself as a good communicator. Why hadn't she just *told* him what she was thinking and asked what was bothering him? They could've cleared up their misunderstandings and... She cared about him deeply. She'd never felt this way about another man. Was she falling in love with him?

No, if she was honest, she already *was* in love with him. She might as well admit it to herself, if to no one else. If she'd told him what she was contemplating, would he have talked her out of it? Would he have wanted her to stay? Who knew where it could have led?

It was too late to turn back. To undo what had been done. She'd made her decision and, clearly, he no longer trusted her. Any idea about where their relationship could have led was conjecture at best; there was no opportunity for them now.

She'd be gone in a month.

She had no choice but to follow through with her move to Honduras.

That night, she drafted her resignation letter for the hospital.

After twenty minutes of tossing and turning in bed, she knew that sleep was impossible. Getting out of bed, she put on her housecoat and wandered through her house, making lists. She'd be gone for at least two years; she needed to decide which of her belongings she would sell, give away or toss, or pack and store. Oh, and she'd have to rent out her little house. She loved it too much to sell.

She had a lot to do before she left for Honduras. She considered that a blessing, since it would keep her mind occupied—and off Cal.

Eventually, when she was lying in bed again, exhausted, she felt a sense of panic. What had she done? She'd been so certain that working for Care Across Continents was the right thing for her, but now she wasn't certain...

She was impossibly sad as she finally drifted off to sleep.

CAL DIDN'T FEEL like sleeping. He sat on his deck nursing a beer, Scout curled up on the bench by his side, head resting on Cal's lap. Cal had watched the sun sink lazily below the horizon, the stars ascend and flicker through the translucent clouds drifting across the night sky. He lost count of the number of couples who'd strolled along the boardwalk, holding hands or arm in arm. It made him wonder if he was the only person on the planet not in a happy, stable relationship, or at least enjoying the first blush of potential love.

Of course, that was ridiculous; he knew the stats. Most relationships—heck, most *marriages*—didn't last in today's society.

And yet he really believed in monogamy and lifelong commitment.

But maybe he was fated to be solitary. Some people weren't meant to be part of a couple. He'd thought Anna had shown him that about himself, but here he was, pining for a woman who was beyond his reach.

He lifted the bottle, took a long, slow sip. He smelled the spicy scent of meat on a grill. He would've assumed it was too late for a barbecue, but this was California and plenty of people kept strange hours. He inhaled deeply, and the scent brought back memories of the first night he'd cooked dinner for Jess.

He wasn't sentimental as a rule, and that only reinforced the depth of his feelings for Jessica. It was different from what he'd felt for Anna. They'd been young, and caught up in the heady excitement of first love. With Jessica, the feeling was much stronger. Steadier. Consuming.

Now he was romanticizing, and that wasn't like him, either.

He stroked Scout's snout. The dog pressed

his head against Cal's hand and snuggled closer.

What if he drove over to Jessica's place right now and declared his feelings for her? Beg her to stay and marry him?

Would she laugh at him? Pity him for being such a sap? Or was there a chance she'd change her mind? What was the point, anyway? She was leaving. She'd made a commitment. Signed the contract. She'd follow through. She had too much integrity not to.

But if she'd had so much integrity, why hadn't she *told* him?

She'd go, and even if she had feelings for him—and that was a huge leap of faith based on how things stood between them—the reality was that they'd drift apart during her time away.

Whatever else happened, he was still in her debt for helping him reconnect with Haley. Because of that, if for no other reason, he would do what was right for her.

What was that old saying—if you loved something, let it go? If it returned it would always be yours, if it didn't, it never was.

The job seemed to be what Jessica truly wanted. He'd let her follow her heart and do what she had to. Wasn't that what selfless love was all about?

He cared about her that much. He'd wish her well.

He wouldn't get in her way; he owed her that.

He'd let her go.

CHAPTER TWENTY-TWO

San Pedro Sula, Honduras

THE SMALL CHARTERED plane banked steeply as it made its final approach to the La Mesa International Airport, located less than seven miles from the city of San Pedro Sula, in the Cortés Department in Honduras. Jessica's stomach lurched at the sharp maneuver.

The Beechcraft carried her, another doctor, a nurse and a quantity of supplies for Care Across Continents' operation in San Pedro Sula.

On their final approach, the Central American coast shimmered like an emerald jewel at the edge of the turquoise-blue Caribbean Sea. From their elevation, it was the beauty they saw, not the poverty.

As soon as Jessica stepped off the plane and onto the tarmac, the heat and humidity smothered her. A driver was waiting for them.

He spoke broken English, interspersed with the occasional Spanish phrase. He explained how long the ride would be, what they could expect at their base camp and that a truck was on its way to transport their supplies. He assured them repeatedly that it was safe to go with him and leave the supplies, which would be taken to the base camp. Nothing would go missing; they had his word.

It was Jessica's first decision in her new role, and she didn't feel entirely comfortable with it. But she lived by the basic principle of trust unless given a reason not to. She chose to trust the driver.

Still, she breathed a huge sigh of relief an hour later when she saw the large canopied truck rumbling toward their base camp in a massive cloud of dust. She was more relieved when inventory was taken and all the supplies that had accompanied them on the plane were accounted for.

She needn't have worried. The Hondurans she met in the next few weeks were an honest, honorable people. They were enormously grateful for the aid provided by Care Across Continents. Although the organization's services were free, Hondurans were a proud people, too, and they often tried to pay her with chickens, eggs, fruit or their own handiwork. She'd accept the small gifts that patients would bring her—it would have been rude not to—but she always politely declined the food they offered. She knew that many of them barely had enough to feed their own families. She didn't want to deprive them of what little they had.

Jessica appreciated the land, its people, and valued the work she did. But her days were long by choice, and lonely. Just a couple of weeks in, and she was miserable.

She buried herself in work to stave off despair. On the plus side, her respect for Care Across Continents grew with each passing day. The organization and all its people, down to the most junior volunteer, were thoroughly committed to their cause. She felt proud to be contributing to the enormous difference they were making in the communities and lives of the people they served.

Their team even had an adopted dog, a small stray, that looked like a beagle. They'd named him Scrubs, and he'd stayed mostly with Tania, one of the nurses, until Jessica arrived. From that moment on, Scrubs had become her shadow.

Jessica's mind was constantly occupied with her work, something for which she felt profoundly grateful. It kept her unsettling thoughts at bay. Until nighttime, when she'd lie on her cot and think about her life.

She missed Cal. She missed Kayla, too. She often thought about calling just to hear his voice, but rejected the notion. A clean break was better, she convinced herself. Somehow her life had become ruled by avoidance. She seemed to be running away from her own inadequacies. She seemed to be running away from Cal.

She wondered if she should've approached things differently with Cal, wondered if there could have been a chance for them.

She'd fall asleep thinking of Cal's smile and his laughing green eyes.

She'd wake each morning sad and restless until she buried herself in work again. That was the cycle of her days.

One morning during her second month in San Pedro Sula, she was roused by a tap on her office door. Helen, the nurse who'd flown in on the same plane she had, was standing there. "Jessica, you're needed in the hospital building."

"Problem?"

Helen's expression was sad. "You need to hurry," was all she said as she turned and left.

Jessica shut down her laptop, shrugged into the lab coat she'd draped over the back of her chair and hurried after Helen.

She knew something was very wrong even before she entered the hospital. She could hear a child screaming and the anguished cries of a woman. She quickened her pace, steeling herself against what she might find.

She pushed back the curtain hung over the doorway and her stomach roiled.

A child, of no more than seven or eight, sat on a bed. The woman, whom she assumed to be his mother, knelt in front of him, arms wrapped around him. Her wails had dropped to a sorrowful keening sound. The boy's left arm was bound to his body by what looked like a bedsheet, but it was stained with blood, as were his ragged shirt and shorts.

An image of Jake—the boy she couldn't save—flashed through her mind. She could see the huge gash in Jake's upper arm, where the rusty survey stake had torn through it. She tried to block the memory as she rushed over.

Her immediate assessment was that there'd been too much blood loss. It was a miracle the boy hadn't bled out or at a minimum passed out.

"What happened?" she asked tersely.

Tania, the other nurse, explained that the boy had been working on his father's farm, when another young boy driving a harvesting machine accidently drove into him, impaling him on one of the sharp tiller blades.

Jessica listened as she injected the boy with a local anesthetic. When Tania was done, she gave orders to the members of her team and instructed Helen to take the mother out of the room. She asked Helen to try to reassure the woman and find someone to stay with her so they could attend to her son.

She knew she projected an aura of focus and control, but inside she was a mess. The image of Jake as she'd first seen him had morphed into one of him lying on the hospital bed, pale and motionless, as she called the time of his death.

Jessica shook her head to dispel the haunting images, but her vision blurred and the memory persisted. She asked where Dr. Lyons, the other senior surgeon on their team, was. She couldn't do this; she needed him to take over.

She was told he'd left over an hour ago, traveling to the village of El Progreso, to assist a woman experiencing complications with childbirth.

That meant Jessica was the only one qualified. She had to do this; she had no choice. When she noticed her hand shaking as she reached for a pair of scissors, she drew in a deep breath and counted to ten before exhaling again.

"You're going to be okay," she said to the young boy as she prepared to cut off his makeshift bandage and shirt so she could examine his wound.

She did what she was trained to do. What she *had* to do. But she questioned each move she made, and questioned it again and again.

Perspiration beaded on her forehead. Her hands were cold and clammy inside the latex gloves. When she raised them, they were still shaking, which concerned her greatly. The slightest slip of an instrument could harm this child.

His injury was bad. The boy was fortunate the blade hadn't severed his arm altogether. She was told the harvester had been working in an area where there would've been manure used for fertilizer, pesticide dust and all sorts of other contaminants that could have gotten into the wound. The wound was dirty and some of the contaminants might have found their way into the boy's system.

Jake was stubbornly rooted in her mind. She tried to ignore the thoughts as best she could and concentrate on the boy before her.

Should she try to clean the wound—torn, jagged and deep, complicated by an open fracture of the humerus? Or should she amputate?

"Please save my arm." She could hear Jake begging her.

"You *killed* our child," Jake's hysterical mother accused her as his father dragged the woman away.

She had to amputate. That was the sure way to save the child. The only way to save the child. "No!"

"Excuse me?" Tania was staring at her.

"What?" Jessica asked, confused.

"You yelled, 'No.' Was I doing something wrong?"

Jessica hadn't realized she'd shouted the word out loud.

"Sorry. You're doing everything fine. Let's save this boy's life," she added with conviction.

TWO HOURS LATER, Jessica pulled off the surgical cap and gown, tossed them in the hamper by the door and washed her hands and face. Then she headed to her quarters. She scooped up Scrubs and sank into the only chair in her room. Hugging the little dog to her, she buried her face in his coarse, scruffy fur. Her body shook with the deluge of tears. Crying was not something Jessica allowed herself to do often, but this time she couldn't prevent it. Even Scrubs, whining and licking her neck and face, couldn't stem the outpouring of tears and grief. When her sobbing finally subsided, she was drained and nauseous. She rose and on unsteady legs padded to her bed. Lying flat on her back, she let Scrubs jump up and curl in beside her as she stared at the ceiling.

Had she done the right thing? Did she save

the boy's arm or would he develop sepsis, like Jake had? What would her colleagues think of her, shouting back at the voices in her head? The voices goading her to amputate the boy's arm. *No*, she'd yelled. She would *not* do it.

The field hospital facilities and supplies were rudimentary compared to what she had had at her disposal in San Diego when she'd operated on Jake. She knew that created an added risk. But she'd made her decision. Now she'd have to live with the consequences. If she'd been wrong…again…she didn't know if she could live with it.

As for the bigger picture, she was coming to the realization that she was not suited to providing direct care, regardless of the circumstances or how little time she spent with a patient. She'd committed her life to medicine, but she couldn't keep doing this. The indecision—the second-guessing before and after any procedure—was torture for her, and not in the best interests of her patients. A wrong decision or a split-second delay in making the right decision could cost a patient his or her life.

And if she left medicine and moved back to San Diego, was there any possibility for her and Cal? No, she couldn't keep hoping for something that wasn't meant to be.

Jessica watched over the little boy, Philippe, like a hawk. Each day made her feel more optimistic about his prognosis and gradually eased her anxiety about his wellbeing. But her question about staying in medicine did not go away or diminish. With every patient she saw, with every patient-care decision she made, she knew her own resolve was becoming clearer, stronger.

She was grateful and relieved that Philippe's progress was positive and there'd be no long-term consequences for him because of the accident, but it did nothing to change her mind.

The boy's mother was so grateful, so effusive, Jessica found it embarrassing. She didn't want to think of how the mother would have felt if the outcome had been different.

Jessica knew she couldn't live her life always unsure, always questioning herself. She'd go mad, and it would only be a matter of time that she *did* make a mistake and the consequences would be dire.

It didn't take her long to realize that if one of the reasons for accepting the assignment was *not* to get emotionally attached to her patients, she'd failed completely. She was coming to accept that she might never win her struggle with that ever-elusive "detached concern." She grappled with what that would mean for her as a doctor and a surgeon. She believed wholeheartedly in the work of Care Across Continents, found it far more gratifying than anything she'd previously done, but she just wasn't cut out for it.

Confidence, decisiveness, steady nerves and hands—these were all essential traits of a surgeon. She feared she'd never have them again, if she'd ever had them to begin with. That meant she was destined to make a wrong decision sooner or later, at the expense of a patient's life. She couldn't live with that.

But what were her choices? If she didn't practice medicine, what would she do?

JESSICA KEPT PHILIPPE and his mother at their compound a few days longer than necessary, because she didn't want to take any chances. As soon as Philippe was able to, he played outside in their small fenced yard with Scrubs. The boy and dog connected, and Scrubs abandoned Jessica's quarters in favor of being Philippe's ever-present companion. The bond was so obvious and strong that when she finally felt comfortable letting Philippe go home, it was apparent that Scrubs had to go with him.

Sitting in her office, she watched through the window as Philippe and his mother walked toward the bus stop, Scrubs scampering around his legs. It brought to mind a day that seemed so very long ago but in reality had been just months—of a little girl, her curly blonde pigtails bouncing, as she played with Scout on the boardwalk. Her name was Cindy, she recalled. The vision transformed itself into a memory, of walking hand in hand with Cal. They'd been walking back to his house that day.

Instead of dulling with time and distance, her memories of Cal seemed to be becoming ever more intense, ever more frequent. Not a day went by that she didn't think of him, wonder how and what he was doing. She thought of Kayla and Haley, too, and wondered how things had progressed for Cal with both girls.

And with a clarity that couldn't be denied, she knew she loved him. She rested her fingertips across her lips and remembered how it had felt when he'd kissed her that first time.

She'd been in Honduras for just over two months, and it already seemed like a lifetime, being away from Cal. But she might as well get used to it. Whether in San Diego or a continent away, the distance between them would remain unbridgeable.

When Jessica's phone rang, she reached for it absently, her eyes on Philippe clutching Scrubs in his arms as he and his mother boarded the bus out of town. Her thoughts returned to Cal and a much different but no less lovable dog. The view outside blurred as tears filled her eyes.

"Jessica Hansen," she answered.

"Jessica, it's Harold Massey."

Hearing the voice of Dr. Massey, recently appointed as chair of the board of Care Across Continents, brought a smile to her lips. "Dr. Massey. It's nice to hear from you. To what do I owe the pleasure of your call?"

"I wish it was good news, Jessica. You remember Raymond Goulding? Our executive director?"

"Of course." She thought of the middle-aged man who'd offered her the contract, and wondered why Dr. Massey would be calling on his behalf. "Is there a problem with my contract?"

"Oh, no," he was quick to reassure her. "That's not why I'm calling. I'm afraid I have sad news about Raymond. He had a massive stroke. His right side and his speech are significantly impaired."

Jessica was horrified. "I'm so sorry to hear that. Is there anything I can do?"

There was a slight hesitation at the other end of the line. "Yes, actually, there is," he continued. "And that's the reason for my call. Raymond won't be able to continue his duties leading the organization. We had a special meeting of the board of directors last night, and both Raymond and I recommended that we review your credentials to see if there could be a fit."

"A fit for what?"

"Well, let me get to that. After assessing your qualifications, the members of the board were impressed and unanimously authorized me to make you a job offer. To see if you'd be interested in heading up the organization as our new executive director."

Jessica knew her mouth had dropped open. "You mean move back to San Diego?" Her immediate and overriding thought was that she'd get to see Cal again. She could go home to him!

"Well, yes." There was warmth in Dr. Massey's voice. "It'll be a demanding job, because of the expansion and fundraising plans we have in place. I'm convinced it would be that much more challenging if you weren't here."

"I… I'm honored that you'd think of me… but am I really the best person for the role? I have limited administrative experience—just running the trauma unit. And there are many well-qualified people who've been with the organization much longer than I have."

"Yes, of course. We always look for candidates who have a passion for healthcare and have been practicing physicians, so they understand the opportunities and the difficulties. We also look for strong communicators, since the executive director is the face of the organization to the public, the media and our donors. I could go on but, in short, yes, we believe you're well-suited for the role."

"I don't know what to say."

"You don't have to say anything right now. I realize it won't be an easy decision for you.

I understand you're an exceptional surgeon and this would remove you from direct patient care. We'd understand if you said no, but I'd like you to consider it and get back to me if you have any questions. While you're thinking, rest assured the board and I believe in you."

Jessica was in a daze. She'd barely had time to unpack and now she had an opportunity to return to San Diego…and to Cal. That was the first and most compelling reason for her—to be able to see Cal and determine whether they could set things right.

And with the new job, she also had an opportunity to do something that required her skills, knowledge and training, would be rewarding and yet would alleviate the professional issues she'd been struggling with. How fitting that the perfect opportunity, one she'd never even dreamed of, had come her way at a time when she was struggling with what to do with the rest of her life.

Despite her limited experience, she'd always been good at the administrative side of healthcare; now, she'd get better.

But a second chance with Cal trumped even her enthusiasm about the job.

THE MORE JESSICA thought about her return to San Diego, the more she thought about Cal, and the more anxious and excited she became. She'd been wrong to withhold her plans from him. She knew that simple act had hurt Cal. Part of her wanted to call and let him know she was moving back home. How much harder would it make things between them if he somehow found out from other sources that she was returning to San Diego?

But that was assuming it would matter to him. Based on the way they'd parted, the fact that he'd *encouraged* her to go and didn't seem the least bit bothered about it, that wasn't a sure bet. She prided herself on being a principled, honest, direct person. How had things become so muddled between them? She had to tell him she was coming home. But then she thought about how much she had at stake. If she called and poured her heart out to him and he rejected her, how could she deal with that? What recourse would she have then? It had to be face to face.

And she had to be honest with herself, too. She was terrified of not being able to work things out with Cal.

She missed Cal. She *loved* him. She wanted to see him.

It might have just been coincidence, but she'd been given this opportunity to return to San Diego. How could she not see it as a second chance to be with Cal? To see if Cal was willing to forgive her… If the adoption hadn't already gone through, would he still want to try…but this time with her? As a couple, presumptuous though that seemed?

After much agonizing, she finally decided she wouldn't call in advance. There was too much riding on the outcome not to talk to him in person. She needed to see his eyes, his body language. She needed to touch him and convince him that she could be trusted. Convince him of her love.

CHAPTER TWENTY-THREE

San Diego, California

"WE'VE GOT A call for an assist from Tactical," Rick Vasquez shouted over to Cal. "You up for it?"

"Yeah. What's the nature of the incident?" he asked as he rose and got his gear ready.

"Armed robbery at a bank. A teller and a bystander were shot. Neither one of them is seriously hurt, but the shooter took off. The unit responding had his vehicle blocked so he took off on foot. Last known location was Harmony Grove Road and he was heading toward the Elfin Forest Reserve. He's got a history of violent crime. He's armed and dangerous. They need tracking."

Cal put on his bulletproof vest and stuffed what he'd need into his duffel.

Rick went to him, laid a hand on his shoulder. "Cal, there's going to be running through

rough terrain and you know it." He said it quietly so no one else in the room could hear. "There's no shame in passing this one over to Shannon," he said, referring to the rookie handler whose dual-purpose dog was training for search and rescue. "It's up to you, but you can pass on this one."

Cal paused for a moment, tested the weight on his right leg. He slapped Rick on the back. "Thanks, but I'll take it. It's my job. Besides, Shannon is still green. I wouldn't want her getting hurt."

He and Scout jogged to his truck. With lights flashing, he drove to rendezvous with the tactical team.

They were in the parking lot by the entrance to the Elfin Forest trail. Cal knew the trail was just under seven miles long but that there were no more places off the main trail where a person could hide.

The tactical team might have full body armor and be heavily armed, but he and Scout had to travel light and move fast. That was the reason he wore only a vest.

If the shooter was hiding, as opposed to moving, they'd be running right to him, and he'd be able to both hear and see them coming from a distance. If he was so inclined, he'd have a clear shot at both of them. Cal, on the other hand, had no way of knowing if they were almost upon him or still miles away. That put him and Scout in extreme danger.

Cal got a quick briefing from the head of the tactical team. He wasn't surprised to learn that it was more than a bank robbery gone wrong. The teller who'd been shot was the shooter's ex-wife. He hadn't been satisfied with shooting her; he'd threatened to take more people out and said something about a bomb. Since he was a chemical engineer, the threat was deemed to be credible. Brody and his explosives-detection dog, Nitro, had been dispatched to the bank to check for explosives.

Scout got the shooter's scent almost right away, and he and Cal led the tactical team into the forest. For the initial part, Scout took them along the trail, but about a mile in, he veered off into the forest.

"Can you slow your dog down, Tracker?" came the anticipated request from the tactical team sergeant. They would've preferred to move more cautiously and under cover.

Cal didn't bother to acknowledge it with

a reply. He just did his best to keep up with Scout, despite the throbbing ache in his right thigh. The high canopy kept most of the sunlight from filtering down to the forest floor and the closely spaced tree trunks provided some cover as they continued through the forest at a rapid pace.

When Scout broke out into a small clearing with a berm on the far side, Cal could feel the dog's energy level escalate. Cal's instincts told him they were in trouble. "Ease back," he called to the cops behind him. "Stay behind cover, if you can."

He attempted to keep himself and Scout to the perimeter, where they'd have partial cover, but Scout was hot on the scent and couldn't be deterred. Cal bent as low as he could and followed.

He heard the discharge of a high-caliber handgun and felt blinding pain when the bullet hit him. He had enough control as he was falling to roll onto Scout's leash, preventing him from yanking it out of his hand and charging at the shooter, which would almost certainly have gotten Scout shot. Cal heard the tactical guys' hurried exchange and saw them rush by before everything went black.

JESSICA LOVED CAL. Since the day she'd accepted the executive director role and knew she was returning to San Diego, she could hardly keep her mind off Cal. She debated over and over again whether she should call him or not. She kept circling back to the same decision. There was too much at stake to call him. What if he rejected her?

She needed to do it in person. To see him, let him see her, let him see the depth of her love…and remorse. She wanted to see firsthand if he still had feelings for her.

Now that she was back home, she couldn't wait to see him.

She was glad she hadn't sold her little Miata, just lent it to one of the nurses at the hospital. She put the top down and drove to Cal's house first. She didn't see his police SUV in the driveway and assumed he must be at work. She picked up the two newspapers tossed on his front porch and placed them in the mailbox, together with what appeared to be a couple days' mail. She wondered if he might have gone on vacation, but decided to look for him at the police division.

The woman at the reception counter would only tell her he wasn't there. When Jessica asked where she could find him, she said she wasn't authorized to provide that information. Jessica explained who she was, but the woman remained adamant that unless she was immediate family, she couldn't discuss Officer Palmer's whereabouts.

As Jessica walked across the parking lot to her car, she recognized one of the other K-9 cops hurrying to his vehicle. She tried to remember his name. Rick. It was Rick, the guy they called Pitbull. He'd probably know where she could find Cal and maybe he'd be willing to tell her.

She called to him, and saw the recognition on his face, too. He gave her a distracted, almost angry look as he climbed into his truck.

Jessica rushed over and rested a hand on the open window as Rick was about to pull away. "Can I speak to you for a minute about Cal Palmer?" she asked.

CAL WAS AWARE of sounds first. He heard vague murmurs and hurried conversation. Next came the pain. His chest was throbbing with it.

When he finally tried to open his eyes, he first saw blurred circles of pastel colors.

He squeezed his eyes shut, opened them, squinted and tried to focus. His sight cleared, and he was staring up at bright institutional lights mounted on the ceiling. The light intensified the hammering in his head, and he squeezed his eyelids shut again.

Someone touched his shoulder. "Cal? Cal? Can you hear me?" The voice calling to him sounded disconcertingly familiar.

He'd been shot. He remembered that, and when he'd started to come to, he'd felt relief that whatever his condition, he was at least alive. But the bright lights and the voice that shouldn't have been there made him wonder if, in fact, he *had* died.

"Cal?" The touch on his shoulder was firmer, the voice more insistent. There was no mistaking it.

He turned his head toward the voice and regretted it immediately as the pain crested. He forced his eyelids open once more, saw a face he'd never expected to see again. Certainly not by his bedside, not in this country.

Jessica looked ethereal. If he reached for her, he was certain his hand would move through unobstructed air. If she was a vision, he didn't want her to disappear. "What…what are you doing here?" he croaked.

"I moved back home," was Jessica's answer.

Cal turned his head away, pain be damned. She'd come back and she didn't even have the decency to tell him about that, either. If he was imagining her, it only proved how much resentment he still had. He kept his eyes closed, his head turned. "Is Scout okay? Do you know if he's okay?"

"Yes. I asked. He's fine. They caught the guy. Thanks to you and Scout."

"Good. Now go away and leave me alone." Cal slurred the words before he drifted off into a drug-induced sleep again.

The next time he woke, he was alone in a hospital room. The pain was still there, but bearable. He felt light-headed, his mind foggy. Lifting an arm, he noticed the IV drip, and assumed he was being injected with a strong painkiller.

He noticed a card propped up on the bedside stand, reached for it and smiled. It was a drawing of him and Scout. Scout had a bone in his mouth and Cal sported a bandage on his chest. Hearts and stars floated down from the sky. Written on the bottom, in a child's hand, was "Get well soon, Daddy. Love, Haley." The drawing had apparently been scanned and emailed, someone had printed it, and tacked it to a piece of cardboard so it could stand on the tabletop.

His little girl *loved* him. He closed his eyes and absorbed the pure pleasure of that for a few minutes.

Then his memory cleared and he remembered first waking up, hearing Jessica's voice and then seeing her. He glanced up at the IV bag. Morphine. He wondered if they'd already been pumping the stuff into him then, and he'd been hallucinating under its influence. The memory was vague and faded; he must have imagined Jessica by his bedside.

Did it take a near-death experience to drive home the fact that he *still* loved Jessica? Even so, there wasn't anything he could do about it. She'd made her choice, and it didn't include him.

Whether it was real or a hallucination, he distinctly remembered telling Jessica to leave him alone.

THEY KEPT CAL in the hospital for several days. He drifted in and out of consciousness for the first few. During his waking moments, he had visits from Logan, Rick, Shannon, Hal Robinson and several of the other guys from the unit. Drew spent a lot of time with him, sat by his bedside so that when Cal had his lucid moments, he was there waiting. Cal even received a call from Anna. After ascertaining that he was up to it, she put Haley on the phone. Getting to speak to his daughter did him a world of good.

When they were ready to discharge him, his doctor cautioned that the pain would continue to be severe for a while, and he prescribed oral pain meds that he could take as needed.

Drew drove Cal home, but they swung by Drew's place to pick up Scout, who'd stayed there the entire time Cal had been in the hospital. The unit had brought Scout back to the division after the ambulance had whisked Cal away; Cal had been speechless to learn that despite his brother's strained relationship with Scout, he'd made arrangements to take the dog home, knowing how much it would mean to him.

Maybe the drugs were making Cal emotional, but he felt inordinately grateful for what his brother had done.

When Drew offered to stay, Cal thanked him and sent him home, explaining he needed rest. What he really wanted was just to be alone.

He settled with a cold can of Coke on his back deck, Scout curled up at his feet.

Cal's head was so crowded with thoughts, he was surprised it didn't simply explode.

He sipped his soda and stared down the length of beach. The sky was an ominous, dense gray. The forceful wind swirled small eddies of sand and propelled waves to batter the shore. The sound of the breakers mimicked his turbulent emotions.

Cops lived with the risk of being killed every single day. He thought of his colleague and friend, Todd, who'd been fatally stabbed in the domestic dispute so many years ago, and considered himself lucky that this was the first time he'd been shot and that he was alive to tell the tale.

He thanked the powers that be that Haley was back in his life. He could, if not entirely understand, at least forgive Anna for how she'd gone about ending their marriage and ensuring she got sole legal custody of Haley.

During a recent conversation, she'd seemed receptive to updating the terms of their agreement to give him joint custody. He'd worried that this incident might have made her rethink that, since she'd claimed it was the dangers of his job that had caused her to leave him. But when they'd spoken a couple of days earlier, he was relieved to discover that she hadn't backtracked. When he'd hesitantly raised the possibility of Haley's visiting him in California, she hadn't ruled out the idea. He got the sense she might be feeling some remorse now.

Added to that, there was a message on his voice mail from Stephanie Lindquist when he arrived home. She was the lawyer who'd been working on his attempt to adopt Kayla. Things seemed more optimistic. Stephanie thought they only had one hurdle left to clear, and that was the fact that he was a single male.

The irony was he no longer *wanted* to be single. He was finally able to put what Anna had done behind him, and realized he wanted to spend his life with Jessica. Hallucinations aside, she was half a world away and lost to him.

He drained the rest of his soda.

He would've expected the drugs they'd given him at the hospital to dull his mind. And yet, he felt he'd never thought about things more clearly.

The beach was nearly deserted because of the late hour and the menacing storm. Neither deterred him. He reached for Scout's Kong and whistled for the dog to follow him. Cal walked along the boardwalk, the sharp wind plucking at his light coat. He threw the Kong repeatedly for Scout.

Suddenly Scout ignored the Kong in favor of sprinting off. Cal whistled to him, but with the howling of the wind, Scout must not have heard it. When Cal realized the dog was running toward a person in the distance, he mumbled an expletive. He took off at an awkward jog toward the dog's intended target, knowing he didn't have a hope of beating him there.

He was relieved to see no indication of aggression when Scout reached his target. Just the opposite—the dog seemed to be offering an ecstatic greeting. Once Cal got close enough to see the person as more than a wavering form, he stopped. With his hands on his knees, he bent over to catch his breath and make sure his eyes weren't deceiving him.

He hadn't been hallucinating in the hospital. Her hand resting on Scout's back, Jessica walked slowly toward him.

She wore faded jeans, sneakers, a yellow knit sweater and a navy blue windbreaker. Her hair was braided, but the strands the wind had tugged free danced around her face.

"I didn't realize you'd be discharged already," she said.

He'd felt a sense of elation that she'd come to see him, but her comment dispelled that misguided notion. "Then what are you doing here?"

She lifted a shoulder, turned toward the ocean and brushed at the hair whipping in her face. "I felt like taking a walk."

He couldn't help smiling, despite the emotions churning inside him as violently as the water pounding the shore. "There are lots of places you could have walked. The beach isn't the most hospitable on a night like this."

Her only response was another jerk of her shoulder. At her silence, he faced the ocean, too.

"You came to see me in the hospital."

"I did, yes. And you sent me away."

Cal nodded slowly. "Yeah, I did." He turned to her. "I'm sorry."

She looked at him but he couldn't read her expression in the muted light. He searched his memory for what exactly she'd said to him in the hospital. That she'd moved back? "What made you come home?"

"You," she said simply.

"I don't understand." He dared not hope for more, only to have his heart torn to shreds again.

"I knew it was the truth but didn't want to admit it to myself. I tried to rationalize that it was because of a job they offered me back here, to be the executive director of Care Across Continents. That it was because I needed to stop treating patients, and this job would let me do that, while letting me use my training. But none of that was completely honest. None of it matters as much as you do. I came home because of you. I missed you and I was miserable without you. The job offer may have been serendipitous, but like it or not, I came back because I love you."

As the first pinpricks of rain began to sting them, Cal took Jessica in his arms, to tell her he loved her, too. He needed that physical contact to assure him he wasn't hallucinating or fantasizing. That she really, truly was here and that she was his, now and forever.

EPILOGUE

"OH, NO. YOU CAN'T open the drapes, sweetie!" Marcia rushed over to Haley and grabbed the curtain before she could yank it all the way back.

"But my daddy's out there."

"Really? Let me see. He's my daddy now, too!" Kayla joined Haley at the window.

Jessica was standing by the full-length mirror that had been set up in Cal's bedroom, her mother fussing with her veil. She smiled at the two little girls in identical white dresses, but with different color sashes around their waists. Haley's was a deep rich brown, Kayla's a bright yellow. The sashes had been the girls' idea. Since they were now sisters, they wanted something to symbolize that. They'd been fascinated by each other's hair from the day they'd met, and decided wearing sashes representing the other's hair color would be a nice connection between them.

"Let them have a look, Marcia. Girls, open the curtains just wide enough for you to take a peek. We don't want your father seeing us in our wedding dresses before the ceremony."

When her mother was finally satisfied with how the veil fell over her long French lace gown, Jessica hugged her before joining the girls at the window so she, too, could take a peek at her fiancé. Not used to wearing heels quite this high, she wobbled slightly as she stepped on the edge of the carpet. She made a mental note to walk carefully down the makeshift aisle to the wooden platform on the beach, which was where they'd exchange their vows.

Fortunately, it was a clear, calm day, and the red flower petals the girls had scattered over the white runner along the aisle were mostly still in place.

"Ohhh, look how handsome Daddy is in his suit!" Kayla exclaimed.

"That's a tuxedo," Haley corrected her. "I think it's the handsomest I've ever seen him!" The girl beamed with pride and pleasure.

"I have to agree with you both," Jessica added. "That's the 'handsomest' I've seen him, as well."

"Look at Uncle Drew! He looks nice, too."

Both girls giggled.

At a knock on the door, all three of them turned. Marcia let Rick Vasquez into the bedroom. He, too, wore a tuxedo and was grinning from ear to ear. "We're ready to start when you are, ladies. And it'd better be soon," he said to Jessica. "Your father's as nervous as if *he* was the bride getting married today."

"All right, everyone. Let's get this show on the road," Marcia announced.

Jessica waited until the others had left the room, and only she and Rick remained. "Thank you," she said softly, and placed a kiss on his cheek.

"For what?"

"This wouldn't be happening if you hadn't told me Cal had been shot and where I could find him." She brushed a kiss across his other cheek.

"What's that one for?" Rick asked.

"It's from both of us…"

Rick held up a hand. "Whoa, there, pretty lady. Tracker and I are good friends, but I'm *not* accepting any kisses from him."

Jessica laughed. "Okay. Then it's just from me, thanking you on our behalf. Thank you for what you did to bring us together. That also helped make it possible for Kayla to be part of our family. The adoption went through quickly enough that Kayla could be with us to watch her new father and mother get married. So, thank you from the whole Palmer family."

"My pleasure, Dr. Hansen, soon to be Palmer," Rick said as he slipped her arm into the crook of his elbow. "Your father and your groom await you. As Marcia said, let's get this show on the road."

CAL'S HEART ALMOST stopped as he watched Jessica walk toward him in a gorgeous white dress. She was on her father's arm, his two little girls preceding her, scattering more rose petals from small wicker baskets.

When her father took Jessica's hand and offered it to Cal with murmured words of encouragement, Cal smiled directly into her eyes and couldn't help saying the first three things that came to mind. "You're absolutely stunning. And you're remarkably tall!" She was nearly eye level with him in her heels. "And I love you very much."

As Jessica laughed, Cal clasped her hand

in his, and with Haley and Kayla standing on either side of them, they each took the solemn vow that would join them together as a family, forever.

* * * * *

LARGER-PRINT BOOKS!

GET 2 FREE
LARGER-PRINT NOVELS
PLUS 2 FREE
MYSTERY GIFTS

Love Inspired®

Larger-print novels are now available...

LILP15

YES! Please send me **The Montana Mavericks Collection** in Larger Print. This collection begins with 3 FREE books and 2 FREE gifts (gifts valued at approx. $20.00 retail) in the first shipment, along with the other first 4 books from the collection! If I do not cancel, I will receive 8 monthly shipments until I have the entire 51-book Montana Mavericks collection. I will receive 2 or 3 FREE books in each shipment and I will pay just $4.99 US/ $5.89 CDN for each of the other four books in each shipment, plus $2.99 for shipping and handling per shipment.*If I decide to keep the entire collection, I'll have paid for only 32 books, because 19 books are FREE! I understand that accepting the 3 free books and gifts places me under no obligation to buy anything. I can always return a shipment and cancel at any time. My free books and gifts are mine to keep no matter what I decide.

263 HCN 2404   463 HCN 2404

Name	(PLEASE PRINT)	
Address		Apt. #
City	State/Prov.	Zip/Postal Code
Signature (if under 18, a parent or guardian must sign)		

Mail to the **Reader Service**:

IN U.S.A.: P.O. Box 1867, Buffalo, NY 14240-1867
IN CANADA: P.O. Box 609, Fort Erie, Ontario L2A 5X3

* Terms and prices subject to change without notice. Prices do not include applicable taxes. Sales tax applicable in N.Y. Canadian residents will be charged applicable taxes. This offer is limited to one order per household. All orders subject to approval. Credit or debit balances in a customer's account(s) may be offset by any other outstanding balance owed by or to the customer. Please allow 4 to 6 weeks for delivery. Offer available while quantities last. Offer not available to Quebec residents.

Your Privacy—The Reader Service is committed to protecting your privacy. Our Privacy Policy is available online at www.ReaderService.com or upon request from the Reader Service.

We make a portion of our mailing list available to reputable third parties that offer products we believe may interest you. If you prefer that we not exchange your name with third parties, or if you wish to clarify or modify your communication preferences, please visit us at www.ReaderService.com/consumerchoice or write to us at Reader Service Preference Service, P.O. Box 9062, Buffalo, NY 14269. Include your complete name and address.

READERSERVICE.COM

Manage your account online!

- Review your order history
- Manage your payments
- Update your address

> *We've designed the*
> *Reader Service website*
> *just for you.*

Enjoy all the features!

- Discover new series available to you, and read excerpts from any series.
- Respond to mailings and special monthly offers.
- Connect with favorite authors at the blog.
- Browse the Bonus Bucks catalog and online-only exculsives.
- Share your feedback.

Visit us at:
ReaderService.com